"MIGNON EBERHART IS NUMBER ONE" —New York Herald Tribune

"Exciting . . . lush . . . a good story"
—New York Times

"Suspense extra tense. High-test"
—Saturday Review

"Polished . . . superb"
—New Yorker

Other Mignon G. Eberhart mysteries you'll want to read:

THE WHITE DRESS
THE MAN NEXT DOOR
WITH THIS RING
CALL AFTER MIDNIGHT
FAIR WARNING
MESSAGE FROM HONG KONG
DEADLY IS THE DIAMOND
MAN MISSING
HOUSE OF STORM
FIVE PASSENGERS FROM LISBON
UNIDENTIFIED WOMAN
WINGS OF FEAR
WOLF IN MAN'S CLOTHING
ESCAPE THE NIGHT
POSTMARK MURDER
RUN SCARED
THE HANGMAN'S WHIP
THE GLASS SLIPPER
THE CASES OF SUSAN DARE

All available in Popular Library editions

MIGNON G. EBERHART
THE CHIFFON SCARF

POPULAR LIBRARY • NEW YORK

All POPULAR LIBRARY books are carefully selected by the POPULAR LIBRARY Editorial Board and represent titles by the world's greatest authors.

POPULAR LIBRARY EDITION

Copyright, 1939, renewed © 1966 by Mignon G. Eberhart
Published by arrangement with Doubleday & Company, Inc.

All the persons and events in this book are entirely imaginary. Nothing in it is derived from anything which ever happened.
THE AUTHOR

TO ALAN
*With his wife's thanks
for supplying the information about airplane engines
for this story, and in the hope that she
has not taken too many liberties
with her rival
in his affections otherwise known as*
THE CRUISER.

PRINTED IN THE UNITED STATES OF AMERICA
All Rights Reserved

CHAPTER/1

Eden forgot the chiffon scarf. It was queer but in its own way inevitable that after her bags had gone and while the taxi waited she went back for it.

It was a long, gray chiffon scarf—so soft it seemed to have no strength, delicate and clean and smelling faintly of sachet. Altogether inanimate; altogether at her disposal. She took it in her hand, put the two letters in her enormous, flat handbag, looked at herself in the mirror for a long moment and went to the waiting taxi. She held the scarf in her hand all the way to the airport. And in the St. Louis plane, when it flew high and the air was cold, she put the scarf around her throat.

She arrived at St. Louis in time for dinner—that memorable dinner which nevertheless, because of her own preoccupation, it was always impossible to remember in its true perspective.

An hour or so before the plane reached St. Louis, she took the two letters from her handbag and read them again slowly. The first was from Averill Blaine.

"My dear, I'm enclosing tickets and want you to come to my wedding two weeks from this coming Friday, that's June the third. The tickets are for the plane trip to St. Louis. From St. Louis we'll all go together (Uncle Bill has chartered a big plane) to the Bayou Teche place where the wedding is to be. In the little chapel; do you remember it? The man I am marrying is Jim Cady; he's at the plant—so things will work out well that way: he really is brilliant and I'm a lucky girl. He's just finished designing and building a new airplane engine everybody's very excited about; there's to be a trial flight Tuesday; so we hope you can arrive Monday night in time for dinner. Then you can see the flight the next day—it really means a lot to all of us. And we'll leave for the Bayou Teche place that night. Do come, dear; if I were having bridesmaids I would want you; but the wedding's to be quite simple and poetic (I'm wearing ice-blue satin with Grandmother's rose-point veil). Noel sends word he hopes you'll come, too. To think if it hadn't been for you, Noel and I would have been married long ago. I ought to thank you for that, though I don't suppose you took Noel away from me then out of motives of sheer friendliness!—I ought to label that 'joke'; it's so hard to tell in a letter. Wire me when to have you met at the airport. Don't worry about clothes; you looked stunning the last time I saw you. All send love. Creda is here, of course. Now do come. Much love, Averill."

Below was a dashing, hasty but invincibly triumphant postscript. "Darling, wait till you see him."

How little Averill had changed since school days! But then the whole setting and circumstances of her life had not changed—abruptly and completely in 1931—as Eden's had done.

Eden wondered briefly just what those years of job-hunting and of precarious job-holding had done to her, Eden Shore. If she had been trained to a profession it would have been easier. The trouble was that even now the shallow foothold she had won was precarious; she was in no sense irreplaceable. There were too many women, just as able, just as brainy, just as tenacious as Eden Shore.

And she was tired.

She thought back to the time, five years ago now, when simply because she didn't love him and discovered it, she'd refused to marry Noel Carreaux. He'd been rich then; extravagantly rich with houses and yachts and good motors, with polo ponies and unlimited checking accounts. Almost literally unlimited, then. And while life could go on without polo ponies, the bank accounts spelled security. How could she have failed to see that!

Well, she knew better now.

The other note was from Noel himself. He wrote:

"Eden, my lovely: Averill's writing to ask you to her wedding in a little over two weeks. I hope you come. Averill's very happy; Bill Blaine pleased as punch; Creda a little upset at finding herself in any position but that of leading lady. We are all going to fly to the Bayou Teche place—but Averill has told you about it. Do come, darling. Much love, Noel."

When the plane at last circled around the landing field and headed into the wind she adjusted her steel-gray hat, flat and smart with an orange wing upon it, touched her mouth with lipstick and scrutinized her face carefully in the mirror of her compact.

It was a good face, luckily for Eden because it (combined with a really nice figure) had got her her first job as a dress model. She'd had to learn to walk, to stand, to smile infrequently and slowly. Her face had the right planes and shadows; it made up well; her features did not become lost and blurred under the correct fashionable smear of heavy lip paste and elongated eye lines. Her golden-brown hair waved back smoothly from her temples and clung to her head; her eyes were dark gray, well placed and level under slender, thoughtfully arched, black eyebrows.

A sudden, gay spark lighted the gray eyes which stared so earnestly back at her from the tiny mirror.

Picture of a young woman about to do her own matchmaking, she thought, and smiled suddenly and gayly so her whole face changed for an instant as if a ray of sunlight had fallen upon it. Then she was grave again, making quite sure her lipstick had not smeared.

There was of course a certain element of rather wry humor about it; she wasn't at all certain that Noel wanted to marry her.

The plane landed; it was odd that when she walked from the plane, skirt blown tight around her slim legs by the wind from the still whirling propeller, she was carrying the gray chiffon scarf in her hand. And it blew upward against her face suddenly as if it were alive—and putting a warning finger softly, surreptitiously to her lips.

Then she passed the gate and Noel, smiling, was waiting.

He was as spectacularly handsome as ever, his blue eyes blazing so brilliantly from under peaked black eyebrows that it almost startled you. He wore a conventional gray tweed suit with exactly the right shade of blue in his tie and in his handkerchief; he carried a gray Homburg and gray tweed topcoat. And still managed to look somehow daring, audacious, like a gentleman adventurer. It was one of Noel's charms. You always felt as if he would be at his best in balloon-cloth shorts and a sun helmet.

Her heart gave a little pitch of excitement. For that was really the reason she had come: to see Noel.

How did one go about it deliberately to induce a man to propose marriage?

He took both hands and kissed her lightly.

"Hello, my sweet. Lovely as ever, Eden. Come along—the

chauffeur will get your bags. Let me have your checks. Two bags, is that all? Like a cocktail or a cup of tea before we start? It's a longish drive out to Forest Park."

He was piloting her through crowds, past the uniformed chauffeur who waited for them and who took the baggage checks, toward a friendly, bright little restaurant near at hand.

There was a table near a window. He ordered quickly; then smiled and regarded her quizzically.

"Well, my dear. How are you? Do you still love your Noel?"

He said it, however, lightly. Too lightly.

Again her whole project struck her as being grimly funny —except the joke was on her.

"Why are you smiling?" said Noel.

"I was thinking about us—years ago."

She put down her bag. And put down at the same time the long, gray chiffon scarf. Soft, veiling its own merciless strength, spotless.

Noel leaned forward, elbows on the table, blue eyes sparkling and speculative. Eden never saw any change in her own face—change is gradual and is not detected day by day; and indeed at twenty-six Eden's face was not much different than it had been at eighteen except it had lost its girlish chubbiness and had become thinner and finer, with its good modeling a little more marked and thus more beautiful. But Noel, she saw with a little shock, had changed. Not much; no markedly. It was only that the lines around his gay, brilliant eyes were a little sharper; there was a faint brush of gray at his temples, a slightly heavier look around his chin and mouth. That was all. And it affected in no way the look Noel always had of being poised on the brink of adventure. About to step upon the deck of an exploring-bent yacht; about to ride forth upon a galloping charger into conquest, into battle, into romance. He said, smiling:

"Darling, what an enticing topic. As a rule you aren't romantically inclined. I remember it all perfectly. Is there anything you'd like to be reminded of? I can tell you . . ."

"No," said Eden rather sharply—aware it was exactly what she had just told herself she did want. "I must have been a loathsome child."

"You were an adorable child," said Noel instantly. "I fell madly in love with you. If it hadn't been for you, indeed, Averill and I would probably have been married lo, these many years. She wouldn't take me back, you know, after you jilted me. Hello, here's the waiter." The waiter put down a cocktail for Noel, tea and buns for Eden. Noel took his glass and smiled again.

8

"Shall we drink to our mutual memories, Eden? Or can you drink a toast in tea?"

"I don't see why not."

"Here we go, then." Noel put his cocktail to his lips. "To you and to me as we once were. How's that, Eden?"

"More than I could expect," said Eden and grinned a little and lifted her tea.

It was unexpectedly hot and she burned her tongue and put the cup down rather hurriedly. But Noel drank half his cocktail, as one might drink water, thirstily, and ordered another. "Now then, Eden," he said, "how's the business world treating you?"

"It's treated me to a vacation," said Eden. "With, however, a certain complacence. I hope it doesn't mean that it's to be a permanent one."

"Gosh, I hope not. That would be tough." Noel was always readily sympathetic. "Let's see, just what rung have you reached on Fortune's ladder? Last time I saw you, you'd worked up to writing advertising copy."

"I'm still doing it; but I'm not one of the heads, Noel. Not even one of the near heads. It's still a pretty low rung."

"How long will you stay on?"

"Till after the wedding, I suppose. I can fly back the night before I go to work again." She realized she wasn't putting her heart into the business of enticing Noel; how, she thought rather despairingly, could she do it with the single-minded purpose and despatch the occasion demanded?

The second cocktail came and Noel drank it promptly and put down the glass.

"Who's the man Averill's to marry?"

"Jim Cady. He's in the plant." Noel paused and said: "Lucky devil."

"Lucky? Because of Averill, of course."

"Averill and—the Blaine plant. We're getting to be enormously successful, you know, with the manufacturing of airplane engines. And Averill's giving him a large block of Blaine stock as a wedding present."

Nice for him, thought Eden.

"Won't that make rather a lot of family in the company, Noel? I mean—you are the only outside stockholder, aren't you?"

"Yes. But it doesn't matter. Bill and Averill, since Averill's father's death, have owned so much of the stock that my voice is purely moral." He stopped there and laughed a little. "How do you like that? My voice being purely moral?"

"Creda owns stock, too, doesn't she?"

"Oh yes. But not enough for much voting power. Anyway she's Bill's wife—difficult as it is for Creda to remember that."

"I don't know Creda much. Tell me about this Jim Cady. What's he like?"

"Jim? Well—he's a tall fellow; blond originally but always brown and sort of—weathered-looking in a nice way. Looks like a soldier somehow but isn't."

"I means what's he like? He sounds a little calculating."

"Well, Jim knows enough to come in out of the rain. He's doing a pretty good job of feathering his own nest. But that's all right. He's an engineer; crazy about airplanes—always has been, I guess. He's been working on this engine for three years. We're going to make a lot of money out of her. That is, if Jim——" He stopped abruptly.

"If Jim what?"

"Oh—if things go right." He frowned, stared into space for a thoughtful moment, shrugged and said: "Putting on your gloves? I suppose we'll have to make a start. You look sweet—what a nice little hat. Are you pulling it at just the right angle for me? I hope so. The car will be this way."

CHAPTER /2

It was Averill's car waiting for them—long and black and sleek with the smartly uniformed chauffeur driving it smoothly. It was the kind of car Eden had been accustomed to in her childhood, had taken for granted.

The way from the airport to the Blaine house in Forest Park was new to her, however; years ago, when she'd spent vacations with Averill because Averill's home was so near the school, they had come into the Union Station by train.

It was a longish drive. She remembered the gates into the private road which led, among others, to the Blaine house.

She remembered the house when they reached it: huge, a little gloomy, very ugly but extremely comfortable. Velvet lawns, bordered with shrubs, sloped upward toward its wide terraces.

Averill was waiting for them.

It had been two years since Eden had seen Averill. Involuntarily she touched her hair and straightened her hat and hoped she didn't look as tired as she felt.

And stopped on the threshold, as she perceived that Averill stood there, at the foot of the stairs, waiting.

There was a moment of utter silence while they looked at each other.

It was a long look, measuring, instinctively and deeply guarded.

She's not changed, thought Eden swiftly. She's beautiful and poised and certain of herself. Powerful.

The first thought was followed by another, swift, too, and curiously poignant. Averil's eyes had become a little fixed: her white eyelids lowered—then she came forward, smiling. And she was not glad to see Eden.

She said, "There you are," and put out her hands.

She was already dressed for dinner. To Eden in that first glimpse every detail was as sharp and clear as if it were etched in black and white with a steel point. She was as always almost incredibly small and neat and sleek, with her soft dark hair parted precisely in the middle so you saw the white, regular part and folded demurely and neatly upon her small skull into a smooth roll at the back of her long slender neck. She wasn't pretty but she was indubitably chic and so well articulated physically that every attitude and every motion she made seemed carefully planned, part of a pattern. Her face was slender with the flesh stretched rather tightly over a somewhat prominent and high forehead and cheekbones; sometimes her nose and chin would be angular and a little sharp, now they merely gave her small, extraordinarily demure face a certain character. She was always dressed with extreme smartness, liking styles that set off her long neck and slenderness. She wore that night a gown of white dull silk, with a great splash of scarlet across the front; it was almost arrogant in its simplicity of cut and in its daring of design. Only a woman as perfectly poised and as slender as Averill could have appeared with a great scarlet—lobster, was it? Eden wondered, dragon?—splashed upon her diaphragm.

"Eden, my dear," she said and offered her cheek to Eden. Since Eden offered her own cheek simultaneously, the result was not exactly a gesture of affection. "You were dear to come. I hoped you would. Your room is ready, darling. Celeste will unpack for you—I hate to hurry you but dinner will be in another half-hour or so. I expected you rather sooner."

"She lured me into three cocktails," said Noel. "She's learned bad ways in the city."

"I don't imagine you needed much luring," said Averill. Her eyes were brown—a shallow brown, with gray and amber lights, and remote, even at her most friendly moments.

"I'll come with you, Eden dear. Noel—there isn't much time."

"She means hurry up and get dressed. And sober. I am sober, my sweet." He took Averill's hand and kissed it. "If I must drown my troubles in drink, it's you that have brought me to this, Averill," he said. "All right—all right, don't frown. I'll go. Excuse me, Eden. See you both at dinner. Averill, if Pace hasn't yet agreed to buy the engine, he will when you persuade him in that outfit."

"Sh." Averill glanced quickly up the wide stairway. "He's here. He's just arrived—ten minutes ago."

11

Noel's face sobered instantly. "Up there? Oh my God. Well, here's hoping." He ran up the stairway ahead of them. Averill put her arm through Eden's; it was a light, indescribably remote touch, as if there were distance between them. They followed, more slowly.

"Noel's staying here just now," said Averill. "So is Jim. We'll live here, of course, after the wedding. You'll—like Jim. He'll go far. You remember Uncle Bill, of course."

"Of course."

"And Creda. They'll move into a small house after the wedding. Everything is done; all the arrangements have gone wonderfully so far. Now if only this Pace——" Averill's voice never shared the vivacity of her words; it was remote, shallow, unrevealing. It became still more remote when she said: "He'll be stopping here tonight too, and tomorrow. He arrived a few moments ago. Eden, perhaps Noel told you, it's really awfully important to please Pace. I'm putting him between you and me tonight at dinner." She broke off abruptly as footsteps came along the hall above. They reached the top of the steps just as Bill Blaine, big, ruddy-faced, smiling so his cheeks made mere slits of his eyes, loomed up before them—huge and bulky in his dinner jacket.

"My God, it's going to be hot tonight, Averill," he said. "My collar will be gone in five minutes——" He perceived Eden and stopped. "Good heavens," he said, peering. "It's little Eden Shore. Grown up. Kiss me, my dear—or are you too old for that? You used to, you know; and I'd take you and Averill to the movies and feed you on ice-cream sodas."

"How are you, Uncle Bill?" She put up her face dutifully for his kiss and patted his fat shoulder affectionately. And thought, in spite of herself, I would scarcely have known him if I'd met him on the street. Has he changed so much—or have I?

Yet she remembered his extravagant, bluff good humor.

And she thought how intensely alive he seemed—alive, and full of energy and vitality. As if he would go on forever; as if nothing could stop him.

He said then, gayly, as if there were no such thing as mortality, as fate, "Come downstairs when you've changed, dearie, and I'll give you the best cocktail this side the Mississippi. Did you see the old lady as you flew over?"

"She could scarcely miss the river. We'll hurry," said Averill coolly. "I imagine Major Pace will be down soon, Uncle Bill."

"Oh. All right, my dear. All right."

He went down the wide stairs, puffing and singing to himself.

"This way, Eden, the room you always had. Remember it?"

How well she remembered! It was like coming home to a place of luxury and beauty. A maid, fluttering white organdy

12

apron strings above trim black, was already deftly unpacking. A soft green evening gown—a good one, selected with care from the store's French-import room but sold to Eden at cost—lay on the bed. Water was running in the adjoining bathroom and there was the scent of lavender and geranium —clean and clear and sweet.

Averill followed her inside the room and the maid went out, closing the door. Her departure left a sudden, rather strained silence. Eden walked to the mirror, took off her hat and put it down.

"How good it seems to be here," she said. It was a little unnerving to discover that in the sudden silence of the room her voice sounded hollow and false.

Averill said nothing; she was looking at Eden thoughtfully. As if probing again—measuring.

Regretting? Was that it? Did Averill regret having invited her to come, having sent her tickets, having made the trip possible?

But Averill had done it voluntarily, had urged Eden's acceptance.

The thought was not reassuring. Eden was uneasy. She pushed her hands through her hair, watching herself in the mirror, loosening the flattened waves. Conscious of Averill's still regard.

"You've not changed much," said Averill suddenly.

She came nearer Eden, walking as always smoothly but quickly in her white silk, and put out a white small hand and jerked on a dressing-table light so the glow fell directly upon Eden's face.

"You've not changed at all," she said.

Eden smiled a little nervously.

"What did you expect in two years, Averill? Crow's feet? Gray hair?"

Averill didn't smile at all.

"Your job must not be a very hard one."

"Why, really, Averill!" Eden checked her rising irritation. "It's hard enough," she said. "But it hasn't exactly made a physical wreck of me yet."

"It doesn't seem very long," said Averill slowly, "since you were here last. Remember?"

Eden wanted to move away from the mirror—away from Averill. But Averill took a step or two nearer so she stood directly beside Eden, adding her own cool, poised reflection to what the mirror already held. Eden was aware of her own image—her trim gray traveling suit; the jacket long and buttoned in front like a basque, the wide-shouldered gray sleeves faintly leg-o'-mutton; a narrow white band tight around her throat at the collar, her brown hair brushed upward like an old-fashioned print. She was aware of Averill's figure beside her—of her white gown and slender white shoulders and the fantastic scarlet dragon across Averill's incredibly slender body—of her smooth dark hair and the neat white part in it; of a faint odor of lilies—a perfume Averill had always used. She was aware of the glimpses of the room behind them, mahogany and yellow chintz and a green dress carefully laid across the bed.

But the eyes of the two women met in the mirror. And all the rest was only a frame for Averill's small, white face, her shallow, enigmatic brown eyes, holding Eden's fixedly.

"You do remember, don't you?" said Averill.

"I—yes."

"It was a Christmas party. We came on from school."

"Yes."

"You had a crimson skirt and a little moleskin coat and cap and you pinned a sprig of mistletoe on your cap."

"I don't remember that," said Eden—and did remember perfectly and wondered why she had said she hadn't.

"Noel was here," said Averill, her eyes unwavering, holding Eden's in the mirror. "He was waiting for me. We were engaged. Don't you remember? He was waiting for us at the steps and took me in his arms and kissed me and then I said, 'This is Eden, Noel, come to spend the holidays'; and he took your hands and then saw the mistletoe in your cap and kissed you, too."

"That was so long ago."

"Before the Christmas holidays were over—you were engaged to Noel and I had been quite neatly jilted."

"Averill—you were twenty; I was eighteen. And an insufferable eighteen at that," said Eden, striving for lightness.

After a moment Averill smiled, too, quite deliberately and painstakingly.

"Yes, of course," she said. "It's odd how one does remember. I was so proud of showing off Noel to you—you had just won the leading role in the class play. I wanted it. Noel—a Prince Charming in those days and with that fantastic amount of money—seemed to even up the score between us."

"It was Rosalind," said Eden uncomfortably. "Oh, Averill, do you remember the English teacher; the one with the nose?"

"Miss Beecham." Averill's mouth continued to smile; her eyes did not move from Eden's. "Yes. But you got on top again—taking Noel away from me."

With a ridiculous effort, Eden took a long breath and wrenched her eyes away from the reflection and turned face to face with Averill.

"We were children," she said, laughing a little nervously. And added, again striving for lightness, "You know you said in your letter that if it hadn't been for me you wouldn't be marrying your Jim now. You ought to thank me, then."

Her sudden and inexplicably frantic clutch for lightness merely achieved a kind of nervous flippancy.

"Yes," said Averill, still smiling. "My Jim—I must go and see to the table. If you want anything, you'll ring. I'll send Celeste in."

She went away abruptly, except that Averill's motions were never abrupt but always graceful and tidy as a cat's.

The door closed neatly, precisely, behind her. "Ouch," thought Eden. But she was perplexed and uncomfortable, too. She thought back to the affectionate terms of Averill's letter; certainly there was no affection in her greeting. Yet Averill wouldn't have asked her to come if she hadn't wanted her. She shrugged her shoulders and opened her dressing case.

If they had been rivals, then they were so no longer because Averill had won. Had far outdistanced her. Lucky Averill.

Smart Averill, she thought finally—splashing milk-white froth in the enormous tub.

But what a long and extraordinarily exact memory she had!

Slipping the soft folds of green over her shoulders and surveying herself in the long mirror, she found herself curiously pleased because she had taken pains in selecting the gown; there is a certain subtlety in cut and fit and line of a really good gown; it shows off its wearer as the setting of a jewel adroitly flatters the stone it holds.

Celeste, helping her, adjusted the girdle with its long floating ribbon of silver and of violet. She set out silver slippers; she touched and patted Eden's hair. She was silent, unobtrusive, helpful. Eden couldn't remember when she had last been assisted in dressing by a trained and skillful maid. Lucky Averill.

In the corridor outside her door she met Creda.

"Darling!" said Creda. "How wonderful! But, my dear, you look simply sttunning! From what Averill has said I expected you to be quite worn down and aged by the business world! What a perfect gown! You must be terribly prosperous! My dear, you're so marvelously slim!"

After that, "Hello, Creda," seemed inadequate.

"You're looking very stunning yourself, Creda," said Eden. "But then you always do."

Which was true enough. Creda's long lashes dropped over her brown eyes—pansy eyes, soft and warm. She was so very pretty and so very conscious of it that it was curiously obtrusive; it came between you and Creda. She had light blonde hair; she had the most doll-like, round and dimpled face; she had a small, rosebud mouth—she had delicate, fat little hands which fluttered quite a lot; she wore girlish clothes. Inevitably there came a time when one looked at Creda and realized with a kind of jolt that she wasn't a girl in her teens, she was a matured and, perhaps, an extremely selfish woman. For her round, girlish face could suddenly grow a little fixed and hard and her eyes could gleam rather shrewdly from those soft, long eyelashes. She weighed at least thirty pounds more than a girl in her teens would be likely to weigh.

She was, however, very much younger than Bill Blaine; Eden knew that. And so far as Eden knew, their marriage, which had lasted now for five or six years, had been a reasonably happy one.

Creda was, that night, very youthful in a ruffled marquisette, black over white with a demure little-girl collar, and Creda's entire, plump white back was visible through the fine black mesh. She slipped her arm through Eden's and began to talk. Creda's incessant talk, too, was deceiving; it seemed like the frankest, most indiscreet babble—and never told you anything unless Creda wanted you to know it.

Tonight it was sheer babble.

The wedding was going to be simply lovely. It was grand of Eden to come; Averill so loved having her. Averill had always adored Eden—in spite of their differences. Eden would adore Averill's young man. He was too marvelous. He adored Averill. In short, thought Eden rather tersely, everybody adored everybody else and wasn't everything just too ducky!

The others were having cocktails on the terrace just outside the library. Creda fluttered across the room toward the open french windows, beyond which were brightly cushioned chairs and the murmur of voices and the soft clatter of glasses and ice in a cocktail shaker. Eden followed.

Averill was talking vivaciously, a cigarette in her hand. Bill was dispensing cocktails; Noel sprang toward Eden and Creda as they came out the french windows; he was smiling, his eyes like blue stars under his peaked black eyebrows; he was impeccably tailored and triumphantly handsome.

He took Eden's hand and tucked it under one arm and put Creda's fat little hand on his other arm.

Where—oddly, suddenly, it clenched. As if Creda had tripped and clutched at his arm to save herself from falling.

But she hadn't tripped. She hadn't indeed taken a step and was standing perfectly still.

Eden happened to see that. Then Noel said:

"May I present Major Pace?"

Major Pace was short, fat and curiously buoyant; he was half bald, with knowing, heavy-lidded eyes set in a swarthy face. He bowed and Eden put out her hand briefly. Then he moved to Creda and the little, white fat hand on Noel's dark sleeve slowly unclinched itself, withdrew from Noel's arm and was placed in Major Pace's thick-fingered, dark hand.

"How do you do," said Creda.

They've met somewhere before, thought Eden unexpectedly. And then Noel said:

"And this, Eden darling, is Jim."

She looked up. Into a brown face, straight and, somehow, soldierly. That was her first fleeting impression. Then Jim's eyes caught her own and held them. Neither spoke.

Perhaps three seconds passed. It seemed much longer, for in those three seconds something came to life that was never to be stifled, some boundary was crossed that could never be recrossed, some secret was discovered and could never be undiscovered again.

"Well——" said Noel.

As if it came from a great distance Eden heard Noel's voice, roused and slowly put her hand toward Jim. He took it as slowly.

"So—you're Eden."

"Haven't we——" began Eden. He finished it for her.

"Haven't we met before? No—I should have remembered."

A little ring of stillness encompassed them. There were voices, there was laughter and movement all about but it was outside that invulnerable, encompassing ring.

Not quite invulnerable. For Eden was finally aware that Averill had approached them.

"You're to take Eden in to dinner, Jim. I want you two to know each other."

Eden sought for words and found none. Averill turned to reply to something someone else said; everyone was talking. Quite suddenly the isolation, the enfolding ring of stillness, deeply shared, was gone but it left a poignant memory that was almost like a shock except it was so sweet.

Someone in Eden's clothes, wearing her face, answering to her name, smiled, spoke, drank a champagne cocktail that was put in her hand. Afterwards Eden told herself it was the cocktail and the champagne.

But when they went into dinner and she brushed momentarily against Jim's arm—when they sat at the candlelighted, lace-draped table with the great pool of crimson roses in the middle of it, and her hand accidentally touched Jim's, when they turned and again looked almost searchingly into each other's eyes—she felt actually drunk. So the light pressure of arm against arm, the actually fleeting brush of his hand against her own lasted for moments afterward.

Her heart was confused, tremulous in its beating. Little waves of the maddest exultation ran along her pulses.

Something indescribable had happened to her; it had happened instantly, without warning. The roses were redder; their perfume sweeter. The flames of the candles, the soft talk and laughter, the warm summer night—all of it had all at once a sharp, deep significance that was mysterious. But it was deeply provocative, too, as if she were on the threshold of a new, terribly exciting world.

"I'm drunk," she thought. "It's the champagne. It's———"

And Jim turned to her and spoke.

"You came," he said slowly, "for the wedding. That's why you came———" He stopped, as if only then aware that he was speaking.

But that was right of course; he was to marry Averill. On Friday.

Averill. Who had won when it was important.

Besides there was Noel and her own deliberate, thought-out decision to marry Noel if he could be induced to ask her.

CHAPTER / 3

Dinner must have taken its prescribed, leisurely course; Eden must have moved, eaten, replied when spoken to. Averill, Noel and Major Pace did most of the talking. Bill, as always, drank more than he talked, listened blandly, smiled good-naturedly at everything and offered no opinions that were not of the most general nature. Noel was charming with Creda who sat at one side of him; Averill was adroit with Major Pace who was suave, polished and urbane—unexpectedly graceful in conversation.

Creda, who usually talked a great deal, said almost nothing and was nervous; she avoided Pace's eyes, yet once Eden saw her watching him with almost deadly seriousness from behind her deceptively demure eyelashes.

And Jim, after that one checked remark, said almost literally nothing.

She wouldn't look at Jim. She wouldn't even let herself look at his hand—brown, lean, with strength and perception in its wiry slenderness—which lay on the lace cloth beside hers for a moment. Wouldn't look at it because when she did she so desperately wanted to touch it. To feel it turn so her own hand could nestle within it.

It was a mad thought—as the night was mad. She forced herself to listen to the talk, and they were speaking of the flight the next day.

"I'm going up, you know," said Averill to Major Pace.

His smile complimented her; his eyes remained cold and disapproving.

"Jim took her up when she was first set up in the plane———" began Bill when Averill interrupted.

"The feminine pronoun here refers always and exclusively to the engine," she said to Major Pace.

Bill went on: "Jim and one of the mechanics took the engine up for the first time. Now it's my turn and Averill's."

"You liked the engine's behavior in the air?" inquired Major Pace.

"She's a honey," said Noel. "When you see her actually perform, Major, you're going to be even keener than you are now."

Again there was a cold, remote look in Pace's dark eyes.

"I must see the engine perform, naturally," he said.

Averill glanced once at Noel.

"Naturally," she said to Pace. "Shall you be in America long, Major? Or ought I ask?"

Pace smiled.

"One never knows," he said.

Averill, refusing to be rebuffed, accepted it smilingly.

"We'll have coffee on the terrace," she said and rose. The men did not linger over the table but strolled with Averill and Eden and Creda along the wide wall, across the shadowy library and again onto the terrace. It was by that time a soft, deep twilight. Cocktail glasses had been removed and the butler brought a tray with coffee and another with liqueurs. There were cigarettes and deep-cushioned chairs and soft fragrances from the garden below.

But all at once it was not tranquil.

For Noel almost immediately went into the library and returned with a roll of blueprints.

Eden sought a deep armchair a little at one side. She must talk; she must behave as if nothing had happened; later she could define the wave of emotion that had caught her—if she had to; conquer it as she must. But just now she must be sure that no one guessed.

She was thankful for the immediate interest of all those others when Bill Blaine cleared a place on a long, glass-topped table with a sweep of his big hands and Noel spread out the roll of blueprints, holding them flat with his hands.

For instantly there was a kind of taut little motion among them as if an invisible thread attached to each had given a little jerk and pulled them all upright and alert.

Major Pace walked over to stand beside Noel; he looked curiously strong—almost threatening, standing there with his thick pudgy hands spread out upon the blueprints.

"We'll need these, Mr. Carreaux. If the trial flight is satisfactory."

"It will be," said Noel. "I can assure you of that."

"I hope so."

"There's no doubt of it," said Bill Blaine. He was lounging back in a cushioned chair, his shirt front bulging, his face a little red, the stem of the tiny glass he held looking absurdly

19

fragile in his great hand. "Tell him, Jim, what a superb performance the engine gave us."

"You tell him," said Jim shortly.

Bill Blaine glanced sharply at him, frowned and sat up.

"Now look here, Jim, you needn't act like that. If you don't want to sell the engine, we won't sell it. We've told you that any number of times."

"The engine is yours to sell," said Jim briefly.

There was a little silence. Pace, thick and stolid with his fat hands spread upon the blueprints, did not move and was taking in not only every word, Eden suddenly felt sure, but every nuance of meaning that lay behind words.

Averill turned like a slender, sleek column in white to look thoughtfully at Jim—thoughtfully and a little angrily. Eden knew what that small tightening of her mouth meant. Creda put her liqueur glass to her lips and set it down again with a small clatter.

Then Bill heaved himself out of the deep chair, went to Jim and put his great hand on Jim's shoulder.

"Now look here, my boy," he said bluffly. "We own the engine legally, that's true. But you've made it; we all realize that. And no matter how definitely it seemed to us to be to our mutual advantage to sell it to Major Pace—we won't do it if you don't want us to. You must believe that."

"You know exactly how I feel, Bill. I'm afraid I can't change."

Major Pace removed his hands from the blueprints and they rolled together with a soft little whisper.

"You understand, Mr. Carreaux," he said to Noel, "I've made my best offer. I am not, as you know confidentially, acting for myself. I can't go a penny higher than the price I've been empowered to offer and my offer is, of course, contingent upon the success of the flight tomorrow."

"I understand that, Major," said Noel in a placative way.

"Then may I ask Mr. Cady's objections to selling?" said Pace.

Averill made a little motion with her hands as if to stop Jim but he replied promptly:

"Certainly, Major Pace. It's simply that I hoped to manufacture the engine ourselves. Here in our own plant."

"That means then that your market would be limited."

"Jim——" began Noel uneasily but Jim said:

"Limited to what?"

"Why, to American firms, of course," said Major Pace.

"Naturally," said Jim Cady after a pause.

"Oh. Then your real reason for objecting is not that you object to selling your product but that you object to selling to my country?"

"Just what is your country, Major Pace?" said Jim quietly.

20

"Jim, that's not fair," said Noel quickly. And Bill Blaine said as quickly:

"That was in the bargain. We agreed not to ask and not to try to find out. Major Pace has been absolutely open and frank with us about that. And he has given us the best guarantee of his good faith he could possibly give. He's deposited in escrow the money we've agreed on as the price of the engine pending the success of the trial flight. The negotiations are finished. The deal's closed. Or will be if the engine performs all right tomorrow." He stopped suddenly, as if checked by a sudden thought, his small eyes narrowed till they became suspicious, angry slits and he said: "And it'll perform, Jim. Understand? No monkey business——"

"*Bill!*" cried Creda on a breathless, high note of protest.

Bill caught himself quickly.

"I spoke hastily, Jim," he said with an air of bluff apology. "But business is business. We can make more out of the engine this way than in any other way. Now's the time to sell. A year from now—two years from now, God knows what will have happened! Averill agrees with me. And Noel. If we didn't want to be fair, we wouldn't consult you at all——"

"I know, Bill," said Jim. "You needn't apologize. And you needn't worry. Pace's—money—the money from whatever country he represents—is as good as in your pocket." He walked across the veranda and stopped beside Averill. "I'll let you settle details. Will you come with me, Averill, for—for a walk in the garden?"

There was a little silence. Then she shook her head.

"I'd better stay here, Jim." Her voice was perfectly polite and pleasant and Averill was angry. Furious because he had rebelled. Because he had gone against her wishes. Because he had held his own view. Eden, knowing Averill, knew that. She stood like a brooding queen in her white gown, with the great scarlet dragon blazed across her slender body like a sign of royalty and of despotism.

Averill had never graciously suffered being crossed.

Jim said pleasantly: "Very well—I'll go for a smoke."

He went down the steps, leaving a little, uncomfortable silence behind him. Then Averill moved toward the table. "Will you bring me a chair, Noel?" she said. "Now then— these are copies of the complete, revised plans. I telephoned to the office and asked Dorothy to make sure. They include everything—isn't that right, Noel? Will you tell him——"

Noel's pleasant voice took up the burden of it. And Eden rose quietly, went to the steps nearest her and, unobserved or at least not stopped by any one of the group around the table, went down into the shadowy garden. She had seen the look on Jim's face when he passed her and she wanted to be with him.

21

CHAPTER /4

It was the first time she heard Dorothy's name; Dorothy—that enigmatic, self-restrained, pale young woman.

Dorothy. Eden, only half aware of it, noted the name and realized that she was connected somehow with the offices at the Blaine plant. That was all.

The thick shrubs below the terrace gave place to a wide strip of velvet lawn with steps at the end of it. These steps, again, led into a turf path, heavily bordered with shrubs, leading in its turn presumably to the garden. It was deep twilight now, with a few fireflies, and stars far above. She could barely see Jim's broad shoulders and the light of his cigarette as it vanished into the deeper shadow of the path. She followed, her slippered feet quiet on the cool turf below them.

The path ran between hedges for a way and emerged into a garden—wide, oval, with turf paths among flowers. In the center, barely visible in the twilight, was a pool with a wide balustrade running around it and Jim stood leaning upon the balustrade, smoking.

"Jim——"

She was near enough to see his shoulders stiffen a little. Then he turned and said: "Oh—it's you."

"Yes." She put her arms upon the balustrade; it felt cool to her skin. She leaned over to look into the pool which returned a dim, dreamy reflection of deep blue sky and stars and a blotch of shadow where she and Jim stood.

"Cigarette?" said Jim and held his case toward her. She took it and bent to a light, and as he held it she caught a glimpse of his face—fine and brown. He was frowning thoughtfully.

"Well," he said, "I made rather a scene, didn't I?"

"Rather. But why not? It's your engine."

"That's where you're wrong."

"You made it."

"I was paid for making it."

"But, Jim—wasn't there any understanding about it? I mean—you've worked on it a long time, haven't you?"

He hesitated and then said simply, "Yes. Old Blaine took me in as a kid, gave me an education, gave me a job—started to build airplane engines. This engine is almost literally the—sum of it. Well, I hate to sell it like this. That's all."

"What's Pace going to do with it?"

Jim shrugged.

"It's the armament race. It's a good engine; it's powerful,

light-weight, air-cooled and cheap to manufacture—thus desirable. I don't mean that if any war comes along this engine's going to decide its outcome or any such nonsense as that. No one engine—no one machine—no one tank or gun design can do that. But the next war—if war there is, which God forbid—is going to be a war in the air. Trench warfare, heavy, massed armies are a thing of the past. The whole thing in another war will be mobility. Fleets of lorries and trucks, fast-moving units; planes." He smoked for a moment and then began to talk again. "Defense is made up of one device plus another device, plus another device. It's the old, weighty argument of the majority being made up of one plus one plus one—repeated the most times. Well—my engine is one of those devices. That's all."

"That's—if there's war?"

"That's whether there's war or not. I'm not alone in the belief that war will be fought or peace defended in the air."

He leaned on the balustrade and after a moment went on as simply as if life together stretched ahead of them:

"Sometime we'll go up in the air together. So you can look down with me upon the panorama below—the broad fields and the wooded mountains and silver rivers. Industry; homes; freedom; all material wants spread out freely, lavishly, for the taking. That's America. My country," said Jim Cady, "and yours."

"You're too young to have been in the war."

"My father was. He was killed in the Argonne. I was old enough to remember it. But then, every generation of American families since the founding of the first American colonies has had to breed soldiers. I'm talking a lot."

"Go on."

"Oh, that's all. It just seems to me to be common sense not to sell the thing—like this. Well, they're going to get a good price for it."

"How much?"

"Two hundred thousand dollars for all patents, all plans and the model itself. Free and perpetual and exclusive use of it from now on."

"Are you—will you share in that?"

There was a little pause. Then Jim said in a voice that quite suddenly held reserve and a little strain in it: "Not directly."

Eden waited. Instantly the complete and spontaneous understanding that made their talk possible vanished.

Jim said—again in a reserved voice, the voice of a stranger:

"Averill—is giving me a large block of stock. It—it sounds a bit odd. It isn't, really. Old Blaine and I had a kind of understanding; he intended to give me a share in the company; he told me so and he told others many times. But he died and it wasn't done. I didn't urge it; I was busy—engrossed in work; I didn't care. But it's all right; I really have earned it and I know it; if Averill wants to turn it over to me in just that way, it's all right with me. Noel and Bill both agree. It—it doesn't really matter."

Except, thought Eden with flash of comprehension, that Jim was going to be under obligation to Averill for something he had actually and really earned.

Jim went on rather abruptly:

"You're awfully good, you know—to listen to all this. I—forgive me, won't you. You see you came along at a time when I——" He stopped.

She turned toward him, waiting, and he was looking down through the dusk into her face. She started to speak—and forgot what she'd intended to say. There was a long, hushed moment, deeply expectant.

Then Jim moved and dropped his cigarette into the pool. There was a little hiss as it struck the water; a bird stirred somewhere in the shrubbery.

It happened suddenly, without warning.

Jim all at once leaned nearer, very close above her; instinctively, irresistibly, without knowing she was going to do it, she put up her mouth to meet his. Their lips met quickly and instantly drew apart.

It hadn't been planned; it was an indescribably brief, impulsive gesture. It was less a definite, intentional act than it was a moment of reality, a moment of being off guard, a moment of surrender to a deep inner compulsion. So new a compulsion that neither of them had yet recognized and labeled it as forbidden and set up a barricade against it.

They drew instantly apart. Neither spoke. As if still moved by that mysterious compulsion they turned and walked slowly through the silent dusk together toward the path. Halfway along the path Jim said:

"Eden—please do believe me. I can't apologize."

He was right, of course; apology would be absurd. Explanation would be dangerous. Any possible words were better left unsaid.

"Of course."

He swung around toward her, trying to see her face through the dusk.

"Eden——"

She wished the brief touch of his mouth didn't cling so warmly to her lips. She took a long breath and said abruptly:

"I know. Shall we go on?"

"I wonder if you do know."

She caught herself on the very verge of swaying a little toward him, irresistibly again. As naturally as her breath came and her heart beat. She said a little unsteadily, almost frightened:

"Averill is waiting."

Averill. And a wedding, four days away. Suppose they did feel that they'd known each other since the world was set in motion; that was all wrong. She and the man beside her had met for the first time an hour—two hours ago and he was to marry Averill.

And, now, Averill stood like a sword, like an implacable empress all in white, between them.

Jim said:

"Yes, of course. But anyway, thanks, Eden."

"Thanks——"

"For being you. All right, shall we go on?"

Impulse, Eden told herself, walking beside him. Put it down to impulse and forget it.

But Averill couldn't begrudge her so small, so brief a thing as that unheralded kiss, taking them both unaware and unarmed, had been.

Yet she walked beside him without consciousness, really, of anything but their nearness to each other, of the dusk holding them both, of the air they both breathed.

It hadn't been the champagne at dinner. She hadn't been the victim of a mad delusion. The fact was she loved him.

Queer, she thought presently, how little love concerned itself with time! Or for that matter with one's will. With millions of men in the world, she'd had to fall in love with the man whom in four days Averill Blaine was to marry.

There was a kind of ironic humor in that, too. But it was no good trying to laugh about it, even to herself.

They reached the steps too soon. Averill, poised and certain of herself and of Jim, would be waiting.

However, no one really was waiting except Bill Blaine who was sunk in the depths of a lounge chair with his bulging shirt front showing dimly white in the dusk. Long areas of light from the library windows streamed out onto the terrace and the empty chairs.

"Where's everybody?" said Jim.

"Creda's strolling with Pace; you must have met them. Noel's gone in to telephone the weather bureau again. Averill's somewhere around."

Jim walked over to the table; Eden hesitated and sat down in the shadow near Bill.

"Where are the plans?" said Jim.

"Averill took them inside. Looks as if we'd better make the flight pretty early tomorrow, Jim. Noel says there's threatened rain and fog tomorrow."

"It's clear now. But you can make it any time. Engine's all tuned up. Mike worked on her all day."

25

"Mike's a good mechanic. None better. Well, all differences between us aside, Jim, I'll do my best to show off the engine tomorrow."

"I'm sure you will," said Jim dryly. "I'm going to turn in."

"You're staying here tonight, aren't you?"

"Yes."

The screened door to the library opened and Noel came swinging out from the band of light.

"It's an early flight tomorrow," he said. "Oh—you here, Jim? Or is it Pace?"

"It's me," said Jim. "What's the latest report?"

"Girl says clear tonight; probably early morning. Showers or possibly fog by seven o'clock."

"It's an early start all right." Bill heaved himself out of his deep chair and put down the end of his cigarette. "I'll turn in, too."

Noel found Eden in the shadow and came to her.

"Let's stroll, Eden, shall we?"

He was smiling a little in the dusk and reached out to take her hand. It was with almost a start that she remembered why she had come to Averill's wedding. To see Noel; to—however one did such things—persuade him to fall in love with her again; and to marry him—cold-bloodedly, purposefully.

And nothing was actually changed. She still needed Noel exactly as she had needed him three hours ago. She mustn't allow herself to forget that.

But she said:

"I—I can't, Noel. If we go to the field early to watch the flight——"

Noel said: "And that means early. All right, dear. See you in the morning."

There was a general movement toward the stairs; it was still fairly early but a feeling of drama and suspense in connection with the flight had already caught at them. Whisky, soda water and glasses were on a table in the hall, and they stopped to drink. Averill came in from some room off the other side of the hall, told Jim that she had put the plans away and took a splash of whisky in a large glass of soda water. Curiously Eden found it almost impossible to look at Jim yet she was actually aware of everything he said and every motion he made. While they were talking in a desultory way of the flight and drinking, Creda and Major Pace entered from the front door.

Pace's swarthy face was blank and impassive as always. Creda looked a little pale and took more whisky than Noel, pouring it, expected her to take for he gave her a quick, surprised look. Pace lifted his glass and said, smiling:

"To the flight. And to the flyer."

Averill, touching her lips to her glass, smiled back at Pace and said:

"Uncle Bill is an expert flyer. There's nobody better."

"Good," said Pace and drank—dark eyes cold and expressionless above the rim of his glass.

There was a little commotion of good nights and of general movement toward the stairs.

Once in her own room, Eden closed the door and stood there for a moment, letting herself think.

The room was orderly and peaceful; the bed turned down, the light burning on the night table, a plate of sandwiches and a thermos of milk beside it. Roses from a vase on another table made a soft fragrance that took her back—if she had needed to be taken back—to that unexpected instant in the garden with Jim.

So small a thing. How could she give it emphasis! When Noel had kissed her, when big Bill Blaine had kissed her it was an equally brief little gesture. Wholly casual and trivial, nothing to give a second thought.

But because it was Jim, it was altogether different.

The strangest inner tumult possessed her. She moved at last and drifted to the window and stood there, trying to look down into the starlit dusk. Away down there, beyond that black and shadowy border, barely discernible now in the darkness, she had stood with Jim.

She wished, suddenly and honestly, that he had taken her in his arms when he kissed her. It was the only time it was ever to happen.

And that thought was as dangerous as words between her and Jim might have been. It unloosed other thoughts which must not be permitted existence. And it was again bitterly ironical that at that moment Averill came.

She knocked and came in and Eden went to meet her.

She was still dressed in the clinging white silk. She carried a cigarette and a glass of milk. She said with a smile that she had come for a little gossip.

"As we used to do," she said, smiling thinly. "That is, unless you're too tired. There's milk in the thermos over there. Shall I pour a glass for you?"

She did so and brought it to Eden and insisted on lighting Eden's own cigarette and made Eden take the chaise longue and stuffed laced pillows under Eden's arms.

"There we are," she said. She sat down on the foot of the chaise longue. "No, don't move. I'm perfectly comfortable. This is like old times, isn't it? Did you find everything you need? Ring for Celeste to help you undress. She never minds latish hours. Not that this one is late. Well, my dear, what do you think of my choice for a husband?"

Jim.

Eden drank slowly, giving herself time.

"Do you like him?" insisted Averill, watching her.

She must reply steadily and she must remember that Averill was quick and sharp as a cat.

"Yes."

"I thought so," said Averill after an infinitesimal pause. "I think you can always tell when people like each other. Don't you think so? There's something—oh, something quite indefinable but quite unmistakable in the atmosphere."

"Dear me. That's almost second sight."

"I'm not blind," said Averill. "I thought you and Jim got along extremely well tonight."

Decidedly, Eden thought rather desperately, she must pull herself together. It was always difficult to duel with Averill. It would be more than difficult tonight. She said:

"We had a little talk in the garden tonight—while the rest of you were talking of the plans——"

"I know," said Averill, interrupting neatly and incisively. "That's what I came to talk to you about."

"Really, Averill! Why?"

A little light away back in Averill's shallow brown eyes brightened. She said slowly and in her usual unrevealing, flat voice:

"Jim is wrong about the engine, you know."

It was as if a little voice warned Eden to be careful. She drank again and put down her glass slowly.

"Jim is—Jim seemed to regret the necessity to sell it," she said cautiously.

"You needn't explain Jim to me, darling," said Averill. "I am to marry him, you know."

Obviously there was no answer to that.

"But it was terribly sweet of you to follow Jim down into the garden," continued Averill. "I'm sure Jim must have appreciated it."

For a fantastic moment Eden wondered if Jim's kiss were visible on her mouth. And she had an equally fantastic impulse to say coolly: "Why, yes, Averill, I have every reason to think he did."

She said instead: "Why, really, Averill, I don't think there was much to appreciate. And in any case——"

"In any case, it's nothing to you, you were about to say," finished Averill and laughed softly. "But naturally, darling! How could it affect you! He'll soon forget about it and will see that I'm right. He's——" She stopped and snuffed out her cigarette in the crystal ash tray; her white, slender fingers were very steady. "He's very much in love with me, you know. Seriously, Eden, don't you think I'm a lucky girl?"

"Very lucky."

"And you do like him?"

"Why, yes. Yes, of course, Averill."

"I thought so. I did want you," said Averill quite slowly, "to see him."

Her words, soft, remote, yet full of meaning, hung in the air between them and became significant. Became suddenly so sharp and bright and salient that they clarified the whole situation.

For that was exactly what Averill did want. That was why she had asked her to come, why she had sent her a ticket, why she had insisted. To show her the man she, Averill, was marrying.

It was as if she had said: Look, observe this man, this wedding, all the luxurious and fortuitous circumstances of my life. All mine. Admit that I am enviable.

Thus paying up past scores. Chalked down long ago; stored carefully in her extraordinarily tenacious memory.

Well, if she had wanted to arouse Eden's envy, she had succeeded. How thoroughly Eden only hoped Averill would never know.

Averill smiled and leaned over and patted Eden's arm. "We've always been such friends, darling. I wanted you to see how happy I am. To see my lovely wedding. And I'm so terribly glad you and Jim liked each other." Her fingers stiffened a little. She went on, still smiling: "You look really handsome tonight, Eden—although it never seems to me that green is quite your color. If Jim weren't so very much in love with me, I would be afraid of your taking him away from me. As you did with Noel."

"Don't be absurd! That was very different."

"Very different. Besides, that time, it wasn't just four days before my wedding. No, I don't advise you to try to take Jim."

"I assure you I don't intend to."

"Eden, darling, don't mind my little jokes." Averill was smiling painstakingly. "It's only because I'm so very happy. Tomorrow I must show you Jim's wedding gift to me. An emerald. I chose it myself. Now go to bed, dear; don't sit there dreaming as you were when I came in. Shall I ring for Celeste?"

"No. Thank you, Averill. Good night."

The door closed.

After a while Eden got up and began to unfasten her dress. Her fingers were curiously awkward and fumbling. The strap of her sandal caught and tore.

No more looking out the window, dreaming. Dreaming—Averill had caught that, too.

She went to bed and tried to read and the print was a blur. At last she turned out the bed light and lay there in the darkness.

Curious, she thought once, how extraordinarily restless the house seemed that night. Twice at least she thought she heard someone pass her bedroom door. Once certainly she heard voices below her on the terrace, for her room was directly above the library.

Yet she must have slept eventually for it was with a desperate dragging of herself up from some nether world of unconsciousness that she heard the maid's knocking at her door.

It was barely dawn. But it was clear.

She dressed hurriedly, drinking the coffee the maid brought to her room, putting a warm white sports coat over her green sweater and white tweed skirt.

Averill, neat and smart in a pale blue knitted suit with a thick yellow coat, was waiting with Creda in the hall. There was no hint of the little scene of the previous night in her words or manner. But then nothing had been said—nothing and everything. Outside the luxurious big car was already drawn up at the steps. The others, Averill said briefly, had gone on. And she wasn't going up with Bill after all.

"Jim thought the mechanic, Mike Strevsky, ought to go. He's worked on the engine and he wanted to. It didn't matter so much to me. It was only sentiment."

They said little on the way to the field. It was barely light but the sky was a great clear bowl above them. Creda looked haggard, twice her age, with deep circles under her soft brown eyes; she smoked constantly and nervously. Averill's marked features were sharp and a little stern. But then four o'clock in the morning was not a flattering hour for anyone.

It was, however, nearer five when they reached the field, and much lighter. They went through the gates. There were clusters of men here and there—not many of them. Workmen in brown overalls; a handful of cars.

The field itself was a great rectangular plot of ground, well drained and well fenced, lying behind the sprawling red brick building that housed the Blaine Company plant. It was entered only by padlocked gates, by the factory itself and by air.

There were not many cars and not many people. And at one side, near enough so they could distinguish Jim and Noel and Major Pace among the cluster of men beside it, was the plane.

Eden caught a quick breath at sight of the sleek, silver-colored plane; it was trim, beautiful, almost alive—vibrant and eager to be off, for the propeller was already whirring and, even before the chauffeur cut off their automobile engine, they could hear the smooth, powerful beat of the engine in the plane.

The sun was up, making a clear black shadow of wings upon the field. Jim, head bare and a brown leather jacket tossed over his shoulders, was talking to Bill, who looked huge in his jacket and helmet. Noel was talking, too, eagerly. Major Pace unslung field glasses.

"Let's get out of the car," said Averill. "We can see better."

They did so; the beat of the plane engine seemed instantly louder. Eden had eyes only for the plane and for the tall, leather-jacketed figure there beside Bill. Then, all at once, Bill climbed into the cockpit where another man already waited for him.

Eden touched Averill's arm.

"Isn't there an ambulance——" she shouted above the din in their ears.

Averill shook her head without looking at Eden.

"It's not a test flight."

Bill waved to someone below. Quite suddenly, the little crew of brown figures moved backward, the engine roared and the plane taxied gently across the field like a great dragonfly and then rose.

Smoothly, effortlessly, superbly.

The sun shone against the silver sides; the blue sky outlined its grace.

The plane rose and soared and made a great circle. All below stood as if transfixed, watching. Listening to the more distant, smooth hum of the engine.

It came down nearer, swooped like a beautiful, tremendous bird and rose again in another and greater circle. Rose higher and higher.

Averill said in a hushed way: "He must be ten thousand feet——"

And presently the chauffeur standing beside them said: "He's higher still. It must be fifteen——"

The plane was smaller and still smaller. A black object now moving against glaring blue sky.

A black object that began to grow larger again.

"Bill's doing stunts," said Averill.

"Stunts——" said Creda and stopped as if her breath had caught.

And then the chauffeur said, "Oh, my God." His voice rose and he screamed: "Oh, my God, there's smoke. It's on fire——"

Eden saw it now, too. Smoke; a flame darting became instantly flames, banners of terror, of disaster.

"He's sideslipping—he's trying to keep the flames out of

31

the cockpit—he can't slip all the way down—oh, my God!" shouted the chauffeur and ran a few steps heavily, blunderingly, and stopped. For he could do nothing.

That was the worst of it. There was nothing anybody could do.

Eden couldn't move. Someone—Creda?—clutched hard at one of her hands. Nobody could move except those men running out on the field—and they too were helpless, unable to stop it, unable to do anything but watch.

The flames spread like wind; the thing that had been a plane, that had been a black object in the sky, was nearer, a flaming mass.

Bill Blaine was a skilled and expert flyer. In the seconds allotted to him, he did everything skill and experience dictated.

He sideslipped; he sideslipped again.

He cut off the engine when he could do no more.

Just before it struck someone screamed and screamed again. And then there was an earth-rocking crash at the end of the field. A sickening crash—and clouds of black smoke.

It released that paralysis of horror and helplessness.

Instantly men were running, shouting. Somewhere, suddenly, the scream of a siren rose.

Averill covered her face with her hands. Creda relinquished Eden's numb hand, turned around, took a step toward the car as if she didn't know what she was doing and went down in a stumbling heap on the ground.

Eden must have bent over her. The chauffeur was running toward the smoke, sobbing hoarsely and loudly. Everybody was running—Averill, too. Eden tried to lift Creda and succeeded in half dragging her to the running board of the car where she sat down and put Creda's head in her lap and tried to rub Creda's wrists and could only stare with a horror of fascination at the black smoke out on the field. After a while a red fire truck hurled across the field, men clinging to the sides of it. Somewhere in the distance an ambulance was already wailing raucously, coming nearer.

She was sick and shivering. She put her arm over her eyes and tried not to look. On the ground below lay a key and she picked it up.

It was a key to a Yale lock and Eden fumbled it and turned it in her fingers and then forgot it while she stared in spite of herself at the pandemonium before her, at the black smoke. Away up above in the cloudless blue dome a skylark mounted and sang.

CHAPTER /5

From the first fractional instant when that burst of flame, so swift to envelop the plane, was seen there had been perhaps little hope that Bill Blaine would be able to save himself and he hadn't been able to do so. The end was swift, between two breaths. All of them thought first and mainly of Bill Blaine. And then of the mechanic who had gone with him.

"Both men," said Noel hours later, "died instantly when they crashed. It happened—like that." He was lighting a cigarette as he spoke and he flicked the light from his match with a nervous, quick gesture. "Bill had only an instant or two of comprehension. None of pain; I could swear to that. Do believe me."

Another somber silence followed his words. The hours intervening between the nightmare of the early morning and the scene in the Blaine library later in the day were vague and confused in Eden's memory. She remembered that Averill and the chauffeur had returned at last, alone, to the car where she still sat with Creda on the running board. The chauffeur had looked sick and white. Averill was like a pale automatic doll. She'd said simply: "They are both dead. We'll go home now. The others will come later." And the chauffeur had driven slowly, as if it was a funeral cortege, all the way home with nobody speaking. Once there, Averill had got a doctor for Creda; Creda was now, mercifully, drugged and supposed to be sleeping.

And then they had waited for the others. Once Averill had said queerly: "I intended to fly with Bill. If Jim hadn't stopped me I would have gone."

That was all. It was afternoon when the others came. Noel white, eyes brilliant with excitement; Jim white, too; his face like a mask. Pace apparently unmoved except his little heavy-lidded eyes were so observant.

Dorothy Woolen came along with them and someone remembered to introduce her, Jim's secretary, to Eden; Eden looked at her briefly and without much interest—a plump, phlegmatic, colorless girl, with pale face and lips, pale, straight, blonde hair done with a braid around her head, pale green eyes with no expression in them. She wore a dark, neat suit and was curiously self-effacing.

They had done everything, Noel said, that was to be done. And he tried again to reassure them; the merciful thing had been the swiftness of it.

"Neither of them knew," he repeated. "There wasn't time."

Jim got up and went to the window and stood with his back to the room and his hands plunged into his pockets.

"The thing is," he said, "it oughtn't to have happened."

"Mr. Cady," said Major Pace suddenly, "just what happened? Why did the plane crash?"

Jim turned around.

"I don't know. There was nothing wrong anywhere. Bill wouldn't have taken her up—we wouldn't have let him take her up if there'd been any question. But there wasn't——"

"We've covered everything," said Noel wearily. "There's nothing to account for it. We've had the engine running as long as fifty hours on the testing table. This morning she was in perfect shape. We started her going and she ran for perhaps fifteen minutes or so before the take off. Sweet as honey. You were there, Pace. You heard."

"But you, Mr. Cady," persisted Pace in a gentle voice. "What's your opinion?"

Jim turned toward Pace.

"Opinion! Good God, I haven't any. It's obvious something went wrong. But nothing—nothing could go wrong. Bill was an expert flyer."

Noel rose again and went quickly to Jim and put his hand on Jim's shoulder.

"But something did go wrong, old fellow," he said. "You couldn't have helped it. You aren't responsible. The engine passed all the tests. Don't take it so hard."

"The point is," said Averill suddenly and very coolly, "is Major Pace still in the market for the engine?"

It wasn't what anyone had expected. Jim gave Averill a queer, long look and turned again abruptly toward the window. Dorothy Woolen blinked. Even Pace looked startled, as if pulled up short, and Noel said:

"My God, Averill. What——"

"Listen, Noel. The flight was a failure. But Jim is sure it wasn't the engine." Averill turned smoothly to Pace; she linked her small, calm hands on her knee and said: "The engine can be rebuilt, you know, Major Pace. It will take some time but Jim has all the plans, all the tools; he won't be held up again waiting for patterns and jigs to be made. If time is an element with you, and I understand that it is, it will take only a short time to rebuild the engine. And if this—thing this morning was due to a fault in the engine, that fault will be discovered and corrected."

"Averill——" Jim began and Averill stopped him.

"Jim, darling, I know how dreadful this seems to you now. But I still have faith in the engine. If this was due to some flaw, you can find it and correct it. The main principle of the engine——"

"Listen, Averill," said Jim, "if the accident was not an

accident but some flaw in the engine then I can't rebuild it successfully for I don't know what that flaw is. I would have staked my life on this one being among the best that have ever been developed. That's not boasting, it's just the truth. Do you think I would have let Bill take her up if I'd not known that?"

"You wouldn't let me go," said Averill suddenly and softly.

Jim gave her an incredulous look. He went so white he looked sick. He said:

"Averill—you can't mean I had any doubt——"

"That's a beastly thing to say, Averill," cried Noel, interrupting. "She didn't mean it, Jim. She's upset. She doesn't know what she's saying. She——"

A kind of veil went down over Averill's shallow brown eyes. She rose and went gracefully to Jim and laid her small hand on his arm.

"Do forgive me, Jim. I meant nothing. I was excited. I spoke without thinking. But you see—you see, in spite of Bill's death which we all regret and in spite of the horrible shock of it, life does still go on for the rest of us. And we intended to sell the engine to Major Pace; why should an accident change our plans?"

Pace turned heavily to Jim.

"Cady—you say this was an accident?"

"I don't know what it was. If I hadn't seen it happen, I would say it was impossible."

"How about the engine itself—what was left of it, I mean. Can't you tell from that what happened?"

"It was pretty smashed," said Noel. "It struck head on."

"Lud Strevsky is out there now waiting for it to cool," said Jim. "He's one of our best mechanics. If it was a fault of the engine Lud will make a pretty good guess as to what it was."

Averill said quickly:

"It seems to me the best thing to do right now is to go ahead with our plans."

Jim turned, as if bewildered, toward Averill. "You mean go on to the Bayou Teche place right away?"

"Yes, of course. Bill would have wanted us to do it that way. The funeral will be at the plantation; all the family are buried there; we would have to send Bill there anyway. The wedding will be extremely quiet; we had planned that already. The plane Uncle Bill chartered is ready and waiting. The sooner we leave the better for all of us, I think. And—Major Pace," she turned to him graciously with the air of a hostess giving a purely social invitation, "Major Pace, we would very much like you to go South with us. We leave tonight."

It was typical of Averill and good generalship to announce her plans like that—publicly and with every detail thought out. It made it almost impossible for Jim or anyone else to oppose her. But it had not occurred to Eden until just then that Averill's wedding could be in any way affected by the plane crash. In spite of herself a small desperate hope rose and grew in her heart. She didn't dare look at Jim.

He said: "But, Averill—I ought to be here. I've got to be here when we tear down the engine—that is, take the engine apart. Don't you see——"

"Jim, you just now said this mechanic—Strevsky, wasn't it?—knows as much about the engine as you do. And, besides, surely you," she smiled a little wistfully (Averill was never wistful), "surely you don't object to our wedding taking place as planned. Jim, my dear, I've been thinking it all out while I waited for you to come. I'm sure this is the way——"

Pace cleared his throat and said abruptly:

"Can you rebuild the engine, Cady? And how long will it take you? And will you be willing to sell to me after it is rebuilt?"

Noel replied.

"Certainly he can rebuild it and will. It oughtn't to take more than a few weeks. And he—he agreed to selling last night. There's no need to go into all that again."

"Noel's quite right," said Averill instantly. "So you will come with us, Major Pace?"

It seemed to Eden that he agreed almost before she had finished speaking.

"Yes," said Pace, "I'll come—if you insist. And I—hope I shall not intrude in these family matters."

Averill turned at once to Noel.

"Noel, will you see that they know at the field that our plans are not changed? We'll make a night flight of it exactly as we had planned."

"Yes— Yes, of course, my dear. At once. Will you come along, Pace?"

The door closed behind them and put a stamp of finality upon Averill's neat plans. Dorothy Woolen rose and said quietly:

"Do you want me to prepare statements for the newspapers, Miss Blaine?"

"Newspapers!"

"The reporters have already been at the field. Mr. Carreaux made a brief statement. He said it had been an accident and they were making an investigation. He kept Major Pace out of it. I imagine reporters will be at the house soon——"

"Yes. Yes, by all means, Dorothy. You'd better stay here and deal with them."

"Averill," said Jim rather desperately, "you don't understand. I—I *can't* go."

Averill blinked slowly, as if giving herself time to seek

behind his words and refute whatever lay there. Eden waited, tense. Jim went on: "I've got to see about this thing. I——"

"Jim," said Averill swiftly, "you can't walk out on me like this. Besides, you can keep in constant touch with the plant and the mechanic you think so much of. We'll take Dorothy with us——" She turned, smiling at Dorothy and said winningly: "You will go, won't you?" Dorothy, looking blank, nodded her head affirmatively and Averill turned again, sweepingly, to Jim. "You see, darling. It's all settled. You'll have to come now, Jim," she said in a gentle way. "I can't go through all this alone. And I won't let our marriage be postponed. Will you give that statement to the papers, too, Dorothy? Tell them that my wedding will take place as arranged; only the family will be present. Good—that's settled." She went to the bell and put her slender finger on it.

The little desperate hope in Eden's heart died. Painfully. Settled, she thought, as Averill wanted it to be settled. The wedding to take place as planned.

Well, after all, wasn't it better to have the wedding over with and done? So she could write the end to that chapter; close it, put it away, forget it. Take up her usual life again briskly. Avoid, for a while, the aching memory of a garden at night, a man's lips—so briefly—on her own.

Yes, it was much better to end the thing, since it must be ended, quickly. Finally.

She rose and went rather blindly to the window, looking down upon velvet green lawn with eyes that did not see.

Behind her, she heard Jim speak.

"I've got to go back to the plant now. Averill, what did you do with the plans for the engine? Last night, I mean?"

"I put them over there in the drawer of the table. Why? You don't need them now."

"They aren't here."

"They must be."

"Nothing here but stationery and pens."

Averill, footsteps light and quick, must have gone to look. Eden turned, drawn by some undertone in Jim's voice. She watched and Jim watched and Dorothy Woolen watched, too. Averill ran her slim hand increduously about the drawer; there was stationery, blotters, pens, nothing else.

"But I—I put them here," she said. "I rolled them up and put them here myself." She stopped thoughtfully. "Bill must have removed them." She turned to Dorothy. "Bill didn't give them to you?"

"No."

Averill's sleek black eyebrows had drawn to a fine line.

"It doesn't really matter, I suppose," she said. "It's not the only copy you have, Jim?"

37

"No. There are the tracings from which the blueprints were made. I have them at the office. And when the government tests were passed we deposited a whole set of plans with the government bureau—sealed. Oh, it's not a question of losing something we can't replace. Of course——" He stopped, frowning.

"Yes, Jim?" said Averill.

"I was only going to say, of course our one model is practically destroyed. It will take time to make another."

There was a little pause. Averill bit her thin lip thoughtfully.

"Well, then," she said with an air of decision, "we'll just have to keep Pace here until there is a new model. Jim— you didn't mind my asking him to go South with us? I mean —well, it was the only way it occurred to me at the time to keep him here. Frankly, I don't see why we should let him go to another seller, as long as we have the thing he wants and he has the money to pay for it. You see, Jim?"

"Yes, I see. It was fairly obvious. It's not so obvious why he accepted."

"Because he still wants the engine," said Averill triumphantly.

"And you are still going to sell it?"

"But of course, darling. And you'll be glad, when we have all that money; you'll think you have a very clever wife, indeed. See if you don't."

Jim said: "If Bill took the plans—or Noel—we can soon find out."

"No one else would take them," said Averill positively. "I'll go now and look in Bill's room and question Noel. I'll find them," she said with energy.

She went quickly away, closing the door definitely behind her. There was a small silence with Jim staring rather fixedly down into the empty drawer and the girl Dorothy watching him.

"I'm sure Miss Blaine will find them," said Dorothy at last, soothingly. "And after all, it really doesn't matter, does it, Mr. Cady? Everything's fully patented; and the blueprints were only copies."

A maid opened the door gently and came in. She gave Jim a half-frightened look from swollen eyes which looked as if she'd been crying, for Bill Blaine had always been liked by the servants, and said a little gaspingly that reporters were at the door.

"Miss Blaine said you would see them, please, Miss Woolen."

"I'll come," said Dorothy Woolen competently and went quietly away.

The door closed behind her. In the silence it seemed to Eden that Jim must hear her heart, beating suddenly fast and loud.

She didn't move or speak; it was rather sweet to stand there, alone with Jim, waiting.

Jim turned as if he'd known she was there; as if, all the time, he'd been waiting, too.

"Eden——"

"Jim, Jim, it was an accident."

"Eden—you saw the plane fall. God——"

"Don't, dear. Don't think of it."

Involuntarily she put out her hands and he took them tight in his own.

Instantly, again, it was as if Averill and Noel and all those others did not exist. It was as if there were no barriers and no masks between Eden and the man before her.

"It wasn't an accident. Believe me, Eden, will you? It wasn't an accident. My engine was safe. There was nothing that could have gone wrong. Yet—it did." He lifted his head suddenly and said: "Eden, it was a good engine. It couldn't have caught fire like that. There's no way——" The line around his mouth hardened and Eden watched it change and gauged it as if she had known the changes of expression in his face always. He said: "There is a way——"

She was sure and unsure of what he meant. He went on slowly:

"It isn't crazy. It isn't fantastic. The plans are gone—and Bill didn't take them."

"Jim—do you mean——"

"I mean the engine was fixed to crash. Don't look like that; I'm not out of my mind. There are ways to do it. And if Pace didn't want to buy it, really—in spite of what he says —if he actually preferred stealing it, there are ways to do that, too."

"Pace?"

"Yes, Pace." He released her hands and turned and paced up and down, talking rapidly. Sharing the thing with her as if he had to share it.

As if he needed her. She closed her heart on that thought and listened.

"If he bought it openly it could be used for anything— openly. But if he could steal it, he could sell it to anybody that wouldn't question too much as to how and where he got it. Suppose he was out to double-cross the government (whatever it is) which he says he represents. Suppose he intends to get away with the plans, sell them to whatever country he can sell them to, claim he bought them honestly, convince them of it (I don't know how), then pocket the two hundred thousand for himself. After all, there are always governments that are not too scrupulous about sources from which they buy."

"He'd have the two hundred thousand besides the price he could get for the plans."

"I'm going too fast," said Jim.

He walked again to the window and stood there, hands in his pockets. Eden tried to follow his thoughts.

How much did any of them really know of the man calling himself Major Pace? They knew only that he wanted the engine and he'd offered to pay them, and he'd deposited the money as an evidence of good faith.

But he'd refused to tell them what country he represented. Eden knew that, too. And there was definitely something about the man which suggested that his motives were in all probability sheerly mercenary.

Creda! With a start Eden remembered the sharp impression she'd had that Creda already knew Pace. It might be only a baseless notion; certainly if Creda knew him then it was curious neither of them acknowledged it.

But she recalled Creda's fat, white little hand tightening spasmodically on Noel's arm—the way she avoided Pace's eyes.

Jim turned suddenly again to face her.

"The plane couldn't crash like that. Bill was a good flyer; the engine was good. I'll stake everything on that. There's something back of it, and I've got to find out what it is."

"That would be murder!"

"Yes. Murder. Bill Blaine and—and the best God damn' mechanic——" He checked himself abruptly.

"Murder," whispered Eden with horror. Pace?

There was another silence.

And Jim said as if he'd made up his mind: "I've got to have proof. Before it's too late. Before he's got away with it. I've got to have proof, and I've got to have time."

"Can I—help?"

"Yes," he said unexpectedly, "you can. I can count on you. It—it may seem crackbrained—what I'm going to do. But I believe I can do it and I don't see any other way."

"Tell me what to do."

He smiled a little.

"Thanks. You—you know what it means to me. Eden ——" His face sobered. He put out his hand and she put her own in it. And all at once, irresistibly, his hand tightened. The look in his face changed; he drew her nearer him. That too was as irresistible as the course of a river, the strength of a tidal wave, the whirling of the earth and sun. He said suddenly and in the strangest voice as if words were wrenched from him: "Eden, why didn't you come sooner——"

— 40 —

During a fractional moment she was aware of two things. He was going to take her in his arms; he couldn't help it any more than she could help yielding. And the door opened and Averill stood on the threshold.

CHAPTER /6

After a deliberate second or two she entered; she was perfectly cool, self-possessed and observing. Eden made a violent effort and succeeded in restraining the quickness of the motion with which she turned from Jim. But Averill, always quick as a cat, probably perceived that very restraint. She ended the slight pause and came toward them.

"I couldn't find the plans," she said. "Noel says he hasn't seen them and they weren't in Bill's room. But it doesn't really matter, does it, Jim? They'll turn up somewhere. And if I were you———" She linked her arm through Jim's possessively and smiled up into his face.

"If I were you," she went on quite simply, "I wouldn't say too much of the plans having been mislaid. They'll turn up somewhere. And it suggests———"

"Suggests what?"

She lifted her slender shoulders.

"Oh, all sorts of unpleasant things. Plots, motives. People talk."

"Wait a minute, Averill. Let me get this straight. What do you mean by talk?"

"Oh, Jim, think! It's your engine and everybody knows it. Reporters are practically camping on the steps right now. Suppose some of them got a hint that you hadn't wanted to sell the engine."

"Averill———"

"There, Jim, I didn't mean to hurt you. It's only because I love you that I'm speaking as I am. I——— Good heavens, Jim, we're to be married in three days. Haven't I a right to think of your name?" She linked her arm through his and put her sleek, dark little head against his shoulder. Jim, his face like a stone, did not move and did not seem to be aware of her caressing gesture. But Averill pushed her head against his arm and looked at Eden.

There was triumph and there was complacence and there was warning in her gaze.

Because Averill knew.

Eden was suddenly as sure of that as she was ever to be sure of anything in her life.

Perhaps there had been something too revealing in the scene Averill had interrupted. Perhaps it was an alert sixth sense. Nothing tangible, nothing definable, but she knew. And she was warning Eden and reminding her.

The trouble was Averill was right. And Eden was quite definitely and unquestionably in the wrong.

The butler opened the door and came in. "Excuse me, miss. If I might see the drawer where the blueprints were placed——"

Eden murmured something and went out of the room and rather blindly walked down the hall and stopped at the big bay window. Sunshine poured down upon garden and shrubs. The hall itself was cool and shadowy and empty.

A house of mourning really; but the thing Eden mourned was still alive.

So that was love. The kind that comes once and never comes again. She'd have to stand by, she thought suddenly, painfully, and see the man she loved marry someone else. Averill.

Well, if Averill had ever wanted revenge upon Eden she had it now.

And Jim—why, Jim must have loved Averill. He wouldn't have asked her to marry him, if he hadn't. Then did he still love her? But he'd said—she closed her eyes, the better to hear it again—"Why didn't you come sooner?" That could mean only one thing.

Noel came quickly along the hall, saw her and stopped.

"Well, it's all set. The plane leaves tonight at nine. Has Averill found the plans?"

"No."

He looked at her sharply.

"Steady, my girl. What's wrong? Don't let this get you down, Eden. It's tough. Poor old Bill. But it's nothing that could have been helped."

The butler came out of the library and advanced sedately.

"Mr. Carreaux——"

"Yes, Glass."

"None of the maids have seen the blueprints that are missing. I'm quite sure none of them inadvertently removed the blueprints."

"Oh. All right, Glass. They'll turn up somewhere, I'm sure."

"I hope so, sir. And by the way—it's a small matter but —when Miss Blaine showed me the drawer just now where the blueprints were placed last night I happened to notice that—well, three new sticks of red sealing wax were missing, too."

"Wax? But, really, Glass——"

The butler drew himself up.

"I realize it is a trivial matter, sir. I mention it because I replenished it only last night."

"Thank you, Glass."

The butler, wearing a disapproving expression, went away.

And Eden thought, wax, a package of blueprints, mailing. But there'd been no time, or at least no opportunity.

The door opposite, which led to the small morning room, opened and Dorothy Woolen looked out, failed to see Eden who stood a little in the shadow of the stairway and said to Noel:

"Noel, they've gone." Her usually blank face wore an animated expression; she was for an instant almost pretty. Noel said:

"That's a good girl." He glanced at Eden. "I knew Dorothy could get rid of reporters if anybody could."

"Is there anything else?" said Dorothy. When Eden glanced at her again the prettiness had gone as if wiped off by a sponge; her face was simply a blank, plump expanse showing no expression whatever.

"Yes," said Noel. He murmured something to Eden and went into the morning room and Eden climbed the stairs rather wearily to her own room.

Just here at the top of the stairs Bill Blaine had taken her hands the night before and kissed her.

Bluff, big Bill Blaine.

If what Jim said was true, if he could prove it, it was murder.

She shivered a little and went quickly to her own room.

Jim must have gone almost at once to the plant where he remained. He did not return to the house to dinner and Eden did not see him again until the plane left that night.

And there were things to do.

She packed her own things first, which was simple and did not take long. She did not pack her heavy white sports coat; she would wear it in the plane for the night was likely to be chilly. As she put the coat over a chair she remembered the key that she had discovered at her feet in that horrible moment when the plane fell, a blazing, smoking mass, with human souls going up in that smoke.

Deliberate murder. Cold-blooded. Planned. Was Jim right?

She didn't know what she had done with the key; she felt in the pockets of the coat she had worn and found it. Again she turned it in her fingers but this time looked at it with attention. A Yale key, she'd noticed that. A large substantial key; it might be the key to the house, the key to anything.

There was no way of knowing who had lost it. Creda, Averill or the chauffeur might have dropped it—or it might have been dropped sometime (any time, indeed) previous to that morning. It was bright and clean as if in constant use, but then it was a brass key and not likely to show signs of weathering.

43

It would give her, however, a chance to talk to Creda. If Creda could be seen.

She took the key; she was walking through the hall toward Creda's suite of rooms at the back of the house when she met Noel again.

"Coast is all clear," he said. "I just sent Dorothy home to pack. I don't know why on earth Averill wants her to go along but expect she can make herself useful. Dorothy's an—an efficient young woman. What's that you've got in your hand?"

"A key," said Eden and showed it to him.

"Why that——" He began and stopped. He shot her a quick look. "Where did you get that?"

"Found it. I think it's Creda's. Do you know what key it is?"

"Creda's? Oh, I see." His face cleared. "For a moment, I thought it looked like a key to the plant. Perhaps I was mistaken—I can soon tell." He drew out his own key ring, selected a Yale key and compared them. "By Jove, it is a key to the plant! What was Creda doing with it, do you suppose?"

"I don't know. I'm going to return it to her."

"Wait a minute." He was frowning, thinking. "Oh, all right," he said. "It's probably Bill's key. It doesn't matter anyway. Are you all packed to go?"

"Yes."

"It's too bad, things turning out like this. Averill planned everything so well. She's a great girl; good executive; she'll be better at running things at the plant, as a matter of fact, than Bill was. Did you see how quickly she took hold of things?"

"Yes, I saw that."

"She'll be a good wife for Jim," said Noel. "She'll pull him out of this thing in fine shape. And, by golly, if we let her alone she'll still sell the engine to Pace. Here's my door; I've got to pack——"

"But, Noel, the thing this morning wasn't Jim's fault. You said yourself——"

"I know." He glanced quickly up and down the hall and lowered his voice a little. "And it's true that the engine passed the tests all right. But—Bill was a good flyer, Eden. Accidents don't happen, just like that."

"You mean you think the engine failed?"

He didn't answer for a moment; his blue eyes were dark and thoughtful. Then he turned away with a shrug and a quick smile.

"I don't mean anything, Eden. Forget it. Run along and see how Creda's getting on."

He waved, still with a smile, and went inside his room. Eden, pondering the things he hadn't said rather than what he had said, went on to Creda's door. She knocked and Creda said at once:

"Who is it?"

"Eden."

"Oh." There was a slight pause, then the soft tread of Creda's feet across the rug and the rasp of a key in the door, unlocking it.

"It's you," said Creda. "Come in."

Her face was very pale and without tearstains; she glanced rather uneasily down the hall over Eden's shoulder and closed the door quickly as she entered. Her fat little hand already on the key, she just restrained herself, Eden felt, from relocking it.

The bed was tossed, clothes were everywhere; two large bags stood open and half packed on the floor and the desk looked as if it had been hurriedly and rather frenziedly ransacked, for letters and papers were in utter confusion.

"Sit down," said Creda. She pushed her hands through her soft curls, wrapped the trailing pink negligee she wore tighter around her and sat down tucking her plump, bare little feet under her. Her eyes were shadowy pools of brown that, just then, looked haunted.

"I'm glad you've come," she said. "I'm trying to pack."

"I'll help you. Tell me what to pack."

"Thanks, Eden. Cigarette?"

As Eden, kneeling at the half-packed bags, shook her head, Creda lighted one herself and smoked it in feverish little puffs.

"What clothes do you want to take?"

"All those things. It'll be hot as hell at the plantation. I may stay quite a long time. I don't know what I'll do. I haven't made plans. Wait, Eden—look in that pocket, will you? Is there anything in it?"

"Cigarettes," said Eden, searching the pockets of the jacket she was folding. "A handkerchief. That's all. Do you want them?" She gave the cigarettes and the wisp of linen to Creda who took them listlessly. "Oh, by the way, Creda, I found a key——"

Instantly Creda shot up out of her chair. Her little face hardened.

"What key?"

"This." She held out the key. "Does it belong to you?"

Creda gave one quick look at the key. Then she snatched it with greedy fingers, took a long, tremulous breath and sat down again as if her knees refused to hold her upright.

"Yes," she said, "it's mine. Thank God——" She caught herself, shot a watchful glance at Eden and said: "That is—I thought I'd lost it."

"It's a key to the plant, isn't it?" said Eden, folding the jacket.

"Yes. That is——" Creda's little face was hard and intent. "How did you know?"

"Noel thought so——"

"Noel!"

"Yes. I didn't know who lost it. I asked him about it. Shall I pack this bathing suit?"

"Yes. No. That is, Eden—where did you find this key?"

"This morning, at the field. Beside the car. You must have dropped it."

"Dropped it. Yes. Yes, I suppose I did. Did you tell Noel where you found the key?"

Eden considered.

"No. I just told him I thought you'd lost it. He said it was probably Bill's key. That's all."

"Oh. Oh, I see. Yes, that's right. It was Bill's key."

It was difficult for her to say "Bill"; she brought it out with a kind of thrust. Yet whatever emotion it was that she repressed, it was unlike grief. She went on quickly:

"I happened to have it. He—gave it to me."

It was unconvincing.

Eden folded a dress and said nothing. After a curiously uneasy moment Creda said:

"Listen, Eden; don't tell anyone I had this key. Will you?"

"Why on earth should I tell anybody! It doesn't matter."

"I know, but—promise me. Will you, Eden?"

"I'll promise anything you want me to; don't be silly, Creda. Nobody cares about a key. Oh, by the way"—she folded an organdy dinner dress, much ruffled, in tissue paper—"by the way," she said casually above the soft little rattle of tissue paper, "what do you know about Major Pace? Just who is he?"

There was another little silence and it was again uneasy. She glanced at Creda over the masses of organdy and tissue paper, and Creda said at last, rather stiffly:

"I don't know anything about him. What a queer question!"

Eden accepted it and put the dress carefully in the bag and reached for the next one.

"I wonder what country he really does represent?"

This time Creda replied quickly.

"I'm sure I don't know."

"Perhaps he doesn't really represent any country," ventured Eden. "Perhaps he's just an ordinary, commercial—well, adventurer."

"Adventurer? What do you mean?"

"Well," said Eden, "I suppose there are spies; other airplane manufacturing plants have trouble now and then with spies. I don't know why the Blaine plant should be immune."

"Spies!" said Creda on a quick breath. "Really——" She laughed sharply and nervously. "He's not a spy. He offered to buy the engine. Besides, there's never been any trouble about spies at the Blaine plant."

"I suppose you're right." Eden closed the bag and sat back on her heels to look full at Creda and risked another question which she tried to make sound idle and casual. "Did you ever see Major Pace anywhere before?"

Creda blinked slowly; Eden was sure that she held her breath for an instant or two because the thin line of smoke coming from her pretty little nostrils stopped for a second or two and then went on. And then Creda opened her brown eyes wide and looked straight back at Eden.

"Never," she said flatly.

Yet there was no proof, thought Eden, returning to her room an hour or so later, that it was a lie.

She'd finished Creda's packing; when she left, Creda closed the door promptly again behind her. And as promptly relocked it. It was queer to stand there in that broad, well-lighted hall and hear the swift smooth click of the bolt.

She wondered why Creda was afraid. And more specifically, what there was to be afraid of.

It was already late in the afternoon when she finished Creda's packing. The sun went down, still clear; at eight o'clock, after a quick dinner, they departed (bags following in another car) for the big commercial airport where the chartered plane waited for them.

They did not, however, leave at nine o'clock, for Jim was late. He did not arrive, indeed, until nearer ten and their embarking at the last was hurried. Dorothy Woolen had arrived early by taxi and was already waiting for them in the cabin. A boy steward stored their baggage. Eden had no chance for a word with Jim who went forward almost at once to the pilot's compartment. Perhaps he intended to take the controls during a part of the flight.

And all at once they were settled, choosing, as if instinctively, separate seats. The motors grew louder, roared and there was motion around them. They taxied across the lighted field and began to lift, a little sluggishly, as if the plane carried a heavy load.

Then almost suddenly lights dropped away below them. The motors settled into a deep drone. Pace, just behind Eden, pulled out a traveling rug and hunched it around his shoulders. Dorothy Woolen, across the aisle, turned her face away and appeared to go to sleep as instantly and efficiently as she did everything else.

Averill was in the seat just ahead of Eden; she rose to adjust her yellow cloak around her, gave Eden a long, wordless look, her small, slender face sallow and enigmatic in the halflight, turned and sat down again.

Outside the night was black and dotted with stars.

Inside there was nothing but the sound of the motors, confusing, drugging thought, eventually lulling one to sleep in spite of the things there were to think. The last thing Eden remembered was taking her gray chiffon scarf from her pocket and wrapping it lightly about her throat.

The plane droned on through the limitless night sky.

Far below and behind them now was the sleeping city, majestic and powerfully entrenched above the broad, winding river which was powerful, too, and older.

Somewhere below and behind them was the wreck of what had been that morning a shining silver-colored thing of skill and loveliness. Around it still men with great lights worked; Jim had spent most of the day there, working with them. Until he found what he had found.

The trouble was he didn't know exactly what to do with it. Or rather, he knew what was to be done but not how. It made him horribly uneasy. Suppose things slipped up. Suppose the thing he counted on failed him.

He was uneasy, too, somehow about the plane and the people inside it. What was going on in there? What were they thinking? And what would they say when they knew?

The night went on; he watched the instrument panel. Once, carefully, he disconnected the radio; the pilot saw it and grinned, a brief lifting of his lip which was more like a snarl than a smile.

Jim saw the smile; that, too, quite suddenly gave him a queer pang of uneasiness. Had he unleashed something it might be difficult to check?

Nonsense! That was nerves. Presently he rechecked figures and gestured to the pilot who smiled briefly again. The plane swung a little further west. Due west now and traveling well over a hundred miles an hour. After a while Jim motioned again to the pilot and took the controls himself while the pilot hunched himself inside his leather coat and slept like a strong, young animal—wary and feral even in his sleep.

When Eden awoke it was dawn; gray light struggled dimly into the cabin and the sky outside was a great, gray bowl streaked with lemon yellow.

She sat up straighter; her muscles were tired and cramped. She put her hand automatically to her hair and yawned.

No one else seemed to be stirring.

It was cold in the plane and the air was like wine, stinging and clear.

Eden glanced out the window again and, this time, downward. And instantly sat up to stare incredulously.

For they were flying over the sea. No, it couldn't be the sea. It was gray, dun-colored, formless—stretching out to meet the lighter gray of the sky. It wasn't a sea; it was land. But it was like a desert, flat, rolling, with distant horizons. It was like a great plate spread out below.

There ought to be the shapes of trees. There ought to be towns and lights and blotches of shadow that marked vegetation. New Orleans ought to be somewhere near, or the bayou stretching silver fingers inland.

She caught her breath abruptly. The sun had tipped over the horizon, and it was behind them. And there were jagged peaks lifting up into the sky ahead of them.

Peaks which, when the sun touched them, leaped into crimson—a soft crimson, red as blood against the pale sky. Mountains.

They looked like something out of a phantasmagory. Out of magic. Out of fairy tales. An enchanted range, shimmering crimson against the sky.

The shining crimson peaks were unutterably beautiful. They were at the same time a little terrifying.

The main thing was, however, that they ought not to have been there.

CHAPTER /7

Where were they, then; above all, what had happened while they slept?

She turned again, anxiously, wondering why no one else stirred and shared her alarm.

But no one moved: no one was awake. Pace was still hunched in his rug behind her; Dorothy an inert mass across the aisle. Averill, Creda in the seat beyond Averill; Noel opposite Creda with his adventurer's profile sunk in the collar of his coat—none of them moved. Even the boyish steward slept, with his curly blond head tipped back and his mouth open.

Jim must be in front with the pilot.

She looked out the window again and the mountains were still there, except the plane must have changed direction a little for their position had moved and they were much nearer.

The plane must be going very fast. She tried to estimate roughly the speed of the engine and could not; to her untutored ears there was merely a smooth steady drone.

There was still desert below and they must be very high; but once when the light struck just right, she caught a glimmer of reflected light as from water in a crisscross, checkerboard pattern. Irrigation ditches—it must be.

What could have happened during the night? They must be miles off their course.

Again she turned to seek some explanation and again no one stirred.

She must arouse them, find Jim.

She was cold; absently she pulled her heavy coat closer around her; she'd lost the chiffon scarf—she groped for it and forgot it.

For the mountains vanished. They had turned, then, southward. Or were they simply flying in a great circle?

She glued her face to the window; they must be flying at considerable speed, for when next she saw the mountains they had changed—they were no longer chimerical, beautiful, magical. They were now rocky peaks dotted halfway up with green scrub pine, all brown and green except those bare rocky peaks which still had a kind of crimson glow. They were clearly discernible now as mountains, mountains of the earth and of the three dimensions. But Eden was never to forget her first, poignant impression of unearthliness, of beauty and, oddly, of terror.

They rose again, high into the clear sky; the air was dry and there was not too much of it; she had an impulse to gulp for breath; her nose felt dry and her throat stung. They were crossing some of those peaks now.

She must rouse the others; she must go forward and find Jim.

Undoubtedly the pilot knew where they were going. There was certainty in the speed with which they drove ahead. Jim, who must be with the pilot—who perhaps was piloting the plane—must know, then, too. And that circle, she thought suddenly, had meant that the pilot was looking for an opening, a pass, and had found it.

The peaks were like a wall, like a barrier. She had a fantastic notion that when they crossed that crimson, jagged wall they crossed from a known world where there were rules into a world that was strange and where anything might happen.

Moments must have passed; she felt suspended, as if in a spell, as if she dared not move while they crossed that barrier. She liked flying and was accustomed to it. But the immensity of the spectacle below held her spellbound, awed, a little frightened.

And all at once they were again over a flat country; the plane lost altitude: they were descending—rapidly, too, for the brownish green expanse far below began to take on shape and distinctness.

She realized that again they were circling. Again it was as if the pilot were looking for something on the earth below. A landing field? Or just a mark to guide him?

She must find Jim, she told herself again. She reached to unfasten the safety belt the little steward had adjusted around each the night before.

And just then Jim himself came suddenly, stooping, through the little door, and shouted: "Hey, there, everybody. We're landing——"

She felt for the safety belt; it was securely fastened. And the others, as habitual plane travelers do at a landing, woke instantly.

"It's a forced landing," shouted Jim. "Hang on. It may be rough."

But it wasn't a forced landing; the plane was obviously under perfect control. She had time to think that. Then Noel shouted something she couldn't hear and Averill in front of her apparently looked out the window and cried out sharply above the roar of the motors. And then everybody was silent.

For they were landing.

Earth was rushing up to meet them. She held her breath—would they make a good landing? Would they nose over? Would they——

They didn't. There was a slight bump; the earth was all at once just outside the window—gray-green, covered with short grass and brush. And they rolled gently to a perfect, quiet stop.

The silence in the cabin continued for a moment while they realized safety. Then the engine was cut off. And into the abrupt stillness Averill cried shrilly: "Jim, what's happened? Where are we? Good heavens, there are mountains——"

And instantly everyone, it seemed to Eden, echoed it. Even Dorothy Woolen looked white and scared and clutched at Noel's arm agitatedly.

"Trouble," said Jim rapidly. "But don't be scared. We're all right now."

"What kind of trouble?" that was Noel, out of his seat now, at Jim's side. Pace, emerging from his rug behind Eden, struggling with the clasp of his safety belt, looked very much like a startled and savage bear.

"I don't know," said Jim. "Instruments went haywire during the night; had some clouds; got off our course. Radio's dead, too. We saw a good place to land and did it. Fuel is barely holding out. We had to land."

"But where——" That was Noel.

"I saw a ranch house over that way," said Jim. "Maybe they'll take us in till we can get squared around."

"But what—what an extraordinary accident," cried Averill. "Those are mountains over there—what mountains, for heaven's sake? Where are we?"

"We'll soon find out," said Jim. "I'm sorry, Averill. But we're lucky to land so near a house. After all there's breakfast to think of—I'll go along. Want to come, Noel?"

"No," said Noel. "I'll stay here."

"Don't be long," said Creda.

They watched him leave, striding rapidly along almost as if he knew his way across the sandy, flat stretch of land—a land covered with a kind of coarse, sparse grass and clumps of grayish green growth which Eden for want of more exact knowledge took (and correctly) to be sagebrush. Evidently the tract of land on which they'd landed was not under irrigation for it was arid, flat, desertlike—curiously primitive and untouched in aspect.

"Well," said Averill in a tight voice, "there's nothing to do but wait." She looked at her watch, said, "Five o'clock. Good heavens. And they are expecting us at the plantation!" She sat down again, pulling her yellow cloak around her and staring disconsolately out the window. Creda came to sit beside Averill. Dorothy leaned back and closed her eyes sleepily. Pace got out of the plane and walked up and down smoking. Rather oddly there was little audible speculation, although Noel, with something enigmatic in his expression, went forward to where the pilot, too, was stretching his legs and smoking.

Eden looked rather curiously at the pilot as he spoke to Noel. He was big, young and would be thickset—almost a bull of a man now, with his sturdy thick neck rising from the open collar of his leather coat. He had very thick, strong-looking brown hair; his face was on massive, heavy planes —with a touch of the Slav in his somewhat slanted eyes and rather cruelly curved mouth. He smiled a little, showing extremely white and squarely set teeth. She couldn't hear what they said but he shook his head with a helpless gesture and pointed to the plane and he and Noel walked around it and out of sight.

It was no good waiting in the plane. Eden got out, too, throwing back her face to take in great gulps of the incredibly clear air. Dorothy followed after a while and Averill. There was not much to see—rather there was much, for they could see for miles to the rim of mountains which enclosed them. But off toward the left where Jim had disappeared was a strip of brush and cottonwoods and a cluster of barns and corrals. Behind them and at some distance there appeared to

52

be an area of green—green grass, green shrubs, green pines —and in the middle of it a house, dimly seen beyond the huge cottonwoods.

There was about the place, then and forever to Eden, an extraordinary feeling of remoteness.

New York seemed to be on a different and distant planet. Even St. Louis belonged to a world irrevocably removed. The mountains rimming the horizon became the very limits of existence.

For an instant it seemed to her that there was promise in that distance and division from things past; as if a new life might newly begin for her there.

That, of course, was fancy. It didn't take Pace's figure, trudging heavily across her vision, to remind her of it.

But the feeling of fatefulness remained.

It was half an hour before Jim returned and he was not alone. A tall, lean, lazy-looking man accompanied him, who despite his lazy, loose-jointed walk still managed to cover distance very rapidly.

"This," said Jim, nearing the little cluster about the plane, "is Mr. Sloane."

"P. H.," murmured Mr. Sloane, looking at them with light, extremely keen blue eyes which were completely surrounded by a fine network of wrinkles. His face was brown and hawklike in the sharpness of its features; he removed an enormous Stetson hat—a ten-gallon hat, Eden was later to learn.

"It's awfully good of you," said Noel.

"Glad to have visitors," said P. H. Sloane pleasantly.

Jim introduced them separately. When Eden put out her hand the rancher took it briefly, not too heartily, gave her one smiling, brief look and turned at once to speak to Creda. Yet, Eden thought suddenly, he'll know me again—he'd know me anywhere again and remember me and every circumstance of our meeting.

He wore a khaki-colored shirt that was open upon a lean sunbrowned neck, khaki riding breeches that looked worn and almost white with washing and laced high boots. A typical rancher, she thought—and then wondered if all ranchers had such extraordinarily observant eyes.

"You're up early," said P. H. Sloane. "Well, now if you'll come along to the house I'll see you get some breakfast. Don't bother about your bags. I'll send a couple of boys for them."

"Oh, we'll not need our bags," said Averill swiftly. "It will be only two or three hours at the most."

"Well, that's all right, too," said the rancher. "Glad to have you, I'm sure. But it's no trouble for the boys to bring

53

your bags up to the house. You might want 'em. This way, if you please. It's not much of a walk. There's no need for anybody to stay with the plane. Nobody'll touch it."

"Mr. Sloane," said Averill, "exactly where are we?"

The rancher surveyed her rather quizzically for a moment before he replied, drawling a little:

"Well now, Miss Blaine, that's easy. You're almost in the middle of the Chochela Valley. Over toward the east—you crossed 'em—is the Sangre de Cristo Range. Red. Spanish named 'em; Blood of Christ. Toward the west is the Continental Divide; the Culebra Range is over that way." He gestured lazily with a long brown hand toward a southwestern mountain rim. "Them mountains, west, is the Cochetopa Hills; beyond are the La Ganta Mountains. The Rio Grande lies quite a way to the south."

Averill's small face was stiff.

"Just where is the nearest city?"

"Well, there's Rocky Gap that way about fifty miles. But it's not much of a city." P. H. Sloane paused thoughtfully. "But there's Telluride," he went on doubtfully. "It's north and west of us. And Cimarron. But if you want a city, you'll have to go down to Sante Fe. Or Albuquerque. Or even Denver on the other side. They're nearest, I reckon. But not very near, at that. Cady tells me your destination was Louisiana. You're off your course quite a way."

"We know that," said Averill.

And Jim said:

"Come along, Averill. Mr. Sloane's ordered breakfast for us. Don't keep it waiting."

The coarse grass was unexpectedly firm and springy under their feet. The air was as clear, as crisp, as clean as the morning sky.

As they approached the fringe of brush and cottonwoods, the panorama of ranch houses and corrals began to stretch out, and the cottonwoods seemed to grow taller. There were barns, sheds, corrals; the party circled them and came in view of the house itself—long, low, rambling, flanked on each side by clusters of rustic cabins with native stone chimneys and narrow verandas running their full length.

The oasislike effect of the green in which the house was set was due, Eden discovered, to a swift small creek lying below the house.

"It's a dude ranch," said Jim to Averill, as she lifted questioning eyebrows. "P. H. Sloane is the owner. It used to be a cattle ranch—still is, I guess."

"I don't care what it is," said Averill, "so long as they'll give us breakfast and a telephone. I expect you can telephone for anything you need."

'I don't know what's wrong yet," said Jim, "but, as you say, we can telephone."

Eden, walking beside Averill, looked up quickly at Jim, caught by an undercurrent of meaning in his words. But his face was uncommunicative.

Yet he must have planned the whole thing. She was almost sure of that in spite of the explanation he gave.

"Right in here," said P. H. Sloane, opening the door from a wide porch to a wide hall. "Dining room at the right. And breakfast——" He stopped, sniffed and finished with a smile, "Breakfast is ready for you."

If it was a dude ranch then there were no dudes. The cabins were obviously closed and unoccupied; the long, sprawling house itself vastly empty.

They had a glimpse of a spacious lounge and at the end of the entrance hall, a billiard room. Rusticity stopped short of discomfort; the few Mexican shawls, the handsome brown and black bearskin rugs here and there were in no sense out of place although one faded crimson shawl lay over an old, massive piano—a Steinway and a concert size—laden also with worn sheet music. Along the walls were bookshelves, packed mainly with books, although there were Indian relics, too—flutes, bows and arrows, machetes, feathered headdresses on the shelves beyond the great piano.

They passed through a large dining room with small bare tables and entered a smaller one—evidently their host's own dining room, for the table and chairs were old and beautiful, and there were two or three good pictures on the walls.

It was an enormous place, thought Eden, glancing about —the original old ranch had been quite evidently rebuilt with added wings and porches. It was so obviously and so fortunately able not only to house them all but to feed them for any length of time that that very fortuitousness was suspicious.

Up to then perhaps no one except herself had questioned the accident Jim and the pilot claimed. But there was something too neat, too pat about running by hazard upon a hotel. And a closed hotel—so there was no one else about to in any way interfere.

However, although the silence may have held doubt it was not expressed. And Jim's face remained a brown, self-contained mask. He ate hungrily and drank and said little.

They were all hungry. There were honey-brown flapjacks and enormous platters of bacon and eggs and steaming, fragrant coffee—all served neatly and quickly by a Chinese houseboy whose round face wore a habitual grin.

The pilot ate with them, naturally, but finished sooner than anyone else and went, he said, back to the plane to get to work.

And it was just then that the inevitable suspicion first voiced itself.

For, as sound of the pilot's footsteps along the hall died away and the door banged behind them, Creda said: "Jim, isn't that pilot's name Strevsky?"

Pace, who happened to be sitting beside Eden, froze into instant immobility; she noticed that because he was buttering a hot flapjack and his hand became rigid. But Pace was not the only one struck by that name. For Noel turned as if he were on a wire to look at Jim; and Dorothy Woolen's pale eyes lifted suddenly, too, and Averill said after a queer little silence:

"Strevsky? But—but that's the name of the mechanic—yesterday. The one with Bill——"

"Yes, of course, it's Strevsky," said Noel quickly, replying to Averill but still watching Jim.

And Jim said: "This is Ludovic Strevsky. Brother to Mike. Why?"

CHAPTER/8

For a moment no one answered. Then Noel leaned quite suddenly across the table.

"Look here, Jim," he said. "This—is an accident, isn't it?"

"Exactly," said Pace suddenly and heavily. The small blunt knife in his hand was oddly inappropriate to the threatening grip of his wide fingers. He leaned, like a great sulky bear, across the table toward Jim. "Why have you brought Strevsky's brother along?"

Jim looked at Noel and then at Pace and smiled a little.

" 'Vengeance is mine, saith the Lord,' " he said softly. "I don't intend taking it from His hands if that's what you're afraid of."

"We're not afraid," said Noel. He pushed back his plate and got to his feet. His eyes were brilliant under his black peaked eyebrows; his face intent and angry. "I just don't understand your motive. Look here, Jim, if you have any fool notion of——"

"Of what?" said Jim.

"Of—anything," said Noel. "I mean—oh, Jim, we all know how you feel about the accident. We don't blame you. But if you've got any crackbrained notion to——"

"To do what?"

"I don't know," said Noel. "But I do know this—all this"—the wave of his hand included plane, ranch, flapjacks—"is too—too slick. Too much coincidence."

"Don't quarrel with your luck," said Jim gravely and in an unperturbed way. "Have another flapjack?"

Noel put both hands on the table and leaned toward Jim.

"Listen, Jim—I don't know why on earth you'd purposely bring us all out here. None of us had anything to do with what happened yesterday—if that's what's on your mind. That was sheer accident; I only mention it because I know your faith in your engine and I can't think of any other motive for your bringing us out here. But even that has no sense. You couldn't possibly accomplish anything by—by plunging us in this——"

"Sit down then and shut up," said Jim.

"Noel, you're being very mysterious," said Averill. "Exactly what *do* you mean?"

Noel sat down again slowly.

"I don't mean anything, Averill." He sighed. "I apologize. As Jim suggests, it was the very access of good luck we were having that roused my lurid suspicions. I apologize all around and hope everybody is satisfied."

Jim passed him a plate of flapjacks; Creda, who had been sitting in complete silence staring at her plate, moved and lifted a cup of coffee to her lips.

But Pace got to his feet deliberately with a kind of threat in the slow movement of his heavy body.

"I'm afraid I'm not quite satisfied," he said. "At least I see no point in staying here indefinitely. I suggest that you tell that pilot to start the plane and take us back to St. Louis."

"Suppose I refuse," said Jim.

"You won't refuse," said Pace. "You don't dare."

"It isn't quite a question of daring," said Jim. He put down his fork and looked at them with a kind of weariness. "If you can fly that plane as she is now back to St. Louis or on to Louisiana or any place in the world, you're welcome to try it. But I won't go up with you."

Pace blinked slowly, like a lizard. He looked at Noel.

"Can you fly? Do you know anything about planes?"

"I've—got a license," said Noel rather hesitantly. "I've flown a little but I don't know much about the—the engine or the mechanics. However, Jim's on the level about this, Pace. Aren't you, Jim?"

"Why on earth wouldn't I be?" said Jim. "What do you think I'm trying to do?"

"I don't know," said Pace slowly. "I can't imagine. But I do know there are ways to get out. I can wire for a plane to pick us up. I can telephone."

"Certainly you can," said Jim coolly. He took another flapjack deliberately. "Go ahead and wire."

Noel said: "It's all right, Major Pace. I talked out of turn. Sorry."

"What's that man Strevsky here for?" said Pace.

Jim poured syrup on the flapjack lavishly. "Because he's a good pilot," he said. "And luckily for us, a good mechanic. Look here, if any of you really want to leave, Sloane's got a couple of cars. He said town was only fifty miles away. You can make it easily."

"How long will it take to get the plane so it's safe to leave?" asked Averill coolly.

"Honestly, Averill, I don't know. We may get out by night —we may have to send for some new parts. I don't know. I'll go down right away and get to work on it."

"Do you think it would be better to take the train?"

Jim shrugged.

"Just as you like. We could leave the plane here. Strevsky could fly it back to St. Louis when it's repaired."

The rancher strolled past the open door and Jim called to him.

"Oh, Mr. Sloane——"

"Call me P. H.," said the rancher parenthetically. "Everybody does."

"When can we get a train from—Red Gap—Rocky Gap——"

"Rocky Gap," said the rancher. "The train's gone."

There was another moment of silence. Then Averill said incredulously: "*The* train!"

"It went through Rocky Gap at five-thirty sharp," said the rancher calmly, "and there won't be another for three days. It's the off season here, you know. In another month they'll put on a train a day. That's when I get my tourists. But just now it doesn't pay the railroad to run more than two trains a week. It's tough pulling, crossing the mountains. But you're welcome to stay as long as you like. My first guests arrive next month. I guess," he added without apology, "we're a little off the main traveled road."

It struck Eden as being almost a stunning understatement.

But she couldn't help rather admiring Averill's rally, for Averill said after a moment, quite coolly:

"In that case we'd better have the bags brought up from the plane. I suppose Mr. Sloane can supply us with rooms."

"Glad to," said the rancher. "At the usual rates. They are a little high."

"At any rates you like," said Averill not to be outdone. "I suppose you have a telephone, too."

"Certainly. It's the country line but it's a telephone."

"Very well. Will you send some telegrams, Dorothy? After you've finished breakfast, of course. Now—if you'll show us to our rooms, Mr. Sloane."

He clapped his hands smartly and another Chinese boy came running.

'Chango will show you, Miss Blaine," he said. "The best cabins, Chango. Tell Charlie to take the light truck over to the ship for the baggage."

Averill sighed.

"At any rate," she said, "we'll have baths and a sleep."

It ended, for the time being at least, any further questioning although there was no way of knowing what anyone actually thought.

Only Dorothy Woolen seemed to think nothing at all. Her bland, blank face was impassive, her pale eyes observed constantly but reflected nothing; apparently she was chilly in her silk jacket and had borrowed from the steward or from Noel, for a man's brown sweater hung apathetically around her shoulders. She seemed utterly unmoved and incurious. Yet she was not unintelligent and certainly she had followed the whole conversation with most minute attention—as if she were making a neat record of every word in her efficient, secretary's mind.

With again a kind of suspicious fortuitousness the cabins proved to be extremely comfortable; their rustic look was not intrusive and did not extend to such things as beds and plumbing.

Each cabin was equipped with two long, fairly wide bedrooms, two fireplaces and two bathrooms. Eden shared a cabin with Averill; Creda shared the cabin directly beside it with Dorothy. Eden didn't notice just how the men were disposed for the airy, chintz-decorated and comfortable room was too welcome a sight. She had a vague impression that Jim and Noel disappeared almost at once in the direction of the plane and that Pace's cabin was at the end of the little row, but that was all.

The water in the tub was hot and there were plentiful bath salts to relieve its indubitable harshness. It was inexpressibly restful. Eden thought dreamily that she would talk to Jim at the first chance she had—and barely reached the bed before she fell asleep.

She never knew much of what happened that day.

Certainly Jim and the pilot spent some time working at the plane; certainly Dorothy sent the necessary telegrams announcing their continued delay and the reason for it.

It must have been to the outward eye quiet and restful with almost nothing of any importance happening. Yet sometime during that long, lazy day, two things must have taken place.

Someone—unobserved and undetected—went to the plane and—still undetected and very efficiently—cut the fuel line leading to the engine.

And sometime that afternoon Creda Blaine took a long walk, leaving and returning alone.

These things happened.

The damage done to the fuel line was not discovered that afternoon because Jim and the pilot, after busying themselves about the plane all morning, had at last wired to Denver for a part they said they needed and had gone to their cabins to sleep. The boyish steward (whose name proved to be Roy Wilson) gave up early in the day and passed most of it sleeping calmly in a hammock hung at the south end of the long porch.

And Creda's departure and late return were observed casually by the drowsy steward, scarcely remembered, and at the time wholly without significance.

It was after dinner that Eden had her talk with Jim—and had likewise, later, her unexpected interview with Averill.

It was a rather quiet and not unpleasant meal except that, even without Creda's presence to remind them, it was not quite possible to forget that Bill Blaine ought to have been with them. Once Noel started to speak of him and caught himself. And once Averill mentioned him, too, and then, with a quick look at Creda, also caught herself.

Creda, though dressed carefully and youthfully in the organdy evening gown—her curls soft and childish around her forehead and her lips made into a perfect, pink Cupid's bow—was unwontedly silent, with small pouches under her gentle brown eyes. So far as Eden knew she had not spoken to Pace, nor Pace to her. Yet Creda's silence was unusual with her, and there was something taut and anxious in that silence.

It was cold. P. H. Sloane, turning out unexpectedly in a perfectly tailored dinner jacket (although none of the other men changed for dinner) and sitting, host fashion, at the head of the table, said it was always cold at night.

"It's because we are practically in the mountains," he said. "We'll have a fire lighted in the lounge."

They had coffee and liqueurs, poured by a gracious host, in the lounge—the enormous room with the great piano; a log fire roared in the fireplace opposite the piano.

It was probably about ten when Eden went quietly out onto the porch and stood for a moment at the railing, looking out into the still night.

Behind her in the lounge their host was telling stories of the ranch country—telling them calmly, not unpleasantly, as if it were a part of his recognized duty; certainly there was a flavor of familiarity about the stories, of oft and extremely well-told tales.

She had changed into a printed silk dinner dress and because of the cold had put her big white coat over it; she pulled the coat tight around her and walked slowly toward the far end of the porch, her slipper heels making little taps of sound along the wooden floor.

She stopped there. Through the pines between she could see lights glimmering from the nearest cabin window—could see even the writing table and chair beside it for the shade was up. It wasn't more than forty or fifty feet from the porch, but an outcropping of rocks covered with thickets of pines intervened.

She lifted her face to the deep night sky. It was a starlit night but so clear that she almost thought she could see the rim of mountains glimmering distantly like silver in the starlight. The loftiness and grandeur of the night caught at her again irresistibly.

Old worlds and old quarrels and the threat of war were inconceivably remote. Struggle and the race for armaments could not, she thought, reach out and grasp at them there.

Someone inside touched a piano—and touched it again. A cascade of silvery notes fell into the night; she listened; it was Debussy, played by a musician. Their host, of course.

Where and how had Jim known him?

The door onto the porch opened and closed.

She heard Jim's footstep when he came along the porch behind her.

He stopped beside her: and as he had done that first night —how long ago it seemed and how distant—offered her a cigarette.

"Thanks." She took it and, as before, bent to the light he offered. The small flame lighted his face for a moment and vanished.

"Let's walk," he said. "Steps are over here."

They left the porch and strolled along a gravel drive. It was so still the sound of their feet on the gravel was distinct, the music behind them clear and lovely. The drive led through dense, black clumps of pines, away from the house; it was irregular, sloping here and there; eventually paths (taking the long way around because of the rocks and pines) led from it, branching right and left toward the two groups of cabins, one at each end of the long house, but the drive itself went on between pines and firs, toward the mile-distant gate. They passed the dividing paths and strolled on.

The house lay behind them—only the distant mountains ahead. There was the bittersweet fragrance of sagebrush at night. The sound of music grew more distant. As if by agreement, they had walked and smoked in silence, until they were some distance from the house. It was Eden finally who said:

"Have you found the plans?"

It was as if he expected her to ask it. He shook his head. "They're not here."

"How do you know?"

"Never mind. I know." He glanced over his shoulder but they were altogether alone with only the still night around them. "Of course you guessed it wasn't an accident. Our landing here."

"Yes."

"The trouble is the rest of them guessed, too. It's fairly obvious. In spite of the way things calmed down there at breakfast. I wish——"

"You wish——" She said as he didn't speak for a moment.

"I wish they didn't know or guess," he said. "I'm afraid it means trouble."

CHAPTER/9

"What kind of trouble?"

"I don't know exactly. I don't like the way Pace took it."

"Jim, who is P. H. Sloane?"

"Oh, you guessed that, too. Well, he's a detective. Rather was a detective. One of the best."

She stopped short.

"A detective!"

"Yes. He—that's it, you see. He's the only man I could think of who can help me. If he can't discover who was responsible for the crash and the death of two men, no one can. We—everybody who was involved in the thing, were going on the plane last night. It seemed a good idea just to—to bring them out here. Keep 'em all together. Sort of simple—but I'm not sure it was such a good idea."

"No one else knows P. H. Sloane?"

"I don't think so. I knew him ages ago. He was a friend of one of my professors in school; we used to meet at his house. I was going to school, then, of course, at Chicago U.; P. H. Sloane was then a consulting detective. He'd been with the police for years—had a row with somebody political in a famous case. I don't remember details. In the end he left the police and set up shop for himself; he prospered and as soon as he had enough money he gave up his profession, came out here, bought this land and set up a dude ranch. He'd always hated his work; he's taken on color like a salamander; you'd think he was born here."

"You've told him about the crash?"

"Some. We had time for only a few words. I'm going to have a long talk with him tonight. He may refuse to do it—but I don't think so."

They had been standing still in the shadow of a clump of pines. They walked on, now, slowly.

"Then what's the matter with the plane?" asked Eden.

"Nothing," said Jim. "That is, I disconnected the radio, and when it was safe, the compass."

"Doesn't Noel know the truth?"

"He could easily discover it. But he's a good egg. He'll keep quiet. Strevsky's the only one who knows much about a plane. And he's with me."

"You mean he knows?"

"He doesn't know P. H. is a detective. He knows the crash oughtn't to have happened. He knows I'm after something and I can count on him." Jim paused thoughtfully, thinking of Ludovic Strevsky, wondering just how much he could actually count on him.

"He looks a little primitive," said Eden. "I hope he doesn't go out for wholesale revenge."

"Lud?" Jim laughed a little shortly. "Lud's all right. He's pretty worked up about his brother, naturally; they were very close to each other, always worked together, shared everything. But he's not the type to start a vendetta of his own. No—I can count on Lud." He hoped he was right.

"What will Mr. Sloane do, exactly?"

"I don't know." He sounded worried. "I—I suppose it's a faint hope of mine that he can do anything. But I didn't know what else to do; the whole thing is so nebulous really—no real evidence except my own conviction. But if anything can be done P. H. will know what. And do it." He stopped short. "What's that?" he said sharply and listened.

Eden listened, too, but there was only the distant tinkle from the piano, nothing nearer. Jim laughed a little.

"I'm on edge. Thought I heard something rustling in the pines." They walked on in silence for a few steps. Jim said in a different voice, musingly, "It seems a shame to bring our quarrels to a place like this. It ought to remain unsullied, apart from tragedy and the shadow of war. Look at those mountains, Eden; they're earthly somehow—and yet at the same time elemental, wise, as if they know old secrets of life and living."

He stopped again in the heavy shadow of the pines and Eden stopped too and her sleeve brushed against him and their shoulders touched.

For a long moment they both looked at that distant lofty line, lifting into the night sky, touched to silver by the starlight, mysterious. It was almost breathlessly still.

Then quite deliberately Jim dropped his cigarette in the path, stepped on it, turned to look down through the night into her face and then quite slowly, as if there were finality about it, took her in his arms.

"Eden," he said. "Eden——" and kissed her.

The night was as quiet as if its heart had stopped too, as

Eden's had. The stars looked down and paused in their course and were so near and clear that it was as if they could reach up and pluck them down. And hold their stars in their own hands.

Stars, thought Eden, fate. And closed her eyes, breathless again, shaken by his nearness, by the hard, tight circle of his arms, by his mouth upon her own.

He kissed her again slowly. And said: "Eden—you know. I loved you the first moment I saw you. I—knew it was you."

Her face was warm against his sweater and his tweed coat smelled of smoke and she wanted her head to remain there. But he lifted her face.

"Did you know, too?"

She couldn't answer. He said urgently: "Did you know? Tell me."

"Yes," she whispered. And remembered.

They didn't really hold their stars in their hands. Stars were already set in an inexorable course and couldn't be altered.

There was Averill.

There was, even, Noel.

"What is it, Eden?"

"Averill," she said. "This is all wrong, Jim. I didn't realize——"

He continued to hold her but he was thinking.

"Yes," he said at last, "there's Averill. And I know what this makes me. But I—I can't help it, Eden. There are such things as broken engagements."

"Not—two or three days before a wedding," said Eden. "Not like this."

She must have spoken with rather desperate conviction for Jim's hands went to her shoulders in a tight, hard grip and he said quickly:

"Eden, you're not going to be silly about this. I'm going to marry the woman I love and that's you. And thank God you came when you did—and not a week or two later."

Eden took a long breath.

"I can't do this to Averill. Jim, I can't. I feel so—guilty. It —you see the same thing happened before—only, of course, it wasn't the same thing, because I didn't really love him. But, Averill——"

"Pull yourself together, my child; don't gibber. Now then, what do you mean?"

"I mean Noel—a long time ago—was all but engaged to Averill; and then he—I——"

"You jilted him; I know that. What of it?"

"But, Jim, I can't——"

"Listen, my girl, is that the extent of the desperate barrier you're trying with bated breath to tell me about? My God, I love you, dear, but you really are being very silly. Now listen, and get this straight in your crazy little head. I love you. I loved you the moment somebody trotted you out on the terrace and said 'This is Eden,' and you looked at me and I looked at you. I don't know what happened; I just instantly, then and there, loved you. And I love you now; I'll always love you. How's that for a declaration?"

"Jim——"

"Shush. I'm doing the talking. I love you and we're going to be married. I know it's not very—nice about Averill. If I'd had any sense I'd have waited till that was all over and in the past. But I didn't."

"It's—it's only been two days——"

"Time has nothing to do with it," said Jim in a simple statement of fact.

"If—if we could have met another way—without Averill——"

"I'm sorry about Averill. I—well, I hate that part of it. But I'm not a fool. I'll settle with Averill; and I'm going to marry you. If you'll have me."

It was just exactly then that both of them became aware of quick, light footsteps along the gravel drive. Involuntarily Eden moved away from Jim, who would have held her. A woman's figure, light cloak distinct in the starlight, came rapidly toward them—rapidly and certainly as if she knew where to find them—and it was Averill.

Her small face, framed in black neat hair, looked extraordinarily pale in the starlight. She said at once but with the utmost composure:

"Jim—oh, it's Eden with you. Eden, I want to talk to you. Won't you come with me—it won't take long."

"Averill," said Jim, "I want to talk to you myself. Something has happened——"

"Later, darling," said Averill and linked her cool, slender hand around Eden's arm and drew her toward the path leading to the cabins. "Later, Jim. No—no, you mustn't come along. It's a very private conversation." She laughed a little, lightly, when she said it.

She was perfectly friendly, perfectly calm and restrained.

"But I really do want to talk to you, Averill. Now. I'll come along," said Jim.

"If you insist," said Averill, still lightly. "But Mr. Sloane was asking for you. And Eden and I will be only a moment; then you can talk to me as long as you like."

"Oh," said Jim, "all right. It'll keep. I'll go and see what Sloane wants."

"I'll be along in five minutes," said Averill, with nothing in the world except gayety and confidence in her voice. It struck Eden as queer that with such gayety in her voice, still

65

her hand on Eden's arm was exactly like a small band of steel.

They separated at the place where the two paths branched from the gravel drive. Jim said briefly, "See you after I'm done with Sloane," and walked rapidly toward the lighted house.

And the two women turned along the path that led to the group of cabins at the south end of the house. Pines cast a heavy shadow over it and obscured the lights of the main house although they were so near it now that they could hear the piano clearly—could have heard voices perhaps had there been conversation instead of music.

A single light burned above the door of the cabin nearest the house which Eden and Averill shared. They entered the cabin silently. There was a tiny hall and Eden's room was on the left, away from the house; the door was open with a small light burning above the bed.

"I'll not take a moment," said Averill and drew Eden inside and closed the door.

Her face in the light was extraordinarily pale; her eyes had suddenly retracted so they were small and wary. She too had pulled her heavy sports coat over her dinner dress. Her small black head rose from the wide fur collar venomously somehow. Like a small snake waiting to strike.

Unexpectedly it gave Eden the strangest sensation that was like—but couldn't be—fear.

Averill said, almost lisping as if her mouth had gone dry, but very distinctly:

"Listen, Eden. We've known each other long enough—and too well. People don't change, after all. I'm engaged to marry Jim Cady; we'll be married in a day or two. My marriage will take place exactly as it has been planned. I'm not going to be humiliated—jilted at the altar."

"Averill——"

"I won't talk of loyalty or friendship or decency. We've known each other all our lives—and really, in spite of pretense, hated each other. You're jealous of me, now. You're trying to take him away from me because you're jealous, because you want to hurt and humiliate me. To show me you can still—but you can't. You always won in the past: well, that's over. You can't do this to me. I won't let you. That's all."

Her dry voice shook a little; her fingers worked as if actually they wanted to claw. She gave Eden one still, concentrated look that despite its hatred had something thoughtful and purposeful in it, and turned without another word and left the room. The door closed behind her.

But the really singular thing about that terse, altogether curious interview was that Eden was left with a sense, mainly, of threat.

She didn't hear Averill leave the cabin; she did hear a door close, and she did hear a murmur of voices—women's voices. It lasted only a moment or two and she was only vaguely aware of it.

Silence followed; and she was only vaguely aware of the silence.

But after a long time she stirred, walked absently toward a chair near the fireplace and then leaned instead on the mantel, her elbow on the low wooden piece, her chin in her hand.

Averill was, again, wholly within her rights. Eden was poaching on another woman's preserves; she was as culpable, really, as she would have been if the wedding had already taken place. She was, altogether, indefensibly in the wrong.

And in a definitely strong sense she was the more culpable because of what had already gone on between her and Averill. Because of those years of rivalry—because of Noel.

Jim had taken a perfectly simple, perfectly straightforward, slightly rebellious masculine view. But Jim was wrong.

And she was wrong and Averill—bitter though it was to admit and contemplate it—was right.

Moments must have passed when she heard a kind of jar in the next room. It was loud enough to rouse her from her reverie—yet not exactly loud and sharp either. It sounded as if Averill had opened or closed a door—perhaps dropped something—or jerked hard at a sticking drawer.

She listened simply because it was so still, after that sound, in the next room and because she was standing so close to the fireplace and could hear in that position so clearly. Evidently the fireplace in her room and the one in Averill's room were built on the same chimney.

Hadn't Averill gone, then? She tried to recall what sounds she had heard but there was nothing clear and definite.

But she did all at once hear the door of the cabin open and a second or two later, the door into Averill's room.

It closed quietly and she heard that, too.

As she heard footsteps which crossed the room, very quiet footsteps. It struck her that they were cautious.

There was a long silence before the footsteps recrossed the room.

She heard that quite distinctly. She heard the door to Averill's room close very softly and then softly, too, the outside door of the cabin. And there was certainly a quality of stealth in the cautiousness of those footsteps, in the soft closing of both doors.

It was completely silent in the next room. A long moment or two passed. Then she went to her own door, opened it, crossed the bare little hall and opened Averill's door. She moved quickly; if she gave herself time to think, some indescribably ominous quality in that continued silence would frighten her.

Averill's room was dark. If the night light had been turned on when the bed was turned down as her own had been, then someone had turned it out again.

The room was perfectly quiet—but it was a laden kind of quiet. Ominous again. As if someone were there, waiting, observing.

She started to speak and her throat was dry. She reached inside the doorway and found the electric light switch and turned it on.

And froze there—fingers still on the little brass plate.

A woman lay on the floor; the yellow cloak was flung out around; there was a small spreading mass of crimson—wet, shining dreadfully in the garish light. Over her face and tight around her throat in strong knots was a gray scarf.

A gray chiffon scarf that belonged to Eden.

A window across the room was open and the shade was up and there was no screen over it—so the stars looked in, too, and the waiting night. Breathless and still with horror.

Beyond the pines lights in the main house were visible— so near yet, just then, so dreadfully far away.

Her knees were dissolving under her; she took a fumbling step or two and knelt. Her knees struck something hard and painful and without thinking she reached for whatever it was, thrust it aside and bent over the figure on the floor, stretching out her hand as if to pull the scarf away from the face.

But the gray scarf was so horribly blotched and stained that she couldn't touch it. However, it was then that she saw that the dead woman was not Averill. It was Creda Blaine.

CHAPTER /10

Most of the face mercifully was covered by the gray folds of chiffon. But there were soft yellow curls in wild disarray above it and one white fat little hand lay on the floor beside the yellow outflung cloak with its fingers doubled over. And it was Creda.

Not Averill as Eden had thought in that first horrified, incredulous instant.

But Creda couldn't be dead. It wasn't possible.

She tried to speak and whispered: "Creda." And then cried aloud: "Creda . . . *Creda!*"

Her own voice was unrecognizably thin and high.

There was no flutter of motion in the inert mass there at her feet. No sound in the room but the thud of her own heart.

No one could be hidden in the room for there was no place to hide and the door upon the bathroom was open, revealing its emptiness. Eden remembered that but she didn't, then, consciously make note of it.

Eden had never seen violent death before; it was only deep instinct that warned her of its presence. There wasn't time to explore the fact, to consider why and how, to think of murder. She leaned over Creda again, forcing her fingers to touch those stifling gray knots, to try to unloose them. to seek a pulse on Creda's soft wrist, to try to find her heart. And to fail. The knots were tied with desperate tightness; there was no breath, no flutter of pulse, no motion. She pulled the scarf at last away from the upper part of the face and quickly, almost frantically, covered it again. Her scarf. That wasn't possible either. She never thought of removing it.

A wave of sickness swept over her. She turned blindly toward the window, thinking, if she thought of anything, of fresh air, of fighting off nausea.

And someone moved away from the open window. Someone outside it with a white blurred face looming from that darkness beyond.

She caught only the motion. She had an impression only that it was a face. That therefore someone stood outside the cabin and watched her and the dead woman and vanished when she turned.

She started toward the window; she could call for help. Yet whoever it was must have seen Creda—must have known——

She put her hands to her mouth as if to stifle words on her lips.

This was murder.

It wasn't suicide. Creda herself couldn't have tied those horrible knots. And if it was murder then someone did it.

That white face, vanishing silently like a ghost face into the darkness outside the window! Why hadn't whoever it was called out to her, come to her assistance, demanded at least to know what was wrong!

Terror was in her very veins like an icy stream. She must call the others—rouse everyone—spread the alarm. Would they come if she screamed for help? Dared she leave the gastly, lighted little cabin and venture into the darkness toward the main house?

There was no telephone in the cabin. She turned toward the door. There was no key in the door.

It was then that, photographically, she saw that the small chest of drawers near the door had been pulled out a little from the wall but it meant nothing; she saw it and no more.

If she screamed would they hear her? But she hated to approach the window, with that blurred face, unrecognizable save that it was almost certainly a face, waiting perhaps outside—lurking in the shadow of the pines, aware of her every move.

Actually only a few moments had passed since she entered the cabin but it seemed to Eden that she had strayed far into a morass of incredible ugliness. Murder?

She went toward the window; her fingers were wet and sticky; with a sick kind of shudder she wiped them on her handkerchief and thrust the scrap of linen, marked with her first name, back into her pocket. A small writing table stood near the window. Still terrified and conscious of that unrecognizable white blur that had to be someone's face dwindling into the darkness beyond the window, she approached the window cautiously and stopped at one side of it to listen. The tinkle of music no longer sounded from the main house and it couldn't be far across that thicket of pines and rocks. Certainly in the blank stillness of the night they would hear her scream for help. She leaned against the writing table, one hand spread upon it. Paper crackled like a whisper under her fingers and she looked down. Creda had been writing a note. Words in Creda's flowing handwriting leaped to her eyes: "Cold-blooded murder is too much. I won't do any more, I can't. Jim . . . you must believe me . . ."

Words stopped there and the ink was blurred as if a hand had brushed over it. And just beside it on the painted green table was a drop of a dark, thick substance which had spattered lightly when it fell.

Jim. She read it again, swiftly, and clutched the little paper and crumpled it and thrust it in her pocket. That, as every act of Eden's so far had been, was dictated by sheer instinct. It was no good letting anyone see Jim's name in that dreadfully interrupted note. If Eden had been questioned she would have given that as her reason. At the moment of taking the scrap of paper her reason actually did not operate.

She shrank away from the little table, sinister now because it was a peculiarly telling witness to the dark thing that had happened there. She tried, now, to scream but her throat was dry and no sound came from it. And then someone in the main house came out onto the porch and banged the door loudly and cheerfully and she tried again to scream and did.

It was a dreadful sound, somehow, piercing the darkness and silence of the night. Her own voice—screaming—she heard it with a kind of curiosity. Had she ever in her life before screamed?

Sanity, order, things as they were and ought to continue being, all that normal state of being, was rapidly dissolving. The scream threatened to release her own rigid self-control. Or had it been self-control; hadn't it been simply the paralysis of shock? In another moment she would collapse sobbing on the bed—she could scream again and gibber and——

She gripped the edge of the writing table with both hands and didn't scream or sob or do any of those wild and threatened things. And whoever was on the porch heard her and stopped some vaguely whistled tune and cried out sharply:

"What's that? Who—what's wrong——"

It was Noel. Miraculously she found her voice: "Noel—Noel——"

Her voice must have told him of horror, for he called sharply to someone inside the house. And then footsteps came running along the path, crashing through the thicket.

Noel arrived first and flung open the door and stared, eyes like blue jet, and then ran across to kneel as Eden had done beside Creda.

"Eden, for God's sake——"

"She's dead."

"How—are you sure . . . what happened . . ." His hands, too, were touching Creda, hunting that nonexistent pulse, seeking to pull that stifling, merciless chiffon from Creda's face.

"She's dead, she's dead, she's dead——" Eden heard her own voice as eerie and distant and monotonous as an echo.

He got up and came to Eden and took her in his arms. "Stop that," he said tensely. "Tell me, what happened? What do you mean? What—Eden, tell me——" He turned her so she need not look, so she couldn't stare at Creda. "Eden, for God's sake——"

And then the others came. Strevsky, the pilot, was first, oddly enough. Then Jim and Pace and Averill. And Dorothy Woolen, too, face as flabby and white as a piece of dough.

Someone—Noel probably—had put Eden in a chair. Everybody was talking. Everybody was questioning. Somebody screamed thinly and sharply. She closed her eyes against the turmoil, against horror, against sickening reality.

It wasn't a nightmare. Five—perhaps three minutes—in time had made a gulf none of them could ever recross.

Noel was still beside her, holding both her hands, patting them a little as if he didn't know what he was doing. There was talk and they were lifting Creda and saying she was dead and there was nothing anyone could do and what had happened. They kept repeating that. What had happened? When? And at last Jim's voice said: "Who did it? It wasn't suicide. It couldn't have been suicide. Who——"

"Eden found her," said Noel. "Give her a moment. She can't talk yet. Has anybody got any brandy or whisky or——"

"Chango, go to the house. Get some brandy——" Dimly Eden thought she didn't recognize that voice and then recog-

71

nized it. It was Sloane, the rancher. No, no, the detective. But no one knew that except herself and Jim. A detective—what would he do?

And who was Chango? Oh yes, she knew perfectly well, it was the Chinese houseboy.

She was, then, sensible; all that dizziness and confusion didn't mean that she had fainted or that the black waves of sickness had completely submerged her. She was perfectly sensible. But her eyes were closed and her muscles like lead and the voices of all the others were blurred and only now and then a clear phrase or word came to her ears out of the hubbub.

Moments must have passed without her consciousness of time for all at once someone was holding a glass to her lips.

"Drink this," said a voice. She opened her eyes and the rancher—no, the detective—P. H. Sloane was bending over her, his face a queer ash gray in the bright light, his eyes two bright points of light. He was telling her to drink. She drank and choked on the fiery brandy and drank again, still choking.

And there was something she had to tell him.

"There's blood," she said, coughing. "There's blood. On the table."

"Finish the brandy. Yes, I saw that. Can you talk?"

She opened her lips again and he tilted the glass. Jim was standing beside the rancher; she saw Jim now, and felt, through the curious haziness around her, that he was trying to speak to her. Yet he said nothing; it was only that there was some message, some urgent message in his eyes. And something she couldn't understand. And she must talk to him, though just as that instant she couldn't remember what she must tell him.

The brandy was like a flame. Already it was running along her pulse; her head was clearing a little. She still wouldn't look but was conscious of Creda, on the bed now. Of others crowding the little room. Of Dorothy Woolen, pasty-faced, sitting as flaccid as a pillow on a chair, hands gripping its arms. Of Noel's warm hand, encouraging, on her own shoulder. Of Pace standing in the far corner of the room, face a blank, livid mask, little eyes darting suspiciously here and there about the room. Strevsky was beside him, thick neck and handsome Slavic head thrust forward above Pace's short broad shoulder. The little steward was there, too, shrinking in a corner behind Pace, frightened, pale as a shadow. And the Chinese houseboy was there too, and—why, cowboys, of course. Several of them; blue jeans and flannel shirts and brown faces which wore exactly the same expression of intense but extremely guarded interest.

And Averill.

She stood beside the little writing table as erect as a knife; she clung to Jim's arm but that was the only sign of weakness about her. She wore now a silk coat—pale pink with glimmering swirls around her feet; her face was extremely white and rigid but her eyes were very much alive. And Averill, too, seemed to be saying something to Eden, mutely, with her eyes.

Averill. Whose yellow cloak was wrapped about that lifeless thing on the bed. They shouldn't have moved Creda, Eden thought suddenly. You weren't supposed to move a murdered person until someone had given you permission to do it. Who, then; what official? But this Sloane before her was some kind of official. No, that was wrong. He was retired. But he expected her to reply to a question he had asked.

She put her hand to her head which seemed extraordinarily light and said:

"Yes. Yes, I can talk."

Jim said: "Easy there." He looked from her to Sloane. "She's had a shock——"

"I know," said Sloane, watching her, "but I think she's all right. I think she can talk. And I've got to know what happened, quick."

"Nothing—nothing happened," said Eden. "I just found her—like that." She felt all at once quite clear and lucid and the nightmarish, confused quality of the scene was leaving her. Struck by a sudden thought she put her hand upon the rancher's brown, hard wrist. "She *is*—dead, isn't she? There's nothing I could have done——"

P. H. Sloane straightened a little, his face looking very bronzed but still pale under the bronze, his white shirt front and black tie appearing curiously orthodox somehow, orderly in all that debauch of disorder. He said rather quietly:

"Was she dead, then, when you found her?"

"Oh yes. Yes, I made sure. I touched her wrist."

"What for?"

"Why, for—for the pulse, of course. There wasn't any."

"You did nothing else?"

Jim was looking hard at her again as if he were trying desperately to make her understand something he could not say. Warning—was it? But why? She hadn't killed Creda.

She had thrust a note into her pocket. She'd done nothing else. She said:

"No. I—I was frightened."

There was a catch in her voice. Sloane said: "Of course you were. But now suppose you tell me quickly how you happened to find her. Where were you—what were you doing? I suppose you"—he hesitated—"you didn't actually see her killed, did you?"

Eden shrank back and put her hands over her face. "No,

73

no," she cried. "I—I just came in. Only a few moments ago. I was in my room, you see. Next door. And I—it was so silent in here——"

A cowboy entered, glanced at Sloane and said quietly: "I got the sheriff. He'll start in an hour or so with a deputy. Ought to be here by two or three o'clock . . . Boys haven't found anybody yet."

"All right. Take lights into the pines. Get both cars out along the roads."

"Sure." The cowboy disappeared again. Sloane said to Eden: "Now you were in your room next door. It was quiet in this room. Why did you come in here? Did you know she was here?"

"No, no, I didn't know it. I—there were footsteps, you see."

"Listen, Miss Shore, I realize you've had a shock. We've all had. It is imperative for me to know at once exactly how and when you found her. Will you please try to pull yourself together and tell me?"

"Yes." Eden swallowed hard. "Yes, of course. I was in my room you see. I don't remember hearing anything. But all at once there was a sound from this room as if—as if something had been moved. As if a drawer had stuck and someone pulled it out. Then it was quiet—but of course I thought someone was here. Then—then all at once I heard the outer door open and footsteps enter this room and then after a few moments tiptoe away again. It was after they'd gone that I—I came. And she was there. Just as you found her. That's all I know."

"Did you hear the sound of voices?"

"No. That is, not then. I——" She glanced at Averill whose small white face was as hard as that of a marble statue. "I had come to the cabin with Averill; we talked in my room for a few moments, then Averill went away. I don't remember hearing her leave—or hearing in fact anything that was clear and definite. I do have a kind of impression that I heard voices——"

"Men's voices, or women's?"

"I think—women's. I can't be sure. I didn't notice anything at all until I heard the—the sound——"

"What kind of sound?"

"I told you. As if a drawer had stuck——"

P. H. Sloane said, "Wait a minute," glanced once around the room and went to the small chest of drawers which stood a little away from the wall. It was at an angle, obviously out of order. He said: "Did it sound like this?" and pulled the chest a little further from the wall.

It made a distinct, scraping sound.

"Yes," said Eden. "It was like that. It might have been that."

P. H. Sloane stood for a moment beside the chest.

"I see," he said. "Well, it doesn't help us much. You're sure she was—dead?"

"Yes—yes——"

"She didn't speak to you?"

"Oh no," cried Eden on a sobbing breath. Noel took her hand again and patted it absently and Averill stared at her with bright, enigmatic eyes, and turned suddenly to the detective.

"Creda is wearing my coat. She's wearing it now."

P. H. Sloane glanced at her, said, "Yes, I know that," and came back to Eden. "Then what did you do?"

"After I came in here, you mean? Well, it was so quiet after those footsteps had gone—it—there was something—I can't describe it. I had to come. So I—I did. The light was turned out. I found it and turned it on and there she was." It was rather dreadful to tell it. She fastened her eyes upon the detective so she need not look at the room—at the floor —at the dark splatter on the little writing table.

"And you——"

"What did I do, you mean? Why, I—I suppose I called out. Spoke to her. She—she didn't answer. I was kneeling beside her then. But she was dead. I—I got up and went to the window and screamed."

And that glimpse of what looked like a white face. She must tell them that, too. As she started to speak Sloane said:

"Listen, Miss Shore, when those footsteps, as you say, tiptoed out of the cabin, you are sure whoever it was really did leave the cabin?"

"Yes—oh yes. Besides, there was no one here. Except Creda."

"And you don't know who it was that entered and then tiptoed out again?"

"No. I didn't see him."

"Him?"

"Whoever it was," amended Eden hastily. "I don't know who it was."

There was a little silence.

P. H. Sloane glanced at one of the cowboys.

"Slim, you and Harris stay here. Don't let anybody touch anything. Now then, folks." He turned to the others. "We'll go up to the house. The sheriff will be here soon as he can make it. Meantime we'll wait where it's more comfortable. By the way, Miss Blaine—when you left Miss Shore in her room where did you go?"

Averill drew herself up deliberately.

"I did not leave Eden in her room," she said distinctly. "I was not there with her. I met her on the path, talked to her for a moment and went directly to the house. I did not come to the cabin at all."

Eden gasped with the shock of it.

"Averill, that's not true," she cried, starting to her feet. "Tell him the truth."

"I am telling him the truth," said Averill quite coolly. "I can't imagine why you lied to him." She turned again, coolly, to the detective. "I saw nobody and heard nothing. I went directly to the house, stood for a moment or two on the porch, smoking, and then went inside. You must have seen me there with the others."

"But, Averill——" cried Eden and stopped. For to her dismay the detective nodded slowly.

"Yes, I remember you were there. You mean Mrs. Blaine could have been dead for some time before she was discovered. In that case it becomes more and more important to discover just who it was that Miss Shore heard enter the cabin." He took out a package of cigarettes, withdrew one, and turned it in his fingers for a moment before he said: "If that person will step forward and explain——"

Instantly there was almost unearthly silence in the crowded little cabin—with Creda lying there on the bed, stained gray chiffon unknotted at last but replaced in light folds over her marred face. With her fat white little hand hanging limply downward.

After a moment P. H. Sloane shrugged a little. He said dryly: "I expect it's too much to ask. However—Miss Blaine, as you remarked, Mrs. Blaine is wearing the yellow cloak you were wearing earlier in the evening. Can you explain that?"

"Certainly," said Averill instantly. "As you see, I'm wearing her evening wrap. I met her on the porch, just as I walked out of the house. You were playing the piano, Mr. Sloane. I walked out for a breath of air and because the night was so beautiful. I met her on the porch; she said she was cold and I wasn't; we traded coats. Mine was warmer than hers and I'm never cold. She went away then. I didn't notice where. I walked on down the path where I met Eden—Miss Shore. We talked for a moment and I went back to the house as I've told you. I was not near the cabin. I don't know anything of this."

"Averill, that's not true. You were here with me. And you were wearing that yellow cloak." Eden turned almost passionately toward Sloane. "I swear it," she cried. "I'm telling you the truth."

Sloane put up his hand as if for silence. He said: "You noticed the yellow coat when you found Mrs. Blaine dead?"

"Why, yes, of course," cried Eden. "I thought——"

76

"You thought what?" said P. H. Sloane very softly. Again it was silent in the packed little cabin with all these faces watching. And again there was a kind of warning in Jim's eyes. Noel said suddenly: "Take it easy, Eden."

And Eden said: "I thought it was Averill. Until I saw it was Creda."

"I see," said P. H. Sloane slowly.

And Averill, with a swirl of taffeta, swept suddenly across to P. H. Sloane and put both her hands upon his black sleeve and lifted her white face and cried: "Don't you see? Don't you see that it was I they meant to kill? My coat—my room —the veil was over her face so they couldn't see it was Creda. They meant to kill me."

"You can't say that——" cried Noel, and Jim said: "Averill —stop——"

But Averill wouldn't stop.

"Ask Eden whose scarf that is. Ask her if it belongs to her. Ask her why she did it."

CHAPTER/11

Jim had taken Averill by the arm and was shaking it and shouting: "Averill, that's monstrous! That's crazy! Don't listen to her, P. H. She doesn't mean what she's saying. She wouldn't make any such crazy accusation if she was herself. It's the shock—it's—Averill, tell him you didn't mean what you said. Averill——"

And Noel was talking, too. Stepping between Averill and Eden so she could no longer see Averill's slender, tense figure, swathed in billowing silk.

"Eden didn't kill Creda. Averill doesn't realize the thing she said. She didn't mean it. Suppose it is Eden's scarf around her throat; that doesn't mean anything. Why, Eden couldn't have killed her; she's not strong enough. They would have struggled, Creda would have called for help, someone would have heard her. Besides, Eden had no quarrel with Creda, no possible motive. Eden—oh, it's absurd, don't listen to Averill."

Again P. H. Sloane put up his brown, lean hand. The gesture induced silence and he said in a quiet and measured way:

"We'll go to the main house and wait for the sheriff. Meantime, if, on consideration, any of you remember or discover any evidence you think ought to be known I'd strongly advise you to tell it. You may not have had time to comprehend the seriousness of this thing. And the importance of telling anything you know or observed." He stopped rather abruptly, turned and said to Chango: "You have a flashlight. You go ahead, Chango, and light the way for the ladies. Now then——"

He waited until they all filed slowly from the cabin—all, that is, except two long, brown, capable-looking cowboys who remained. Eden herself was conscious of Noel's arm around her; it was a light touch but sustaining; without it she doubted whether she could have risen and walked out of the horror-freighted cabin and along the path. The night was still, the stars as clear as they had been half an hour ago. Ahead Chango's flashlight glanced here and there eerily, lighting the pines, lighting the path in flashes. Behind her someone spoke and then was silent. Where was Jim? Oh yes; there he was ahead with Averill whose light, long skirt looked ghostly, glimmering in the half light from Chango's torch. The coat she wore was obviously a coat belonging to Creda, one Averill couldn't possibly have chosen; pale pink taffeta with ruffles, pulled in slenderly at the waist and then billowing downward in yards and yards of the silken, whispering stuff. Sometime certainly between Averill's short, ugly interview with Eden in Eden's own room and (a few moments later) the discovery of Creda's body, Averill and Creda had changed coats. For Averill was wearing the yellow cloak when she came upon Jim and Eden in the shadow of the pines and went with Eden to Eden's cabin. Eden remembered that clearly. Therefore that meeting with Creda and exchange of coats took place in the short interval following Averill's talk with Eden. Why, then, had she lied?

But why, then, had she burst out with that sharp, ugly attack upon Eden? An attack so unexpected, and so plainly virulent that it robbed itself of its own sting. Or did it?

Was there stirring question in the eyes that turned toward Eden? Jim had tried to defend her and Noel had done so instantly, too. But what really did all of them think?

She had found Creda. She had been by her own admission alone in the cabin with Creda. And it was her own gray scarf knotted with murderous tightness and strength around Creda's throat.

That scarf. Where had she last seen it—on the plane, of course. She had put it softly around her throat and gone to sleep. And when she awoke to the amazing sight she awoke to (only that morning?) the scarf was gone and she looked for it briefly and forgot it. Then had whoever murdered Creda been plotting murder even then? Exploring ways and means, deciding on the scarf not only as a means of murder, but as a means of confusing any possible clues?

Noel at her side said nothing; his arm warm and steady upheld her. They had reached the steps—they were crossing the wide porch. Incredibly the lights inside fell upon utter order and normalness. The room was exactly as it had been;

nothing out of place, nothing changed except perhaps the chairs were pushed about a little as if people had sprung from them hurriedly when she and then Noel shouted for help.

He put her swiftly into a deep, cushioned armchair and stood there for a moment looking down at her.

"Can I get you anything?"

"No. Noel—that scarf—how could Averill——"

"You know Averill. She's always that way with you. Averill's a—a stubborn hater. You ought to know that by this time. Eden dear, don't look like that. You poor kid. Stumbling upon Creda——"

"Don't——"

"I know. I won't. Only, Eden, isn't there anything you can think of that will sort of—well, distract the sheriff when he comes? I mean—good God, Eden, everything you've told up to now could be used (if the sheriff's a knothead as he may be) actually to incriminate you. You couldn't possibly have done anything like that. That's just absurd. But you do realize, don't you, dear, that the sheriff——"

"Noel, you can't mean anybody suspects me——"

"There, now, Eden. I mean—oh God, what a mess. Listen. You've told them you found her; you've told them you were alone in the cabin with her. You've told them you didn't hear a sound—and, Eden, don't you see there *must* have been some sound? Murder—a murder like that—there had to be a—a struggle of some kind. Creda must have called for help."

"There wasn't anything, Noel. I've told everything——"

"I know, Eden dear. That's just the trouble. That's what I'm trying to tell you not to do. I mean—just don't say any more than you have to. But if there's anything in the world to—to give the sheriff an idea of what happened, who murdered her, for God's sake tell it."

"But, Noel—there's nothing. I—it's not real, any of it. Things like this just don't happen to—to people like us."

Noel smiled a little.

"A very snobbish remark, my child," he said. "Murder can happen anywhere. But the really charming thought about this is that you have to know anybody pretty well to want to murder them. Murder is a plant of slow growth—and I don't think any of these cowboys—or Sloane or Chango or the cook—took such an instant and violent dislike to Creda they had to murder her."

"You mean—oh, Noel, none of us murdered her! That's horrible."

"It's not a nice thought, no." His eyes traveled slowly around the room. "Not at all nice," he repeated. "There's the lot. Averill and Jim. Dorothy. Pace, who's in the same category as Sloane inasmuch as he met Creda only a night or two

79

ago. You and me—I'll have to retract, Eden. I can't see any of us doing murder. What do you think?"

With a new and dreadful question in her eyes she followed his look. The others were grouped in little clusters. P. H. Sloane was at the door, giving Chango low-voiced orders probably, for the little Chinese was listening intently, his black eyes shining, and nodding briskly at every word. Averill was standing with Jim and Dorothy Woolen before the fireplace where the fire had burned down to ashes. Averill's face was ghastly above the pale pink taffeta, her mouth as brightly and heavily crimson as if she had dipped it in blood. Jim was talking to her, swiftly and in a low murmur which Eden could barely distinguish. Dorothy was like a blank, wooden statue painted in the palest pastels—ash-blonde hair with its great braid around her bland, blank pale face. Pale blue eyes staring fixedly at Eden. Pale lips, never touched with crimson make-up and now almost gray, lent a kind of flabbiness to her whole face. As Eden met her eyes she came forward, slowly, and said:

"Is there anything I can do, Miss Shore? It must have been a dreadful shock."

Her words were kindness and friendliness itself; her voice and pale eyes utterly blank and without expression. But Eden was about to take the words at their face value and thank the girl when Dorothy spoke again. She said calmly, almost monotonously:

"It seems too bad to make such a fuss about Mrs. Blaine's death. I mean this talk of murder. It's so obvious that it was suicide."

There was an instant's silence. Then Noel said sharply: "Suicide! What do you—— By God, I never thought of that!"

Dorothy's pale eyes went to Noel.

"Why, yes," she said. "Of course. Mrs. Blaine—on account of what happened yesterday. It's so clear. After the crash, I mean, with Mr. Blaine killed."

"But, Creda——" began Noel and stopped. And Eden thought: "But she didn't care—much. She didn't love Bill. Nobody believed she really loved Bill."

Dorothy went on blandly: "I think the sheriff when he comes ought to be told that she had a motive for suicide."

"But—those knots," began Eden and Noel caught her up: "Exactly. Those knots. She couldn't have tied them herself. I saw Sloane untie them. She couldn't possibly——"

"Suicides have extraordinary determination sometimes. I would—explain the whole thing to the sheriff when he comes."

Again there was a little pause while Noel stared at the girl. Then his eyes lighted and he said with an air of decision: "Dorothy, my dear, you're right. Bless you. It's an idea."

Dorothy replied something but Eden didn't listen. For she was thinking Creda, Bill, the crash and now Creda's murder. And for the first time she thought of a connection between the two. The unexpected airplane crash which Jim was convinced was purposeful; the vanished plans, and Creda's murder. Put together it added up irresistibly to Pace.

And the very name itself was like a brilliant flash of lightning serving for an instant to light up a darkened scene.

If Pace had stolen the plans, if Pace had been behind that crash and thus Bill's death, had Pace murdered Creda?

Creda had known him. Almost certainly she had known him in spite of her denials. Her denials indeed had only served to further convince Eden of her acquaintance with the man.

But why? Had she been about to denounce him? If so she would have had to be able to prove an accusation she made against him.

The instant of clear perception had gone as quickly as it flashed upon her. If it was Pace how could it be proved?

Yet there was no one else who could conceivably have murdered Creda. For there was no motive. And none of them were homicidal maniacs, killing without motive—for the sheer pleasure of killing.

"Well, Eden, what's your conclusion?" said Noel suddenly.

"Where is Major Pace?"

Noel's bright eyes narrowed. "He's out there in the hall. With Strevsky. Why, Eden? Is there something you remember? What makes you think of him?"

"There's no one else who could have done it," said Eden, forgetting Dorothy's presence and her habitual air of listening and recording.

"Have you any evidence? Try to think, Eden. Any little scrap of evidence?"

But there was nothing. And the feeling of clarity, of comprehension, of the imminence of truth had gone again. Eden shook her head wearily. And Sloane walked toward the fireplace, stood there for a moment beside Averill, looking at them thoughtfully, and then said:

"I've just had a telephone call from the sheriff. There's been a bad accident at the other end of the county; he's got to go—it's a railroad affair. A couple of cars went through a bridge. He can't get here now; he's not sure when he can come. But he's made me deputy. Me and a couple of my boys. Swore us in over the telephone. It's not the first time——"

There was a faint stress upon the last few words; a definite significance. It was because he was really a detective. Eden knew it and Jim knew it, but no one else. Was he going to tell them? Warn them? Throw down the gauntlet? Or was it to give himself official authority?

Averill picked up the words sharply. She said: "Not the first time? You mean you often act as his deputy? And that now you—you, yourself, will conduct an inquiry——"

"An inquiry into murder. Yes," said P. H. Sloane. "I'm a detective, you know."

He said it easily, almost casually, but Eden had a quick impression that he was watching the effect of his announcement.

It came at once.

There was a second of utter, complete silence. Noel's hand paused on its way to a cigarette box, Pace (just entering the door and followed by Strevsky) stopped so abruptly to look at Sloane that Strevsky brought up short against him and stopped, too, to stare with those bright, animal eyes, narrow and watchful, at Sloane. And into the silence Averill said suddenly and thinly:

"You—a detective. You must be joking."

"I was never more serious in my life."

"But you—you can't be! I mean you're a rancher. You own this ranch. You—why, you're our landlord really."

"I'm a rancher and I'm at the moment your landlord. But I——" He glanced at Jim. "I think you better tell them, Jim."

"Jim——" repeated Averill in a kind of whisper and turned questioning eyes to Jim.

"But, P. H.——"

"Go ahead. We've got to begin at the beginning. And I very much think the beginning was as you believe it to have been."

"You do believe me, then," said Jim quickly. "You didn't at first——"

"I do now," said Sloane. "And I also advise full explanation to your friends, Jim——"

Averill interrupted sharply.

"Jim, you came here purposely. You knew him. You knew he was here. Why did you do it? Was it because of the crash—— Oh, Jim, you're out of your mind! You can't believe him, Mr. Sloane. There was nothing about that crash——"

"Hush, Averill," said Jim. "I've told him everything about it. And now he believes with me——"

"Believes what, in God's name?" flashed Averill.

"That it was a phony crash," said P. H. Sloane almost casually.

Noel walked toward him.

"Why do you believe that, Mr. Sloane?" he asked. "What has Jim told you?"

"What he knew of it," said Sloane. "Why?"

"Because we—none of us but Jim even thought of it being,

82

as you say, phony. There was no motive. No one had anything against Bill Blaine; he was a man with no enemies. And as for the engine, Major Pace had openly offered to buy it; well, then, he wasn't likely to have anything to do with wrecking the very thing he was buying. Granted Jim hated it about the engine failing, still it did fail. There's no dodging that. If Jim brought us out here, lying about the plane, lying about you——"

Noel was white, his eyes blazing, his head up like a war horse scenting smoke of battle. Averill was white, too, and angry.

She whirled again toward Jim.

"How dare you do this to me, Jim Cady! How dare you bring us here—enlist a detective—delay our arrival at the plantation—Jim——" Her voice choked. She was almost literally too angry to speak. Jim said:

"Forgive me, Averill. I had to do it. P. H. was the only man I could think of."

"Jim, let's get this straight," said Noel. "In spite of everything you still believe that that crash was—well, as your friend says, phony?"

"There's nothing else for me to believe," said Jim. "I told you that from the first. I tried to convince you. Nobody would listen to me."

"You think the engine was fixed?"

Jim took a long breath.

"I know it was," he said.

"You know——" Noel stopped short. Averill cried: "What do you mean, Jim? If you have proof—if you know who did it—— Oh, but that's impossible." She turned swiftly to Sloane. "You can't believe him."

"Yesterday," said P. H. Sloane deliberately, "the trial plane crashed and two men were killed. Tonight—just now, not an hour ago—a woman in my house was killed. That was murder. It couldn't have been anything else. It was not suicide so there's no use trying to make me think it was suicide—if any of you had that intention. It was murder. Well, then, how do I know that other thing was not murder? Suppose those two men were cold-bloodedly, designedly murdered."

"But—but even so——"

"Even so it would be nothing you could concern yourself with," said Noel.

"But I intend to do so," said Sloane, all at once speaking in a silken tone. "Can you stop me? Do you want to stop me?"

"Good God, yes," shouted Noel, suddenly letting out his anger. "Do you think I can't see the stinking mess this is going to be? Jim, you're a fool! You've started all this. Can't you see what it may mean——"

"Then you think it's murder, too?" said Jim.

83

"I—I think it was suicide. I think that crash was accident. I think Creda killed herself because of it. Because of Bill's death. And—and even if I don't really think it," said Noel with sudden candor, "I think it's better for us to think it. Look here, Sloane, you're a good egg. Let us all go. Tell the sheriff it was suicide—you can't prove it wasn't. Let us go without all this horrible mess of inquiry. You'll get nowhere. The crash yesterday really was accident——"

"Look here, Noel," said Jim suddenly. "You'd better know. It wasn't accident. The fuel line was cut."

"Jim——"

Strevsky, Eden was aware, had pushed past Pace who still stood like a swarthy fat statue, unmoved, blinking only at the mention of his own name as an obvious and first suspect. There was no way of guessing what was going on behind his swarthy face except that there was no suggestion of fright or even dismay. The pilot came quickly across the room; he was graceful and powerful as a leopard.

"He's right, Mr. Sloane," he said. "I saw it myself. It had been cut and mended with something like wax. The wax wouldn't melt and give way until the engine became heated. I can swear to that. I think it's almost the only way it could have been done. Flames like that—all at once."

Averill turned around and sank into a chair as if all strength had gone out of her slender body. Dorothy Woolen said something, Eden didn't know what.

Noel didn't move or speak. Only his blue eyes blazed into Strevsky's. And Sloane said quite deliberately again:

"Thank you, Strevsky. We'll go into that later, Jim. Just now, the main thing is the murder of Creda Blaine. It is murder. And it happened not more than an hour ago. Here in my house. Murder is not a thing apart. It's done by hands. It's done for motive. It's done usually because of the most urgent necessity. We'll stick to this just now. Mr. Carreaux——" He extended his hand toward Noel and the hand held something in its grasp.

It was a revolver. And the detective held it carefully, gingerly, with a handkerchief between his palm and the dully glowing surface of the revolver.

He said: It's your revolver, isn't it, Mr. Carreaux?"

"My——" Noel stopped, eyes riveted to the revolver. "Where——"

"Then it is your revolver?"

"Let me look at it."

"By all means."

There was an instant's pause. Then Noel tore his eyes from the revolver and flung up his head.

"Yes, it's mine. Where did you find it?"

"It was beside Mrs. Blaine. In the cabin. On the floor."

CHAPTER/12

"But she wasn't shot," said Noel after a moment. He spoke stiffly. "She—was strangled. Wasn't she?"

"Then it is your revolver?" repeated the detective.

Noel shrugged helplessly.

"Of course it's mine. At least it looks like mine. And I had one in my bag. But I don't know how it got there."

"Why did you have it with you? Is it your custom?"

"No, it isn't. I just happened to have it and when I was packing saw it among my things at Averill's—I'd been staying there for a few weeks and naturally took it along rather than leave a loaded revolver there——"

"You knew it was loaded?"

"Certainly. If a shot's been fired from it—well, I mean if no shot has been fired from it that proves she wasn't shot with it, doesn't it? And besides she—she wasn't shot. She was strangled——"

"You saw the blood, didn't you?" said P. H. Sloane. "And if the revolver is fully loaded as you see it is, that doesn't necessarily prove it hasn't been fired and reloaded. However——" He paused thoughtfully and then continued briskly: "However, there's only one thing I'd like to know now—about this revolver at least. And that is how it came to be there."

"But I don't know," cried Noel. "I tell you I haven't the faintest idea. It was in my bag—I remember slipping it into a pocket when I was packing. But I—I simply don't remember seeing it since."

"It's impossible to tell just what was the cause of her death —the direct and immediate cause, I mean—until we've had a doctor look at her and had a post-mortem. And as you say the gun is still loaded and I'm inclined to think we would have heard a gunshot. We in this room might not have heard it because of the piano but Miss Shore couldn't have failed to hear it——" He paused there and looked inquiringly at Eden.

"I didn't hear a shot," she said. "There was nothing—except those footsteps and the sound that drew my attention to the presence in the next room——"

"Look here," said Noel abruptly. "I want to know just where I stand. I mean—that revolver. Am I suspect?"

"You want it straight?" said P. H. "All right. You are. And not only you. Everybody on the place is suspect until we get at the truth. No one here at the ranch knew Mrs. Blaine, it's true. Murder is usually a last resort of some intensely personal and desperate urgency. That would seem to exclude me and my boys, but I've got to make sure of it. The most reason-

85

able answer to this thing would be a tramp, an intruder—we can't exclude that, either, until daylight when we can make a more intensive search."

"But—but you cannot ever altogether exclude that possibility. Can you?" It was Dorothy, calm, dispassionate, observing.

P. H. Sloane smiled briefly.

"Yes, we can. It's a large county but a scant population. I'd venture to say there's not a soul in the county whose presence has been unobserved and whose business is not known. This may seem incredible to you; you'll just have to take my word for it.

"Well," he concluded unexpectedly, "there are things that have got to be done. If I were you I'd go to bed—all of you. Chango and one of the boys will move your things to the main house; the bedrooms here are not quite so desirable as those in the cabins but I imagine in view of what's happened you—at least the ladies—would rather spend the night in the main house."

"Oh yes, yes," said Eden with a gasp. Averill agreed, too, not quite so eagerly, but Dorothy Woolen demurred.

"I'm quite comfortable in the cabin," she said. "I'd rather not move."

"But, Dorothy—it's better," said Jim and Noel agreed: "Don't be silly, Dorothy. Murder——"

In the end she was persuaded by Sloane's coolly giving an order to Chango to move Miss Woolen as well as Miss Shore and Miss Blaine. Dorothy did not again object but there was a blank, stolid look in her face.

"The boys have been searching the grounds as thoroughly as is possible tonight," said Sloane. "There are things I will have to do; in the morning perhaps the sheriff can get here, certainly the coroner. Chango—you'll see that the ladies are comfortable." The Chinese boy bowed and bobbed away. And P. H. Sloane said simply: "Good night—try to rest. Tomorrow will be a difficult day for you all. Jim, will you come along with me, please? No, thanks, I won't need anyone else."

He walked quietly out of the room. Jim glanced once at Eden and followed.

Always to Eden it marked a kind of division.

It was as if, going along a deep but swift and steady stream, she had plunged unexpectedly over a rocky precipice and into a seething, twisting cauldron below. And then fighting her way through that indescribably confusing and bewildering trough she had at last emerged from the first shock of it, into the stream again. It was a treacherous stream full of hidden rocks and deep and powerful currents of human motives which then she was only dimly aware of. But Sloane's disappearance, his terse advice, the abrupt silence that followed his departure marked in her mind a grateful emergence from those first half-answered, half-asked streams of questions, of speculation let loose, of horror. Indubitable horror. That was, just at first, the worst of it.

It is always difficult to adjust one's self to death. The irrevocability of it is always a too amazing phenomenon for the mind to grasp immediately. The nearness of Creda's presence, the mere fact of the shortness of the time which had elapsed since Creda, alive, sentient, had been one of them was in itself baffling. Creda, plumply pretty and aware of it, adjusting her youthful gowns, glancing at her rosy fingernails, powdering her pretty nose and putting lipstick with the utmost care upon her rosebud mouth. Creda with her pansy brown eyes, demure behind those extravagant lashes. Creda with her soft, childish curls.

Yet since the airplane crash she had been a different Creda; she had been silent, with that childish babble—which yet, oddly, didn't tell anything Creda didn't want told—still. Creda herself quiet, as curiously unobtrusive as, usually, she was coquettishly obtrusive.

Why had she so changed? Was it due to Bill Blaine's dreadful death? Or was there another reason—a less accountable reason, one that lay more deeply imbedded in Creda's selfish, secret little nature.

The change in Creda, however, showed at least one thing and that was that she had a capacity for silence and for secretiveness.

And there was a kind of cruel exasperation in the sense of her continuing nearness, in their inability, yet, to comprehend the enormous reticence of death. If only she could tell them what had happened. If only she could explain those footsteps and the silence in the cabin where she must have died.

Eden, alone in the room allotted to her in the main house, sat dully on the edge of the bed and considered it.

With, in her pocket, the letter Creda's fat little fingers had begun to write and tragically stopped.

She must see Jim; she must give him the letter.

Her own gray chiffon scarf in tight hard knots around Creda's soft throat.

She was shuddering, curiously cold and trembling. Chango came to the door and she started violently when he knocked and asked if he might bring her bags into the room. She said "Yes" and did not move while the little Chinese trotted into the room, put down her bags and pattered quickly about, seeing there were towels and soap in the adjoining bathroom, seeing the windows were open upon the still starlit night, seeing there was water in the little carafe beside the bed.

"Sleep well, missee," he said and pointed to a key in the door. "Here is key, missee. Good night." He chuckled and smiled himself out the door again. And Eden rose as if she were a doll pulled by wires, went to the door and locked it with a nervous strong jerk of her fingers.

Jim had followed Sloane instantly from the room. Noel had gone with Chango to get his own bags. The men, then, too were to be moved to the main house, for protection? Or to give Sloane a better chance to watch them?

There was no possibility of getting away even if any of them had wanted to leave. Sloane had made that abundantly clear. Fifty miles to the nearest town. Only two cars on the place. "There's not a soul in the county whose presence is unobserved and whose business is not known."

She remembered the enormous expanse of flatland, no cities, no stream of human traffic along highways where one might lose himself, which she had seen from the plane. She remembered the barrier the mountains made. Sangre de Cristo—red in the morning light.

No, there was no escape. And anyway you could not escape anything geographically. Simply by removing yourself. You had to fight through—even when it was murder.

Jim.

She wondered what he was doing. Why had he gone with Sloane? Wouldn't his old friendship with Sloane incline the detective in their favor?

Her own gray scarf.

She kept coming back to that. And remembering Creda flung upon the floor in Averill's yellow cloak.

She must rouse herself, move about, arrange her toilet things—go to bed.

But she moved in a daze. Eventually she got undressed and into bed. But with her hand stretched out to turn off the lights she couldn't, although never in her life before had she been afraid of the dark.

If there were sounds of search about the place, then she couldn't hear the sounds. Once or twice she thought she heard voices and feet on the porch below her window, but if so the sounds were too well muffled to be heard distinctly. What would the next day bring? Why hadn't she removed the scarf from Creda's throat? Her own scarf. She intended to think, to try to assemble and consider the chaotic circumstance of Creda's death. But the facts were too incomplete, too little explored. Too much left in abeyance, inconclusively, pending Sloane's own activities and decision.

Of one thing only she was certain and that was that the first hurried plunge into inquiry had brought forth only the barest shreds of fact.

What, then, lay deeper?

She was thinking desperately of Pace when, because she was physically and nervously exhausted, unconsciousness possessed her like a faint.

She roused dazedly, dragging herself from sleep as from a drug, when someone knocked sharply at her door.

"Who—who is it?"

"Averill. Let me in, Eden. Hurry."

The light, of course, was still on, glaring in her eyes. But almost instantly she remembered sharply why she had left the light turned on and had gone to sleep as she must have done with the bright bulb glaring into her face. She rubbed her eyes, realized that there was urgency in Averill's sharp whisper, and got up and went to the door in her thin white pajamas. She caught a queer glimpse of herself in the mirror over the bureau at the end of the room; a slender woman, looking tall in the long, full white trousers, her brown hair disheveled, her face white above the tailored white collar of her pajama coat. Her eyes were wide and dark and looked frightened. She unlocked and opened the door.

Averill came quickly inside, turned and closed the door herself and said:

"Why didn't you answer me sooner?"

"I was asleep. What do you want?"

Averill's slender jet-black eyebrows went up.

"Asleep. Good heavens. Lock the door. I don't want anyone to interrupt."

"Very well." She locked it again. "Averill—I want to talk to you."

"That's good," said Averill calmly. "I want to talk to you. That's why I came. Do you have any cigarettes?"

"There on the table." Beside Eden's cigarette case her little traveling clock pointed to three o'clock.

Averill walked across, took a cigarette and lighted it. She was as self-possessed, as calm as if she had been paying a social call. She turned, blowing a small cloud of smoke from her mouth, and sat down composedly in a small chintz-covered chair. She was wearing a crimson dressing gown, high-necked and long-sleeved, with a train; she crossed one knee over the other so her lace-trimmed nightgown was like a ruffled petticoat around her bare ankles. One crimson mule dropped from her small white heel. Her dark hair was neat and unruffled. Only her altogether colorless face, bare of lipstick and make-up, and the intensity of its expression suggested any anxiety or any hint of the horror the night had held.

"Averill," said Eden. "Why did you lie? How could you have done it? You've got to retract what you said and tell them the truth."

There was a lambent flash back in Averill's dark eyes. She said:

"We both like to come straight to the point, don't we, darling? I should think you would know why I lied. It's fairly obvious. I believed then and I believe now that whoever killed Creda actually intended to kill me."

"Averill, you can't sit there and say that I thought of murdering you. No matter what you think of me you don't really in your heart believe that, and you know it."

Averill's demure face looked suddenly a little pinched about the nostrils and there was a shadow around the corners of her thin mouth. She said:

"Let's not talk of that, Eden. Perhaps I don't think you— would kill anyone. I've known you so long. Yet the fact remains that Creda was murdered while she was in my room— wearing a cloak everyone knew as mine—her face veiled in a chiffon scarf. Your scarf, Eden. How did it get there?"

"I don't know."

"Or won't tell."

Eden put both her hands on the railing at the foot of the bed, clutching it. She said, her voice shaking: "Averill, there's no use in our talking like this. Can't we forget our own feelings toward each other——"

Averill laughed shortly.

"Is that a proffer of peace at any price?" she said. "All right. As a matter of fact that's what I've come for."

"Do you mean you'll tell Sloane the truth?"

"I don't know. Listen, Eden—Jim and I have had a long talk. Just now. In my room, if it interests you to know it." She waited a moment, watching Eden with narrowed, lambent eyes. "Jim told me about tonight."

"Tonight?"

Averill's eyes flashed.

"Don't pretend innocence. He says he—you rather flung yourself at his head and he—manlike, was a bit flattered and carried away by it for a moment, but it meant nothing to him."

Eden clung to the bed, this time for support.

"Jim—said *that?*"

"Certainly. How else would I know?" said Averill, coolly watching her.

"But, Jim——" It was as if her body had turned to lead. She said heavily: "I don't belive you. I don't believe Jim said anything like that."

Averill smiled.

"I don't care whether you believe it or not. It's true. I imagine you will shortly be convinced of it. The point is Jim and I have come to a real understanding. He regrets this little passage with you, Eden; he's really sorry about it and for you.

He asked me to apologize. I don't think myself that Jim is the one who ought to apologize. After all, when a woman throws herself at a man as you have——"

"Averill, that's not true."

Averill stood up and smashed her cigarette in the tray with a small savage gesture.

"Can you deny it?" she said quickly but softly as the swish of a garment. "Can you deny you've had eyes for no one else since you first met him? That you've acted like a moon-struck child, hanging on every word he uttered? You thought I didn't see it. But I did. You thought I didn't see you follow him into the garden that first night in St. Louis. Listening, watching, always planning and trying to be near him. My dear child—your methods are jejune. You've only succeeded in making a fool of yourself and greatly embarrassing Jim."

Had she done all that, thought Eden, aghast. She'd followed him to the garden; but why not?

"You were unfair to Jim, Averill. The engine was important; you refused to see his side of the thing or to support him as you could so easily have done. You don't love him yourself. Why are you trying to keep him?"

"Listen, Eden. Jim loves me. We are going to be married and you can't stop it. He's sorry for this little affair with you and glad it went no further. He loves me and doesn't want me to break off our engagement, or even postpone our marriage. He told me all this. I tell you we've had a long talk. And he asked me to come and tell you this. Now will you believe me?"

Eden took a long breath. Only that night in Jim's arms, with his mouth warm and hard upon her own, she'd thought they held their stars in their hands. She'd thought love was the answer to every question and every perplexity and every doubt of human existence. She said:

"No, Averill, I don't believe you. I love Jim." She paused and put up her chin and said clearly: "And he loves me. I— I'm sorry—we were both sorry about you."

Averill walked quickly toward her, stopped within six inches of Eden and slapped her face.

"You——" she said in a throbbing, panting whisper that itself was shocking. "How dare you——"

The suddenness of it and the ugliness stunned Eden.

"Averill——"

"You can't even defend yourself," said Averill, still in that shocking unsteady whisper. "You have no courage—you know you're in the wrong. You let me strike your face and don't try to defend yourself. You——"

"Averill, stop that. If you say another word, if you come a step nearer me, I'll scream. Do you understand? Control yourself——"

"Me, control myself! What about you!" But the words had their effect nevertheless. Averill's breath still came quickly but the moment of white, mad fury had passed. She said, still panting, but marvelously drawing herself up again in a semblance of her usual poise: "No one would believe you. My word is as good as yours."

She looked at Eden and actually laughed a little and said: "If either of us looks upset, Eden, it's you. Not me."

Probably she was right. For Eden was so swept and shaken with incredulous anger that it was itself frightening in its strength. She must control it; she must not permit that rising tide of something dreadfully like hatred to give itself outlet. Her hands were trembling, her breath coming quickly. She turned half away from Averill and saw her own white coat lying across a chair and, suddenly, remembered Creda's letter. Creda's letter, so dreadfully interrupted, mentioning Jim. Averill was incalculable; she was also quick and curious as a cat. She must not learn of the existence of the letter; Averill could be trusted with no secrets, not even a secret which must in some inexplicable way concern Jim.

The thought of it and the thought of Jim was steadying. All at once she saw herself and Averill as they were—two women, rivals all their lives, over trivial things—rivals again when it was important. So terribly important. Averill must really hate her; nothing else could drive so deep below Averill's glacé surface, nothing else could so devastate and shatter Averill's studied, demure and civilized façade.

Curious how one thought of hatred as being at least polite.

She said, thankful when her voice emerged quiet and controlled:

"I'm not going to engage in a childish and vulgar kind of struggle with you. But I'll tell you this—if you ever dare touch me again I'll——"

"You'll what?" asked Averill with a nice blend of derision and curiosity.

"I don't know what I'll do," said Eden quite honestly. "It's not exactly a precedented situation. But I'll do something and it won't be pleasant—remember that——"

Without warning Averill took a new course.

"I didn't mean to do that, Eden," she said with an effect of contrition and frankness. "I'm not like that as a rule; I was angry and forgot myself. You must admit I had some provocation."

"I don't believe anything you've told me about Jim, if that's what you mean. Oh, Averill, there's no use in our talking like this. It's—it's all so horrible with Creda dead like that——"

Averill ignored that and said silkily: "Come now, my dear. I've apologized neatly. Let's sit down quietly and talk this over. I came here in the friendliest possible spirit. I only wanted to tell you that I—I'll tell Sloane the truth about last night."

"You——" That, too, was surprising; in its way as much of a shock as Averill's savage, sharp blow across her cheek had been. "Why?"

"Why? Well, really, Eden, what a question! Do you think I'm going to enjoy telling him that I have to retract a statement I made? That I did it because we had had a misunderstanding and I thought you had taken me to be Creda and had been impulsive——"

The anger Eden had felt before was nothing to the cold rage that possessed her then. She walked over to where Averill sat again in the chair, her bare ankles swinging in a froth of lace, her small pale face demure and secret.

"Averill, you wouldn't dare——"

"That's the second time you've used the word dare, Eden." She said it as lightly as a song. "Don't be childish. I'll tell Sloane I lied; that I was with you in the cabin for a short time. That we had quarreled—no, I won't tell that. I promise you. So that clears the slate between us. Shall we be friends?"

Eden said quite slowly: "You must take me for a fool, Averill."

And Averill laughed softly.

"No, darling. I only want you to see quite clearly that your —love as you call it, for Jim is out. Definitely out, my dear. Jim doesn't want you—he may have been a little carried away last night, there in the shadow of the pines; men are only men and you're a very pretty girl and it was starlight and romantic. But he doesn't love you, really; this thing—Creda's death—is serious. So serious that he realizes now that his little affair with you was only a trivial—and if you don't mind my saying it—a rather unpleasant little flirtation. He regrets it and he wants you to understand that. Don't pretend to be so obtuse, Eden. After all, when a man asks you to end a thing, even a trivial kind of affair——"

"Jim looks quite capable of defending himself against unwelcome feminine advances," said Eden in a cold voice that didn't sound like her own. "You are lying to me, Averill." She groped for half-glimpsed motives, whose presence she felt without being able to define. "I don't know what you expect to accomplish. But I don't believe a word you've said about Jim."

"Very well," said Averill. She rose. There was a curious secret smile in her eyes; a shadow of it on her lips. She drew herself up, her slender neck at its full height, her small demure face somewhat triumphant. "If you don't believe me, ask him. He'll tell you it is the truth."

"I will ask him," said Eden slowly.

CHAPTER / 13

But nevertheless when Averill had trailed her crimson gown away, Eden thought of the certainty and assurance in her manner, of the look of demure triumph in her small face. "Ask him," she had said promptly and had smiled.

After a while Eden bolted the door, glanced at the traveling clock which said now three-fifteen—only fifteen minutes had that struggle with Averill lasted; again briefly a sense of the amazing suddenness and inexorability of a moment in time touched her and went on—and this time she turned off the light before she returned to bed.

She lay for a long time staring into the darkness. Uneasily aware of a growing conviction that somewhere, somehow, Averill had a basis for her statements.

Yet that wasn't possible either. The things Averill had said sounded like Averill—not like Jim.

And Jim loved her, Eden—as she loved him. She deliberately permitted herself to live over again every instant of those moments in the shadow of the pines—in Jim's arms, with his lips on her own. She repeated to herself every word he had said, and every word still held an almost unbearably lovely truth. "I fell in love with you," he'd said, "the instant somebody trotted you out on the terrace and said this is Eden." And she herself had looked at him and the whole world and all her life had changed its beat and its rhythm for this was love.

She turned restlessly, putting her face upon her crossed arms, thinking of Jim and the starlit sky and the hushed and tranquil night. Refusing for the moment to think how horribly that tranquillity had so soon been destroyed. Holding one memory out of that night intact and untouched.

How strange it was to be suddenly touched by and then swept irresistibly into that gigantic current! To be all at once a part of the deep pulse of being and life instead of an onlooker. All her life up to that moment became pallid and without meaning in comparison to the exciting significance every heartbeat now mysteriously possessed. It was, she thought suddenly, like a key with which to open doors of tremendous experience and (curiously, in the distance) doors that held promise of the deepest content.

Jim loved her. How could she doubt the strength of the thing that swept them together?

Yet—yet Averill had been so certain. Ask him, she'd said, smiling.

The night went on. Stars passed serenely and distantly

above, tracing their precise course through the dark sky. Stars that had seen many strange things.

Lights were on in the old ranch house all night and in one of the cabins. In the gray, cold hour before dawn coffee was brewed in the low-ceilinged kitchen for men who had been up all night. They were tired and low-voiced, talking laconically among themselves as they did not talk when strangers were about.

"Well, I'll bet anything anybody wants to bet that one of them murdered the woman."

"You got no takers, Bill. It's a cinch there wasn't anything but a coyote and some jack rabbits around the place tonight. And they weren't what you'd call strangers."

"I say there's something behind it all. Coffee, Charlie?"

"Sure, there's something behind it. Got to have a reason for murder, don't you? Pass the sugar."

"He means something important. Something about this airplane engine that crashed. That's why they came out here to see the boss."

"Who told you?"

"Pilot. Strevsky."

"Yeah, and he might've done it, too."

"I don't like the looks of that Italian fellow myself."

"Who? Pace? He's not Italian, he's English."

"If he's English I'm an Egyptian. I think he's plain American myself. More doughnuts, Chango."

"Tough on the girl that found her."

"Tough on the girl that was killed, if you ask me. What's the matter, Charlie? You're not eating."

"I'm all right, not hungry."

"Charlie had to help the boss. What really killed her, Charlie, did you find out?"

Chango, still smiling, serving them.

Sloane himself and Jim had about that time a prolonged talk in another room—a small, crowded room which was P. H. Sloane's own study and held, packed in cupboards and along shelves, all the slowly acquired paraphernalia of a profession he had once disowned. A light burned, too, all that night in the cabin where Creda Blaine still lay.

And sometime that night Sloane talked, also, to Noel and to Strevsky and even to the boyish and frightened steward, Roy Wilson. It chanced that Eden herself was present when he had his first interview with Major Pace.

The day then slowly dawning, with the shapes of sagebrush growing gray, and the tall black cottonwoods looming like sentinels against the pale sky, and the cry of a coyote off in the distance was to have its influence and its weight upon many lives and among them Eden's.

About five the sheriff telephoned from the other end of the

county and held a long conversation with P. H. Sloane. At six, fortified with breakfast, three cowboys carefully wrapped the thing that was left of Creda Blaine, lifted it gently into a car and drove slowly away along the fifty-mile route, scarcely more than a car track in places, toward Rocky Gap.

"Where do you suppose Miss Blaine will want the body sent, when the coroner is done with it?" asked P. H. And Noel told him Louisiana and added wearily that they'd send telegrams.

"Better not be in a hurry about the telegrams," said P. H. "There's only one newspaper in Rocky Gap and the editor of it is also its crime, weather and society reporter and occasionally sets type, when his typewriter goes on a spree as he does once in six weeks. But the Blaines have a certain importance. The moment the news gets on the wires there'll be reporters from St. Louis."

"Right," said Noel apathetically. "Okay, no telegrams till we have to send them—— God, what a night."

It was, however, full morning by that time with the sun tipping suddenly over the black ridge of mountains toward the east. From the east they made a shimmering crimson wall, but from the ranch the wall was black and looked impassable, as if it hemmed them all rigidly inside its confines.

"You'd better get some rest," said P. H. "There's nothing more you can do just now."

He disappeared, alone this time, still in dinner jacket and black tie, into the study at the end of the hall, beside the billiard room; Jim and Noel talked a little, wearily and without conclusion, and at last went to their rooms, upstairs now, in the main house, where Chango had brought their bags. Tiptoeing carefully past closed doors so as not to wake anyone.

The sun had reached the top of a clear blue sky, and the shadow of the cottonwoods lay short and thick upon the sagebrush when Eden awoke.

She lay there for a moment, thinking again and instantly of Jim, of Averill, of Creda's death and the horror into which that death plunged them. Sunlight lay across the floor; she rose finally and went to the window. The air was clear and dry; the sun poured down from a cloudless sky upon the ranch with its oasis of green, and upon the vast flat reaches of, she supposed, grazing land. Away in the distance the mountains were now vaguely blue and hazy-looking in the heat.

Near at hand so far as she could see there was no movement and no activity except for a squat, thick figure, the thicker for its foreshortening, which waddled out from the porch below and along the paths. It was Major Pace, in white linen which obviously and amazingly had been pressed;

he was smoking and looking idly about him, quite as if murder and horror by night had no concern with him. His attitude was so completely and elaborately that of an observer that it was too elaborate. It struck Eden rather sharply that the lack of concern in that strolling, ineffably nonchalant figure was assumed, altogether artificial.

And certainly of all the people who might have murdered Creda the most likely suspect was, to Eden's mind, the man calling himself Pace. She watched him stroll on down the path and stop in the shadow of the pines (almost at the spot where she and Jim had stood the night before) to light a fresh cigarette from the end of the one he'd finished.

Only last night.

She turned from the window, pushed her hands wearily through her hair, sighed and went to turn on the shower and rummage in her unpacked bags for clothing.

She looked at herself for a long moment before she opened the door into the hall. As she had done when she was starting from her little apartment to the waiting taxi—how long ago. New York and that small apartment where the last two years of her life had been spent seemed incredibly distant in space and time and completely unreal.

She thought of Noel—and her deliberate plan to marry him—if he could be induced to ask her and that too seemed incredible. It was as if it had been another person seated on the westbound plane, coolly planning and arranging her life as one might plan and cut a bit of dress material. She smiled a little, thinking of it, and the woman in the mirror with the pale face and grave eyes with shadows under them smiled too, wistfully, a little sadly. Yet she could see herself that there was in that woman's face a kind of warmth, a luminous, almost intangible quality of eagerness that had not been there four days ago. Did women in love always show it in their faces?

And then she remembered going back into her apartment on that day that seemed now ineffably distant because she'd forgotten her gray chiffon scarf.

She turned away abruptly and the image turned, a slender woman in a white dress with a crimson belt and the lipstick on her mouth matching the belt. And with the shadow of remembered horror in her eyes.

Instantly the swift marching train of events that had developed since that day marched upon her again, catching her up in the inexorable procession.

At the door she remembered the letter Creda had begun to write and went back for it as she had done, days ago, for the gray scarf.

It was then that she had her first intimation of depths below depths taking their secret course. For the letter was not in her coat pocket. Was not on the dressing table, was not on the night table, was not anywhere in the room.

Someone, then, had taken it; the pocket of her coat was deep, it couldn't have fallen from it.

Averill had been in her room, but had not approached the coat. She stood still, thinking rapidly of the previous night. Anyone, almost, could have taken the letter from her pocket. She had sat perfectly still for moments in the cabin, only half aware of what was going on. Jim had been beside her. Sloane had leaned over her, pressing a glass to her mouth. Noel had had more opportunity than anyone else; he had walked beside her, half-supporting her with his arm all the way from the horror-laden cabin to the house.

No one could have entered her room while she slept, heavy from fatigue though that sleep had been. It would have been scarcely possible for her to lose that crumpled bit of paper. Therefore it had to be removed from her pocket.

More troubled by it than she liked to admit even to herself, she unlocked and opened her door. No one was in the long hall, bisected further down by another hall; no one on the stairway. But in the lounge Noel sat staring somberly at his feet and smoking. She stopped in the doorway. At the end of the hall (back of the closed door to the room she was later to learn was Sloane's study) there was a murmur of voices, the words indistinguishable. Noel saw her and sprang to his feet.

"Hello, Eden. So you're able to navigate under your own steam? I thought perhaps last night was too much for you."

"Where's everybody?"

"Sloane's in there with Jim and Averill. Dorothy's having breakfast, I think. Pace has gone for a walk—and needs it I would say, never having seen a gent look greener around the gills." He took her hand and drew it lightly inside his arm.

"What has been done?"

"Never mind. I'll tell you while you have breakfast. Nothing much really. Come along."

Dorothy, white as the tablecloth and not much more expression in her face, looked up as they entered the dining room, nodded and went back phlegmatically to oatmeal. Noel pulled up a chair beside Eden's.

"I can put it all in a nutshell," he said as Chango, still indestructibly cheerful after his all-night vigil, brought in coffee and orange juice. "Creda was taken away this morning. The sheriff telephoned and had a long talk with Sloane; I don't know what was said but I take it Sloane is still in the saddle and riding high.

"He's turned out, by the way, to be quite a lad. I'd hate to have his clutches on me. He's got all kinds of stuff here—

fingerprinting outfits, cameras, a whole chemical laboratory —my God, you never saw such a lot of stuff. He said he thought he'd never have a use for it again—well, he thought wrong. All the same——" His handsome face sobered and looked suddenly haggard; his peaked black eyebrows drew together. "All the same it wasn't just square of Jim to bring us all out here as he did. Never a word of warning. Intending just to dump the lot of us and all his harebrained notions about the plane crash upon this detective. Between us, I'm not sure P. H. is so hot. If he was as good as Jim claims he was, what'd he leave his profession for? People don't retire while they're successful—not if they can help it. Success is too potent a drink."

Dorothy helped herself to more cream with a reckless disregard for her already lumpy figure which would have dismayed Averill. She said blandly: "Don't be too hard on Mr. Cady. He couldn't have known what the result would be."

Noel looked at her sharply. "Do you mean Creda was murdered because we came here? But why? That doesn't make sense."

"I suppose not," said Dorothy calmly. "Still if we'd gone on to the plantation things might have been different. It only occurred to me that if"—she glanced over her shoulder and lowered her voice—"if Major Pace hadn't felt so far from police and regular detectives and all that——"

"Pace," said Noel. "Well, naturally—who else?" But he was frowning thoughtfully. "I can't get the hang of it, though. If there really was anything crooked about the plane crash— as Jim insists—why did Pace offer to pay us? He was about to get the whole thing, signed, sealed and delivered, to do as he pleased with. Why go to such lengths as to destroy the only model of the engine, steal the plans . . . And besides how on earth could he have fixed the plane to crash? A thing like that takes elaborate planning."

"He hasn't paid you yet, has he?" asked Eden.

"No. But the money's there waiting. Oh, of course, he could now withdraw it and vanish with the plans, if he's got 'em and the money. But—but if that's the explanation, why murder poor Creda? Creda wouldn't hurt a fly——"

"Suppose she knew that was his plan," said Eden. "Suppose she threatened to expose him?"

"Even so—killing her like this only makes things worse. They'll search the whole place for those plans, which are very likely put away in some of Bill's things in St. Louis right now. Besides, Creda never ever knew Pace; the first time she met him was when he came to the house to dinner Monday night."

"Are you sure of that?" asked Eden.

He gave her a surprised look.

"Why, yes. Reasonably sure. They were introduced and

99

neither of them acted as if they'd ever met before. What—exactly what are you driving at, Eden?"

Dorothy, blandly attacking an enormous heap of pancakes, was suddenly as blank and receptive as a stenographer's tablet waiting to be written upon. Eden said, "Oh, nothing really. I don't know what to think." And Noel frowned and snapped his fingers suddenly and said:

"Pace is out. He's got an alibi for the whole time. He was right there in the lounge, sitting in one of the chairs, smoking one cigarette after the other. I saw him. He was there the whole time while Sloane was playing the piano."

Dorothy's languid eyelids lifted and there was a small spark in her light, flat eyes. "Why, yes," she said with a flash of something approaching animation. "You're perfectly right. I remember. He seemed to really be listening to the music and liking it. I remember thinking he must be a musician." A faint shadow crossed her face. "I'm sorry," she said apologetically. "It—it can't be anyone except Pace, can it? But I—I do remember he was there, the whole time. He was there when you screamed, Miss Shore, and we heard it. He was there when Mrs. Blaine walked out of the room perhaps—oh, half an hour before we heard you call out from the cabin. Mr. Sloane had stopped playing then and we were just sitting, not talking much. That's why we heard it so clearly."

Alibis, thought Eden rather drearily. She hadn't thought of alibis. And there were all the other well-known trails of crime detection. Somehow she hadn't thought of them applying or being applied to Creda's murder. It was so far from cities and police mechanism, so completely and entirely in an isolated world that it was as if that world ought to have its own laws.

She wondered what, if anything, Sloane had discovered. She was soon to find out. For on the heels of Dorothy's disappointingly firm recollection Sloane and Averill and Jim walked into the room.

Eden looked up and straight at Jim.

She was aware of P. H. Sloane, fresh and brown as if the night had held its usual rest for him, newly shaven and clad again in faded khaki riding breeches and boots, and a blue shirt open at the throat. She was sharply aware of Averill, too, as trim and poised as a catbird in a pale gray linen dress. She wore green beads at the base of her slender neck and a lovely square emerald on her right hand, and there was not a hair out of place on her small dark head.

But Eden looked straight into Jim's eyes. And experienced a shock. For Jim Cady was looking directly at her and his look was as distant, as remote, as impersonal as if he had never seen her before.

CHAPTER/14

Luckily there was a little commotion of voices and movement and it covered any change of expression; but her hands made a small involuntary clutch at the edge of the table as if to brace herself against an unexpected precipice looming under her feet.

She hadn't believed Averill; she hadn't really had in her heart any doubt at all about Jim.

She told herself a little frantically that Jim looked like that because others were there. Because he was not alone with her. Because he did not want others to have any hint of how things stood with them until—well, until his engagement to Averill was officially at an end.

Sloane had said "Good morning," and she supposed she had replied along with Dorothy and Noel. They were all talking and Sloane and Averill seated themselves at the table and somebody rang for Chango. She permitted herself to glance at Averill, and Averill was smug and demure and was looking at her with again a faint, secret smile in her shallow eyes and touching the corners of her mouth.

They were again talking of alibis and of Pace, and Eden listened.

For Major Pace did have an alibi. An airtight, waterproof, hard and fast alibi, to which P. H. Sloane himself subscribed as well as Dorothy Woolen and, with a rueful look, Noel.

"It's like this," said Sloane and took a pencil and drew a diagram on the tablecloth. Chango glanced over Sloane's shoulder, stopped smiling instantly so his face was an impassive yellow mask with slitted eyes, and put down the coffee he was carrying with a clatter. Sloane glanced up and said: "Oh. Never mind, Chango, it'll wash off," and resumed his drawing as Chango, disapproving, pattered sulkily away.

"Here's the lounge; here's the piano along the wall opposite the fireplace. When I began to play the piano, Miss Shore," he looked briefly at Eden, "had just left her chair by the fireplace and walked out onto the porch. And in a moment or two Jim followed her; he tells me he met you, Miss Shore, on the porch and that you talked a little and strolled down the path where Miss Blaine, who left the lounge ten or fifteen minutes later, came also. Is that right?"

"Yes," said Eden huskily. Jim was looking straight at the detective, his face a little grim, altogether enigmatic. He must be thinking of that moment in the shadow of the pines; he couldn't fail to be thinking of it. But if so his expression gave no hint of it and he did not look at her. The detective went on slowly, drawing as he talked a little outline of the long lounge; a triangle showed the location of the piano on the west wall, with the player facing the wide door along the north wall, which went into the hall. Along the eastern wall, opposite the piano, was the fireplace with a long divan before it, its back to the piano but fully visible to anyone seated at the piano. There were chairs before the fireplace, too; chairs in the deep window embrasures opposite the hall door. Pace had been sitting in one of those chairs, facing the room, his back to the deep, curtained window, a table with an ash tray on it at his elbow. He was in the shadow, said Sloane, but Dorothy and Noel had been constantly aware of his presence.

"I'd have known it if he left the room for a moment," said Dorothy with the utmost matter-of-factness.

But the detective had not finished. Eden realized suddenly that it was not only Pace's alibi he was concerning himself with. It had been almost a foregone conclusion with her, and she thought, with the others, that Pace was the only logical suspect. But to the detective it was not perhaps so instantly evident that none of them (except Pace) were the kind of people to do murder.

She caught herself on that; what kind of people did murder? And she thought of Averill's astonishing burst of fury of the previous night. Well, then, perhaps there were among them other hidden capacities for cruelty; hidden fears perhaps; desperation so deep and so harrying that the only recourse was murder. No matter how civilized, no matter how well known people were to you, still underneath ran universal human passions and needs that might result in the undertaking of desperate expediencies.

Averill; but Averill couldn't murder. She couldn't have killed Creda. Yet she must have been the last to see Creda. She had been wearing that yellow coat shortly before Creda, wrapped in the coat, was found dead.

The detective was talking again.

"This left Miss Woolen, Pace, Carreaux, Creda Blaine herself and me in the lounge. After a few moments Mrs. Blaine got up and went out; I believe it was just as Jim returned——"

"That's right," said Jim. "It's as I told you. I met her on the steps, we talked a moment or two, then she went down the steps toward the path and I came back into the lounge. I sat down. . . . I think on the sofa opposite Dorothy." Dorothy nodded slowly. Jim went on: "Pace was here when I came in and I didn't leave the lounge again until we heard Noel call us."

"Time is always difficult," said Sloane. "If we could know exactly when she died——"

Noel was leaning forward: "Mr. Sloane, exactly what killed her? Was it my revolver? Because I swear to you——"

"I don't know. My opinion is that she actually died of strangulation. But there were knife wounds, a number of them. Made by a small and I would say single-edged blade. We haven't yet found the knife. And it's barely possible that among the wounds there is a bullet wound; there were several wounds at her throat; and it's difficult to tell without more detailed examination than I was able to give. The coroner is going to do a post-mortem; Miss Blaine has given her permission. If we find a bullet——"

Noel was looking drawn, his brilliant eyes no longer gay.

"But, Sloane, I swear I didn't shoot her——"

"No one said you did. Anyway there were fingerprints."

"Whose?"

Sloane did not reply directly. He said: "Arrangements have been made for you to stay here until—well, until we feel justified in permitting you to leave. I'm sorry; but Miss Blaine at last agrees with me that it can't be helped. The murder was committed in this county and in this state and the simplest, indeed, the only thing we can do is to request you to stay here for, I hope, only a few days. That, however, remains to be seen. I do want to emphasize again that your cooperation will help more than I can say."

"Sloane, do you really mean that you believe Jim's cock-and-bull story about the plane crash?" asked Noel.

P. H. Sloane rose and stood looking down at them from his lanky height. Tall, brown, self-contained, with a suggestion of dry humor in the wrinkles around his eyes, he looked a typical rancher. His eyes had grown so keen, anybody might think, from years of seeing such clear and far horizons.

"It's worth investigating," he said. "Pace is worth investigating; all of you, when I've inquired, have in one way or another indicated your willingness to blame him for what may amount to three murders."

"Three——" repeated Dorothy, barely moving her pale lips.

Averill said: "Mr. Sloane——"

"Yes, Miss Blaine."

"I only want you to say that—that I want to correct something I told you last night. I—the story Miss Shore told you is true so far as I know. That is about my having actually entered her cabin with her. That's quite right. I entered her room with her exactly as she said, talked to her for a few moments and then went away."

There was a little silence. Jim stared into space with completely expressionless gray eyes; Noel made a quickly checked movement, his peaked black eyebrows surging upward in astonishment; Dorothy silently and passively seemed to record every look on the faces around the table—even Chango's yellow face peering inquisitively through the pantry door.

"Do you mean that you completely retract your former statement saying that you did not enter the cabin as Miss Shore said you did?"

"Obviously," said Averill neatly. "I don't remember exactly what she said, but I do subscribe to it; every word of it——"

"*Averill,*" said Jim sharply, turning suddenly toward her. He said only that, and Averill smiled slowly.

"You do understand, don't you, Mr. Sloane? I entered the cabin with Eden and we talked awhile, then I left it."

"When did you meet Mrs. Blaine and give her your coat?"

"Afterward—I think," said Averill sweetly. She turned to Eden. "That's right, isn't it, Eden?" she asked in the friendliest and most agreeable way in the world.

She had again outplayed Eden; her whole retraction, true though it was, sounded false; sounded too friendly and agreeable; sounded as if she were merely backing up Eden's testimony, in order to help Eden. Sounded obviously, flagrantly, a lie.

Eden said: "I don't know when you met Creda, Averill. I know you came to my room with me and when you left me there you were still wearing your yellow coat."

Averill, slender eyebrows lifted, patience and forbearance in her smile, turned again to Sloane.

"Then that is exactly what happened," she said. "Do forgive me for—for not telling the truth at first."

"Why didn't you?" asked Sloane simply.

Averill waited a moment before replying, her faint smile undisturbed. Then she said: "It doesn't matter, does it, Mr. Sloane? So long as I subscribe to Eden's story now."

P. H. Sloane turned to Eden. "When you've quite finished your breakfast, Miss Shore, I'd like to question you. In the meantime—Jim, will you see if you can find Pace and bring him in here."

"But, Sloane, you haven't answered my question," said Noel. "Whose fingerprints were on my revolver?"

"Oh yes," said Sloane. "I want to talk to you about that, too, later. Whose fingerprints? I don't know yet. That's one of the things I want you to do if you don't mind. That is, go into my study and let Charlie take your fingerprints. All of you."

"But we——" began Averill sharply, and Sloane went on without looking at her: "He's taken mine, too, and those of the cowboys. Sorry, but I'll have to ask you to do it."

Jim got up and went into the hall. As he did so a cowboy entered from the kitchen, his sombrero in his hand, and approached P. H. Sloane.

He was tall, lean, brown, like Sloane; laconic, easily graceful and just then his eyes were snapping electrically.

"Just thought I'd let you know I'd got back from Rocky Gap," he said. "Coroner said he'd phone you tonight and tell you whether he got any bullets or not. And—say, P. H.——"

"Well?"

"Didn't know whether you knew it or not but Curly (that is the little blond fellow—the steward, I guess you'd call him, on the plane)—well, he's disappeared. Can't be found, high, low or level. And—well, Chango says——"

Chango mysteriously appeared at his elbow and nodded his head vigorously, his beady eyes like bright shoe buttons. The cowboy said apologetically: "I know it sounds kinda silly, P. H., but Chango says there's a hatchet gone, too. I think myself Curly is kinda young to do any murders. But he's sure as hell run away. With Chango's hatchet."

There was a strange little silence. P. H. and the cowboy looked steadily at each other. Dorothy Woolen sat like a figure carved in soap, and Noel's blue eyes went swiftly from the cowboy to Sloane and back again. Then all at once Averill pushed out her chair with a blundering, scraping sound and got to her feet and cried shrilly: "But you've got to find him. He must have killed her. You've got to find him—this is horrible——"

"He can't have disappeared. There's no place to go," said P. H. Sloane.

And the cowboy nodded and said: "He's gone just the same."

Eden rose, too. P. H. asked how long the steward had been gone and where they had searched for him, and Eden went out of the room. The steward—Roy Wilson; she could barely remember his name and pale face and curly yellow hair—where had he gone? Why?

The obvious answer was guilt on his part and fear of detection. Yet the young, curly-haired steward with his girlish mouth and mildly pleasant manner certainly could have had no possible motive for brutally murdering Creda Blaine. A hatchet had gone, too? Probably it had been lost days ago and Chango had just discovered its loss.

Why hadn't Creda screamed for help? Why had she pulled the little chest of drawers a few inches from the wall and left it there? Why had she written that strange, scarcely intelligible note to Jim?

She must find Jim. She must tell him immediately about the letter that was lost, and she must ask him a certain question. But in the hall she was stopped pleasantly but firmly and fingerprinted. It gave her the strangest feeling of uneasiness to see her own small prints set down in ink and labeled.

Jim was on the porch when she found him; Pace was nowhere in sight nor so far as she could see anyone else. She went swiftly to Jim, who hearing her approach turned toward her.

Was it the sun or were his eyes exactly as cold and impersonal as they had been there in view of all the others in the dining room? She said rather timidly: "Jim——"

"Do you want me?"

"Yes, I—Jim——" It had to come out. She was too certain, still, to take refuge in silence herself; in pride. She said, fumbling and awkward as a child: "Jim—Averill said you asked her to tell me it was over—between us, I mean." She put her hands on his arm and he moved his arm deliberately away, and still she could not believe it, but had to go on: "I didn't believe her. I don't . . . I couldn't. She said you—you wanted to end——" Words stopped in her throat and she couldn't say any more. She had already said far too much.

For Jim, looking stiffly out toward the mountains, replied quite clearly and deliberately: "Averill was quite right. I'm sorry, Eden. We were both mistaken."

CHAPTER/15

This, thought Eden, cannot be happening to me.

Not like this; not Jim.

She put both her hands upon the railing of the porch and looked out toward the blue mountain peaks and did not see them. And she forgot the letter in Creda's writing—blurred with ink, broken off so abruptly.

Jim said, still watching the rim of mountains and speaking in a brisk and businesslike voice: "Averill and I are to be married as it was planned. The only thing I can hope from you is forgiveness."

She still couldn't speak. It was quite literally impossible. And besides, what could she say? She began to hope only that she could get away without having to speak at all for talking was dangerous.

And she had already said too much; why hadn't she let that stirring instinct of warning guide her? Why hadn't she approached the thing more cautiously—giving herself a chance to see ahead, to draw conclusions from what Jim himself said, or conspicuously failed to say? Why need she invite the direct cruelty of the thing?

Averill had been right. Well, she had recognized Averill's certainty; her smile as much as the unmistakable air of authority and assuredness in her tone and manner had been convincing. But Eden hadn't permitted herself to accept it because of her faith in Jim.

So—again—she'd been wrong.

"Will you—forgive me, Eden?"

He was waiting for her to reply. She was poignantly aware of that but she was still shaken, as if the ground under her feet had rocked. Later she supposed she would feel emotion; hurt pride, anger, loss. May as well face that now, for it would be loss. There might be—there would be jealousy, too. That wouldn't be pleasant either. She didn't really, she told herself, feel anything now except regret for her own rash and impulsive directness. Well, probably she was not the only woman in the world to which the inconceivable had happened.

The curious thing was even now that she seemed to have known Jim so long; it was still as if all her life he had been a constant, important, deeply familiar force in that life. It was as if old foundations, tried and true, had suddenly gone out from under her; as if a hand always extended when she needed it had suddenly failed her. It wasn't sensible; in point of fact it had been an incredibly short time since she'd known him at all. But it didn't seem so; deep in her heart there remained that indestructible, strong sense of understanding, of sharing, of being instantly and forever one with the man beside her.

Well, it wasn't true. Women's hearts had made crazy mistakes then. At least she'd had the thing from Jim's own lips; certainly he had hated to tell her. She said: "All right, Jim."

Surprisingly, her voice was fairly steady but she wouldn't look at him. For that matter he wouldn't look at her. She knew he continued to stare, as she did, at that distant blue rim of mountain. She'd looked at them last night, above the warm pressure of Jim's arms, and felt indescribably at peace. She broke off the thought at once.

"All right," she repeated quickly. "You are forgiven. Forget it all as I shall." She turned away quickly, intending to escape while this incredible calm supported her. But Jim made a swift motion and caught her by the wrist and whirled her around to meet his eyes. For a moment his eyes sought with a kind of desperation into her own. Then he said abruptly:

"No, it isn't all. There's something else."

"There—can't be anything else."

"Yes. It—it's about the murder. I hate to—listen, Eden, did you see Noel's revolver last night? When you came into the cabin, I mean, and found Creda?"

It wrenched her savagely back to the thing confronting

107

them. She tried to think back to those frenzied, horribly bewildered moments and could not.

"I don't know. I don't remember it?"

"Think. Are you sure you didn't touch it?"

"Touch it! How could I? It wasn't there—that is, it must have been there but I—it's as I say—I simply don't remember seeing it."

"Eden, you've got to know. A woman's fingerprints are on that revolver."

"But I—you can't mean my fingerprints?"

"I don't know. A woman's. Slim, fine—I saw the print. They haven't been identified yet. Sloane's getting a record this morning of everybody's fingerprints; you heard him say it. He's got mine and Noel's and Pace's. And Strevsky's. There's only you and Dorothy and Averill. And this little steward——"

The steward. Well, they wouldn't be able to get his fingerprints now, until they found him, that is.

"Are you sure you didn't touch it?" insisted Jim. "You see Creda may have been shot—even though the revolver was fully loaded when it was found—and Sloane's morally certain she wasn't shot; he couldn't definitely say without a post-mortem and he isn't qualified to do it. But you see, the presence of the revolver shows somebody thought of using it; somebody perhaps planned to shoot her and then—God knows why—didn't. Perhaps because it was so quiet a night and the sound of the shot would have been heard. But, Eden——"

"Creda," said Eden with stiff lips. "Perhaps Creda herself took it from Noel——"

"Noel says he doesn't think so. He says the last time he saw it was when he packed it to go on the plane trip. That night everybody was asleep. His bags weren't locked; anybody could have taken the revolver——"

"My scarf," said Eden. "Someone took it——"

"Oh yes. Your scarf," said Jim. He was silent for an instant or two, thinking; then he said abruptly: "Anyway, it wasn't Creda. Sloane got her fingerprints, too. Before they took her away. I—I helped him. I watched him compare them with the prints on the gun. I couldn't see much of it but he says they're not the same prints and Sloane knows. Eden, if you didn't even see the revolver until Sloane found it then you couldn't have touched it so that's all right——"

"Wait." Unexpectedly, terrifyingly, a small sharp memory, lost and confused by all the intervening memories, returned to Eden like a stab. "Jim—it must have been the revolver! I'd forgotten it! It had to be that! Jim—what shall I do? I didn't kill her—I had no motive—I wouldn't——"

"What do you mean? Tell me. Hurry!"

His face was suddenly white; his hand went out involuntarily toward her and then withdrew. "Tell me quickly, Eden. What do you mean?"

"I'm not sure it was the revolver. As I knelt by Creda my knee struck something hard and painful; I didn't look at whatever it was. I was looking at her. It was in that first moment when I entered the room and saw her and I——I couldn't believe what I saw. I knelt and——it may have been the revolver. Whatever it was, I remember pushing it out of the way, pushing it from under my knee——but I didn't look at it . . . I never thought of it again. I may have thrust it under a fold of the yellow coat. I don't know. I don't even remember the touch of it. I suppose it sounds incredible, but it's what happened. So if it was the revolver my own fingerprints may be on it."

"That's all you can remember about it?"

"Yes. Everything——except, Jim, there was a letter . . ."

He did not hear it for he said quickly and urgently: "Eden, you'd better tell Sloane. But I hate you to tell him; I know it's true as you tell it but it doesn't sound true. It sounds like an excuse——"

"But, Jim, I didn't kill her. Creda was——there was no way in which she even touched my life. I had no quarrel with her ——there was nothing——"

He looked away from her then and for a long moment stared again at the distant blue rim lifting into the sky. "Eden, in a thing like this no one is safe from suspicion; no one is safe from accusation. And many an innocent man——yes, and woman, too——has paid penalties for something he didn't do."

"But I——"

"Circumstantial evidence still has its weight. Eden"——he turned to her suddenly and with a kind of impatience and cried——"Eden, why in God's name didn't you remove that gray scarf? Why didn't you take it——hide it——do anything with it! There was time——why didn't you?"

"Why should I?"

"But you knew it was yours, didn't you? You knew you would be questioned? You knew——"

"I simply didn't think of removing it. I did recognize it, of course. I even wondered how it had got there——vaguely, not caring much. The whole thing was so——so horrible; I couldn't think. It didn't occur to me that anybody could possibly suspect me on account of it——I don't think anyone does. And even if it had made me think I would be suspected, I'm not sure I would have taken it away. It seems to me the best thing to do was exactly what I did——touch nothing, leave the scarf where it was and call for help."

"But you did touch something," said Jim with a kind of

groan. "And of all things you might have touched, the revolver was the most dangerous. Oh well—I suppose you'd better tell Sloane the truth; he'll find the fingerprints are yours, that's inevitable. The only thing you can do is admit and try to explain it. But if you only——"

"Good morning, Miss Shore," said a suave voice near them. It was Pace, panting a little from his walk in the sun, his olive face glistening, his little eyes squinting until they were smiling slits. He had a handkerchief in his hand and he was wiping his fat neck above his collar, and somewhere he had come upon a scarlet geranium and picked it and thrust it in the lapel of his white linen coat. It looked inexpressibly jaunty and garishly out of place on that day of horror, with the thing that had walked in the stillness of the night before still at large, still unchecked, still undiscovered.

"You wanted me, Mr. Cady. One of the—what do you call them, cowboys—told me you had inquired for me."

"Yes, Major Pace. Mr. Sloane wants to see you."

Pace's small, dark eyes blinked with that lizardlike swiftness.

"I suppose," he said in an unperturbed and good-natured way, "that your detective friend wants to question me. Well, it will be short and I'm afraid not very helpful to him. I know absolutely nothing about this affair except that I wish I had not been involved in it. My business here in America is delicate. I look to you, Mr. Cady, and to Mr. Carreaux to help keep any undesirable publicity about me and the purpose of my visit from the papers. Indeed, I think it would be as well for your factory if you do so. While your agreement to sell me the thing I wish to buy is, of course, perfectly aboveboard, and within your rights, still I'm given to understand there is a well-defined public distrust of foreign—shall I say—buyers? Isn't that true, Mr. Cady?"

"Perhaps."

"But nevertheless—although I realize you are not exactly sympathetic to my errand——" He shrugged as if, after all, it was only a question of differing taste between gentlemen and need not be explored. "Nevertheless I hope I may have your assistance in the matter I mentioned."

"Good God, Major Pace," said Jim explosively. "We will do everything possible to keep as much of the thing as we can from the newspapers. Some of it will inevitably get in; it will have to. But for our own sakes we'll do everything possible to keep the thing quiet."

Pace blinked again, several times, rapidly. He continued to smile.

"Good. Good. It ought to be easy here—it's as if we were at the very ends of the world. Of course, you understand, Mr. Cady, that it's necessary for me to conclude my mission at the earliest possible moment and return to—return. Now then—where is your detective friend?"

It was, however, just then that there was another interruption and an unexpected one. For the pilot, Ludovic Strevsky, came rapidly along the porch. He was bareheaded, his thick, curly hair looking too vigorous to be neatly and smoothly combed; he was a powerful man, striding along with strength and enormous vitality in every motion; he had a soldier's wide square shoulders and slim waist and only his thick, bull neck gave him a look of something not quite civilized, not quite disciplined, as if he were answerable only to himself. There was as always a touch of cruelty in his tilted Slavic eyes and the curve of his lips. He said:

"Jim, wait a minute——"

Jim had already paused to look. "What is it?" he said sharply as if prophetic of trouble.

"It's the plane," said Strevsky. He came to a halt beside Jim. He was excited; the pulse in his bare, thick neck was beating hard. "Wilson—the fellow they sent along for steward —has disappeared. Nobody knows where he went or why. I saw him last night—this morning, rather, about two. He went off to his room and I supposed to sleep. But he's gone——"

"Wilson! But he—— Good God, that kid could have had nothing to do with Creda——"

The pilot shrugged.

"He is a queer sort, dreamy. Maybe he's scared. Anyway he's left and Sloane wants him found."

"What about the plane?"

"The fuel line is cut. Wait—let me tell you! I went out to tune her up. I was going up to see if I could spot Wilson; country like this is awful hard to hide in—unless he followed the ditch down there—what they call the arroyo——"

"Alone?"

"Sure I was alone. But one of these cowboys was going up with me, him and a gun. Sloane, I guess, was afraid I'd just leave once I got the plane up. Anyway, the fuel line's cut. Like the other."

"You're sure? But of course you're sure! No use asking who did it?"

Strevsky shook his head. "The point is, Jim, now we can't leave this God damned place. Nobody."

There was a brief silence and Strevsky said again: "That Wilson's a queer kid. He'd know enough about a plane to know you can't move with the fuel line cut—at least," his curved upper lip twitched upward suddenly, "at least not far. It wasn't mended this time. I looked. The other time——"

"We'll see Sloane. All right, Major Pace; he's waiting for you inside." Jim turned toward the door and Pace, who had

111

listened in complete silence, followed. At the doorway Jim seemed to remember Eden and looked at her and said: "Better come along, Eden."

He said it distantly, as impersonally as he would have spoken to a stranger.

And in the most curious but definite way his manner reiterated the other thing he had said. "Averill was right—we were both mistaken—I'm sorry." It even added a kind of postscript as if he'd added: "Well, it's all over now. We can go on from here. The other is in the past——"

He held the door for her and she brushed so near she could have touched him; could have put her hand on his arm —could have laid her head against his shoulder as she had done so short a time ago.

But that was in the past. Love in the past? Over and done with?

Better—much better—not to think. And not to feel.

Besides there were things that had to be done.

She put up her head and walked into the lounge where Averill waited for her. As she entered Averill looked at her; it was a long look, steady and again smiling. This time the smile was one of open triumph. Averill rose with a neat, catlike motion and walked softly to meet Jim. She put her hand on his arm and smiled again, but demurely, at him.

CHAPTER/16

Sloane was in the lounge, too. Seated at a long table in the center of the room with a sheaf of papers in his hand and a very large pair of horn-rimmed glasses perched on his thin, high-bridged brown nose. Two tall vases of flowers, one formerly placed at each end of the long table, had been removed that morning and it gave the table a bare and oddly official look.

Noel was standing before the fireplace, smoking, watching Sloane, watching Averill, watching the approach of the others with intent blue eyes; Noel's habitual look of the adventurer, the dashing gallant, was that morning a little blurred as if he found adventure seen at close hand less exhilarating than he would have expected.

"P. H.," said Jim at once, "Strevsky just found that the plane has been damaged; the fuel line is cut. We can't possibly take it up."

Averill's hand tightened and her small face instantly became intent and businesslike.

"Cut?" she cried. "But that's what you say happened to

the plane that crashed! But that——" She broke off, stared at Jim and cried intently: "Who did it?"

"I don't know. Strevsky found it just now and came to tell me."

Noel started forward excitedly and P. H. pulled his horn-rimmed glasses down over the bridge of his nose so he could look at Jim over them and said:

"When was it done?"

Jim turned to Strevsky, who lifted his shoulders and eyebrows and said he didn't know.

"It could have been done yesterday or during the night or even early this morning. I think Wilson did it before he left—so we couldn't take the plane up to search for him."

"I see," said P. H. slowly. "Jim—Miss Blaine is right; that's what was done to the other plane, wasn't it?"

"Yes. Except this time it hasn't been mended, which is just lucky——"

"The way it was the other time," volunteered Strevsky. "As soon as the engine heated up the wax melted and then the gasoline leaked and immediately caught on fire. This way the break was clean and the engine just didn't start; gasoline had already leaked. I can show you——"

Wax, thought Eden suddenly. He had talked of wax before. What kind of wax? There had been sealing wax—red, hard sealing wax—missing from the table in the St. Louis house. Could that possibly have sufficed to mend, with intentional, fatal brevity, the break in the fuel line? She didn't know whether or not it would be possible but decided swiftly to tell Sloane of the missing wax.

"I know," P. H. Sloane was saying in a way that suggested he did know. "When did you last look at the plane?"

Strevsky hesitated and his narrow, tilted eyes became a little wider.

"I don't remember exactly. We worked on her awhile yesterday morning. Then we left her—you said it was safe——"

"It was safe from any of us here at the ranch," said Sloane crisply. Strevsky blinked and went on:

"I walked out to take a look at her last night; just to see everything was all right. I didn't look at the engine then—didn't start her up. The break might have been made already —I couldn't say."

"Your brother was killed in the crash when Mr. Blaine was killed—is that right, Strevsky?"

The pilot's beautiful body stiffened as an animal's body stiffens when it scents danger. A dull flush rose in his face.

"Yes, Mr. Sloane. Michael."

"Michael Strevsky," repeated Sloane softly. "All right, gentlemen, won't you sit down? My boys will find Wilson if he's to be found. The plane would have helped." Without any warning his soft voice changed and became as quick and cutting as a whiplash; his drooping eyelids flashed upward. *"Which of you disabled that plane? Why did you have to prevent anyone's leaving? Which of you did it?"*

No one spoke. They were all probably a little taken aback by the unexpected unleashing of force which up to then had been somewhat masked by his leisurely, easygoing manner. He waited, eyes still unhooded and as hard and rapacious as an eagle's. It was curious to see the look on his lean, hard face, in contrast to the grandfatherly and benevolent stance of his horn-rimmed spectacles, still down on his nose.

At last Jim gave a kind of shake to his shoulders as if he were rousing himself and walked across toward P. H. Sloane. He put his hands on the table and leaned over it and said:

"Listen, P. H., whoever cut the fuel line had to know how. I know how—Strevsky would know."

"But I didn't do it," said Strevsky hurriedly.

"Major Pace might know how——"

"I'll add to Strevsky's denial," said Pace instantly and smoothly.

"—and Roy Wilson might know how to do it, but I doubt it."

"It matters more," said Sloane, "why it was done than who did it." In a flash he reverted to his usual easy, leisurely but economic manner. "Sit down, Jim. All of you. I've got some reports from St. Louis here I want you to hear. I talked confidentially to the police there last night; they got some material together and gave it to me over the telephone early this morning. Will you——" He motioned toward chairs. Eden thankfully sank down into a great wing chair which was like a shelter. The others hesitated and then, as if persuaded, overcome by Sloane's suddenly easy manner, sat down, too—in chairs, mainly, near the long table; Jim on the arm of the great divan which faced the fireplace, where Noel still stood and smoked. Dorothy Woolen was in the room, too; so quiet that Eden just then perceived her with rather a shock for she was sitting quite near her, blank and impassive as the wall behind her, strong, bloodless-looking hands clasped in her lap, blonde braid like a coronet above her wide forehead. She would have been a handsome woman, Eden realized swiftly, had a spark of animation lighted that splendidly wooden face. Then she forgot Dorothy. For Sloane had pushed his spectacles up again so as to read and was looking at the sheaf of papers he held in his hands.

And he said: "Eden Shore——"

It pinned Eden's attention.

"Eden Elizabeth Shore; born June 6, 1912, in Lake Forest, Illinois. Father Charles Shore, died in 1931." He glanced along several lines and apparently telescoped them. "Palm Beach winters, Lake Forest or Newport summers—m'm'm. Educated abroad and at Miss Snelle's School (see Averill Blaine)." He stopped, glanced at Averill and then at Eden again and said: "You two became friends at school, then?"

"We—met at school, yes," said Eden, and Averill added demurely: "We've been the best of friends for many years, Mr. Sloane. Since school days."

"I see," said Sloane in a voice that struck Eden as being rather dry. "Well—correct up to that point, Miss Shore?"

"Where did you?" began Eden, her own voice a little husky and then checked her question and said: "Quite correct."

"Good. In 1930 your father lost his money; he died in 1931 and your mother (who was Eden Jane Sothern also of Lake Forest) died shortly after. You went to New York and held—apparently you held a succession of jobs."

"Yes; yes, that's true."

"You kept up your friendship with the Blaines?"

Eden glanced once at Averill and said, "Yes."

"I see. Saw them whenever they were in New York, I presume?"

"Yes," said Eden, still a little huskily.

"Came to St. Louis four days ago to be Miss Blaine's bridesmaid at her wedding?"

The wedding. "Yes," said Eden stiffly, not daring now to glance at Averill, not daring to look at Jim.

"You subscribe to this whole account, then?"

"Yes."

"Good. Miss Shore, in your present position you must come into contact with a great many people."

"Why, I—yes, I suppose I do. Briefly."

"Of," said Sloane, "probably many nationalities."

"I——" Eden was bewildered. "Yes, I suppose so. But still——"

"Miss Shore, please think back and answer a—a rather important question." Sloane paused as if to arrange his words and then said so carefully that the question took on more significance than its words alone claimed: "Have you ever told anyone about your friendship with the Blaine family?"

"I'm sure I don't know," began Eden crisply. "It's nothing to boast of if you mean——"

"Really, Eden," said Averill.

"I don't mean that," said the detective impatiently. "I mean—has anyone ever questioned you about the Blaines? Shown any marked interest? That's a better way to put it."

"No. No, of course not."

"You're sure about that?"

"Positive."

"Thank you. Miss Blaine——"

"You don't mean you have a story of my life there, too! How perfectly absurd! I had nothing to do with——"

"Will you listen, please, Miss Blaine? Thank you. Averill Blaine; born November 30, 1910, in Byton Parish, Louisiana; lived in St. Louis since 1914; daughter of—we all know all this. Educated privately and at Miss Snelle's School; made her debut in 1928." Again he seemed to scan and telescope: "M'm'm—maid of honor Veiled Prophet's Ball; two years in London and Paris——" He stopped and glanced at Averill and said: "You must have a fairly wide foreign acquaintance, Miss Blaine."

"I suppose I have," said Averill icily. "What of it?"

"Accurate so far?" asked the detective pleasantly.

"I suppose so. Yes."

"Good. Now then—engaged at one time to Noel Carreaux—engagement broken—this was apparently some time ago—just after your debut——"

"It was not a formal engagement at all," flashed Averill. "I can't imagine where they got such extremely old and unimportant information!"

"Probably," said the detective, "by inquiring of your friends. The police have their own methods——"

"And very unpleasant ones, I should say," said Averill.

Noel put down his cigarette. "Now then, Averill. We've got to go through a certain amount of this. After all, nobody's going to hold a brief and childish engagement to me against you."

"I didn't mean that, Noel. It's all this disgusting poking into our private lives——"

Sloane resumed: "Engagement to James Cady announced—let me see—a month ago, wasn't it?"

"Yes," said Jim.

"Wedding to be this week. On the death of your father you inherited his property and holdings of Blaine Company stock; right, Miss Blaine?"

"Certainly."

"Very well. Now, then, the police were unable to get much of a record of Creda Blaine. They know, in fact, nothing except that your uncle married her five years ago. The wedding took place in New Orleans; they have got in touch with the police there but so far they've discovered simply nothing of her or her family. Now she didn't drop down out of the sky or come up out of the bay. What do you know of her?"

"Not very much, I'm afraid," said Averill slowly. "She never talked much of her people. I think her name was Hursten; I think she was about forty though she never talked of her age. In fact—well, she never talked of her life previous to her marriage to Bill. She—I think before her marriage she must have had a small income; certainly she had to have something to live on——"

"You don't know where that income came from? I mean —had she been married previous to her marriage to Blaine?"

"No, I don't think so. If so it was never mentioned. She— she had money—not much but some—before her marriage but I don't think she had any profession and if it came from her own people then she never mentioned it. I do know that it ceased about the time of her marriage."

Sloane leaned forward; his brown, lean face seemed to tighten a little.

"Are you sure of that?"

"Oh yes. Creda was extravagant, you know. Loved to spend money. And, after all, Bill's funds were not unlimited. She borrowed of me sometimes when she was low, then she would have a row with Bill and get more money and be very rich for a time and then——"

"Blaine always gave her money?"

"Why, I——" Averill's eyes looked startled. "I suppose so. I never questioned the source of it." She stopped and thought and said: "I always assumed she got it from Bill. I don't know where else it would come from. Creda was really perfectly square with Bill."

"She—forgive me, but it's a routine inquiry—she never had any affair with another man?"

"I would say, no. Definitely, no. Creda was by nature flirtatious but that was all. She—there's no use in not telling the truth; she was vain and loved attention but that's as far as it went. I think—yes, I'm quite sure she was—well, faithful to Bill, if I have to put it like that. Creda had her own notions of dignity, you know. She was——" A thin pink came into Averill's cheeks but she said coldly enough: "She was exactly what she was; I don't know what her origins were and I think if they had been anything to boast of I should have heard. She was intelligent—shrewd, rather. I think she could have lived by her wits if she had needed to. Really that— that is all I know of her."

P. H. Sloane looked at the sheaf of papers in his hand for a long moment. Then he said slowly:

"It must have occurred to you all that the murder of last night may have been no ordinary murder; I mean that it may have a meaning and a significance quite apart from any wholly personal revenge or quarrel. If Creda Blaine had permitted herself to become entangled in an espionage net——"

"Espionage!" cried Averill sharply. "What on earth do you mean?"

117

"Just what I say. Jim tells me, and Noel agrees, that there have been a few attempts in the past to steal plans and new devices and inventions at the Blaine Company plant. They both agree that, occasionally, they have had reason to suspect leakage somewhere, although they could never pin the thing down. It's quite possible that Creda Blaine, through her husband but naturally without his knowledge, was the source of this leakage. In that event why she was murdered or what went wrong it's impossible to say. But it does presuppose that Creda Blaine herself was the object of the attack and not Averill Blaine."

"But I——but she——" Averill lifted her small head higher and said stubbornly: "She was wearing my yellow coat. Her face was covered; she was in my room."

"Nevertheless I——at the moment, at any rate, and failing direct evidence to the contrary——will have to proceed on the theory that whoever killed her knew it was Creda Blaine, and that there was some urgent reason for that murder. It was also someone with whom she felt perfectly at ease and, so far as she knew, had no reason to fear. Otherwise she would certainly have called for help."

"No," said Averill suddenly. "Not Creda. She——she never could speak when she was frightened. It was a nervous kind of thing; any fright or nervous shock seemed to paralyze her throat muscles. If a car skidded, if she had a frightening dream, anything. She used to laugh about it."

Eden remembered a moment of horror, with flames bursting against the clear sky and a falling plane and Creda's sudden, frozen silence.

Noel cleared his throat uneasily. "That's right," he said. "Bill used to kid her about it. He used to tell her she'd make a good——" A quick look of regret flashed upon his face and he stopped.

"A good what?" asked Sloane.

"Well, a good criminal, he used to say. Because she would never give herself away in times of stress. Bill was only joking," he added quickly.

"That then," began Sloane slowly, "would explain——" He did not finish but left the sentence hanging in mid-air for a thoughtful second or two before he resumed abruptly: "Do any of you know of any definite attempts on the part of anyone to buy or steal any information at the plant?"

Jim glanced at Noel and then at Dorothy. Noel said: "You remember the pistol clearance affair." He turned to Sloane. "A rival firm, a foreign one, had our way of solving the trouble a month after we worked it out in the plant."

Dorothy interrupted. She said calmly to the detective: "Yes, Mr. Sloane, there was a definite attempt. I myself was approached. I was offered sums of money varying with the importance of the information I was able to supply. I refused it. I told Mr. Carreaux and Mr. Cady about it. We decided it would be best to keep it to ourselves. It only proved that there really were attempts—as we had suspected in the past—to get information, particularly when we were developing the new engine."

Averill gave a kind of gasp and said: "You didn't tell me——"

"There was no reason to tell you, Averill," said Jim rather wearily. "We didn't even tell Bill. We didn't want to upset you, and Bill always talked too much. It was just one of those things. Almost every airplane plant has its troubles with spies; sometimes they are commercial spies, sometimes simply agitators. You can't tell. Anything, almost, seems to go under the label of espionage. It's true, Sloane, that at least twice a rather important device of our own invention has turned up unexpectedly; once in use and once ahead of us in the patent office. Several times we've had reason to think that some of our plans about this new engine were known. But there was never anything definite—never anything you could put your finger on. The only definite fact we had to go on was this thing Dorothy has just told you about."

"Miss Woolen, exactly who approached you with this offer? And when?"

"About a year ago," said Dorothy composedly. "It was a letter, typewritten, with no heading. It wasn't signed but it gave directions for communication with the writer, the number of a post-office box. I never knew, naturally, who had written it. I—I thought it was a joke," said Dorothy calmly, "until I told Mr. Carreaux and Mr. Cady about it and I could see that they took it seriously."

"What did you do with the letter?"

"I threw it away."

"Do you remember the post-office box number?"

"No. I couldn't possibly remember."

"What exactly did the letter say? How were you to get information and what about?"

Dorothy's pale eyes were as bland as an untroubled sea.

"Why, about the new engine, of course! It just said that the writer was willing to pay for any plans I could copy or secure for him; he would pay generously, I remember him saying, and I was to communicate with him by way of the post-office box. That's all. I was never approached again about it."

"Plans," said Sloane. He swerved suddenly to Averill. "Miss Blaine, Jim says he has told me everything he knows of the plane crash. Consequently I know that the plans for the new engine—one copy of them—have disappeared and that you were the last person to have them. Now then, are you sure you placed them in the library drawer in the St. Louis house?"

"Perfectly sure," said Averill.

"And you don't know what happened to these plans?"

"No, certainly not."

Noel, his peaked black eyebrows drawn nervously together, lounged forward, hands in his pockets.

"Look here, Sloane," he said. "Granted that Creda's death may prove to have a connection with the crash; granted Jim may be right in his explanation of the crash, even so I don't see that you can do much in the way of investigation here. Wouldn't it be better to let us go on to Louisiana, do what has to be done there, and after that—and after the wedding —meet us in St. Louis? I mean . . . Well, if Creda's death was a result, really, of the crash, wouldn't it be better to investigate the crash first, and then Creda———"

"You are quite right," interrupted Sloane. "But in the wrong order. Creda Blaine was murdered in my house. In the county where I live and have some influence. That comes first. The crash of that plane is my affair only so far as it may possibly bear upon Creda Blaine's murder. . . . It is true that I have set certain inquiries in motion in St. Louis but only because of the murder."

"Oh," said Noel rather weakly. Sloane glanced through the papers again. "Mr. Carreaux, you've already subscribed to your own history; Jim—I know yours to be substantially correct. That leaves Miss Dorothy Woolen, Ludovic Strevsky and Major Pace. Miss Woolen's is short; educated public schools, secretarial course at the business college and———"

"And ten years exactly at the Blaine plant," said Dorothy Woolen suddenly. Her voice was as calm and unperturbed as ever, her whole thick body as phlegmatic; yet there was certainly something a little unexpected in the sudden way she finished her own brief, queerly brief, dossier. It startled Eden a little although she could not have said why. It startled Sloane, too, for he shot Dorothy a quick look and put down the paper thoughtfully. But before he continued Chango came to the door, hovered for a moment and advanced a step or two into the room. He looked oddly disheveled; instead of his usual spotless white coat he was in his shirt sleeves, with a long white apron tied around his waist. He said:

"Boss?"

"What is it?"

One hand which had been tucked away under his apron came into view. It held a crumpled white piece of paper. He said, advancing with the paper held gingerly between his fingers as if it might burn him: "Boss, I was cleaning the bedrooms. I found this."

"Give it to me." Sloane took the paper. They all watched while he smoothed it out and read the words written upon it. It took only a second or two. But in that second Eden was suddenly, painfully sure that she knew what the letter was.

She was right, but in an important way she was also wrong.

CHAPTER/17

Sloane's face hardened a little; without lifting his eyes from the note he said; "Where did you find this, Chango?"

Chango's little beady eyes darted quickly around the room and fastened upon Dorothy Woolen.

"In Missee's room," he said and pointed at Dorothy.

"Do you know anything of this, Miss Woolen?"

Dorothy eyed the note dispassionately.

"I don't know, I'm sure. I don't know what it is."

He neither read the note aloud nor showed it to Dorothy. Instead he said briefly to Chango: "Later." The Chinese ducked out of the room and Sloane, a queerly startled and sober look on his usually enigmatic brown face, stood for a moment with the paper in his hand looking at it, then went back to the table and put the note carefully between two blank sheets of paper (to preserve fingerprints, thought Eden; if it was the note Creda had been writing when she was killed then her own, Eden's fingerprints would be on it). With an air of finality, as if there was now something more important he had to do, Sloane began to put together the written notes from which he had been reading.

There was an almost tangible change in the whole atmosphere of the room. Everyone there, perhaps, sensed that change and the reason for it; certainly every pair of eyes was riveted upon the table and the papers so carefully protecting the note Chango had brought. Certainly there was uneasiness and there was an added tensity of extreme, anxious curiosity. But no one inquired, and what was more important no one volunteered information. It was, however, as Sloane gathered up all the papers and was about to speak that Major Pace stepped forward suddenly.

"Before you go, Mr. Sloane," he said quite simply, "I want you to clear me of suspicion concerning this truly horrible crime."

If it took Sloane by surprise then he gave no hint of it. But Noel gave a smothered little exclamation and Averill's hand went up to clutch the green necklace she wore with tight, nervous fingers.

"Well?" said Sloane.

"I realize," said Pace, "that I am in a difficult position here. You are all known to each other; I am a stranger. And I came to buy an engine which is beginning to appear to be the crux of the whole affair. But mark you, I came to buy that engine—not to steal it. I came in good faith. I acted, under orders, as a private purchaser. That engine failed and killed two men. I could have had nothing whatever to do with that. But I was induced to believe that the reason for that failure could be corrected and if so the engine still had the advantages which made it of value to—to the government I represent. Well, then. I agreed to wait. I expected the treatment one reputable business firm accords another—if not what one gentleman accords another. Instead of that I——"

His face was gradually empurpling as restrained violence threatened more and more nearly the suave and pleasant manner with which he began his statement. "Instead of that I was brought out here willy-nilly by a crack-brained young fool and plunged into murder. A woman, brutally, cruelly murdered. A woman I did not know. A woman I met for the first time when I came to the Blaine house in St. Louis. A poor, pretty woman in whom I have no interest whatever. But she was murdered. And instantly the finger of suspicion points at me!"

He was breathing heavily. Averill began, "But, Major Pace——"

He did not look at her or listen but went on rapidly and with growing vehemence:

"I feel it. I am a man of sensibility. I don't like the whispers, the looks, the understanding between you. I feel it here," he said, clasping his heart. "I realize I would be a welcome scapegoat. But I did not kill her. I had no motive. And I can prove I didn't kill her. I was in this room, there by the window, the whole time during which she was murdered. You saw me——"

Sloane interrupted.

"I was at the piano. My back was turned toward the window embrasure in which you sat. The windows were open; you could easily have stepped out that long window onto the porch, followed Creda Blaine when she left the lounge, waited your chance, murdered her and returned."

"But I——" Pace was trembling and purple. "But I tell you I didn't! I would have been seen. Besides there is the other window—over there——" His short thick hand pointed jerkily toward the end of the room. "Someone else sat there. Someone else could have gone without your seeing it, as you said I did. You can't prove I killed her because I didn't do it! I demand that you retract——"

Dorothy Woolen interrupted heavily but with inexpressible conviction: "Mr. Carreaux sat there before the other window. And neither Mr. Carreaux nor Major Pace left the room while you were at the piano, Mr. Sloane. I sat in a chair facing that end of the room. I would have seen either man leave the room."

Noel looked embarrassed.

"I—well, thanks, Dorothy," he said. His face brightened. "Now if somebody would explain my revolver——" he said.

Major Pace gave Dorothy a beaming look of gratitude and a sweeping bow.

"You see, Mr. Detective," he said. "There is my alibi. Perfect. Thank you, Miss Woolen."

It was oddly exasperating and seemed, that time, to have a kind of official weight. Pace obviously considered himself cleared of any ghost of suspicion; his wrath was gone; he was beaming and smiling and gracious.

No one spoke. And Pace bowed to Dorothy again and said to Sloane: "Whether you acknowledge it or not, you have no shadow of evidence against me. I dare you to find such evidence. I—I defy you, Mr. P. H. Sloane," concluded Pace in a grand burst of swagger, turned with a sweeping gesture and walked out of the room. It was a curious gesture which suggested the sweep of a cloak. And as he walked away his right hand rested on his hip as if he expected to find a sword. Or a dagger, thought Eden, for there was certainly a hint of medievalism about the man, and about his public somewhat theatrical defiance.

Sloane looked at his watch and said as if dismissing Pace entirely: "I have very little information about you, Strevsky, and very little about the steward." Strevsky started at the mention of his name and came forward a step or two, wearily. "I had a talk with Wilson," continued Sloane briefly. "Last night. About two o'clock, I think. He said, and I believed him then, that he knew nothing whatever about the murder. That he had seen Creda Blaine leave her cabin yesterday afternoon for a long walk; she went alone and some time later he saw her return, still alone. When I questioned him he admitted that he had thought she looked frightened but he wasn't sure. That was all. Miss Blaine, is there any possibility of this missing steward having known Creda Blaine well at any time?"

"No. No, certainly not. I never saw him before—to my knowledge." She leaned forward, one hand still twisting the green necklace. "Why did he run away?"

"I don't know. But he'll be found. He must have food and he must have water."

"But—perhaps he, too——" began Averill; a faint gray shadow seemed to creep from her dress to her cheeks and she stopped. But Sloane shook his head.

"He is probably merely frightened. Some minor peccadillo in his own life, perhaps, and he dreads police investigation.

We'll soon know. Now then, Strevsky. You are not a naturalized citizen?"

"Well, and if I'm not," said Strevsky insolently.

"You were born in——"

"England."

"This report says Ragusa."

"All right, Ragusa, then. Or Athens. Or Petrograd. Anything you like."

"True cosmopolite," said Sloane but not unpleasantly. "Look here, Strevsky. Nobody's going to accuse you of something you didn't do. You can drop that extremely belligerent manner and tell me the truth."

"I'm telling you the truth. I don't know where I was born. I don't know who my father was. I remember my mother. She worked and slaved and worried, and drank sometimes to forget the worry. She saw to it that Michael and I had food in our stomachs and shoes on our feet. And she died a year after Michael and I got jobs and could take care of her. There was just Michael and me." The sullen look of defiance changed to something threatening, suggesting barely restrained violence. "Michael and me," he repeated. "And Michael was murdered. Like that silly, fat women was murdered. Like big Blaine was murdered and he was as good a boss as man ever had." His great, strong hands were working nervously, his slanted eyes were two gleaming slits. "The woman wasn't important. Michael——" He stopped there as if his throat had closed on the word and then said with the queerest effect of simple determination: "If I could get my hands on the throat of whoever murdered him I'd strangle him. Like that." His hands gave a kind of twist, a shadowy gesture which was nevertheless unpleasantly realistic.

Sloane said rather dryly: "Well, you needn't go that far, Strevsky. At least I trust that if your brother really was murdered——"

"He was murdered."

"——that the law will relieve you of any—duties in that respect. Can you tell me anything of Wilson, Strevsky?"

"No," said Strevsky. "I can't."

"Thank you." Sloane glanced at his watch again, took the papers on the table carefully in his hand and said: "By the way, there's a detail of which the St. Louis police informed me. They say that your house, Miss Blaine, was entered the night you left. Entered and thoroughly ransacked. The police were notified by the servants the next morning but so far have been unable to put their hands on the intruder, whoever it was. Nothing was taken. Did you know that, Miss Blaine?"

"How could I know?" cried Averill. "Who—are they sure nothing was taken?"

"So your servants told the police," said Sloane and started toward the door.

And Eden thought swiftly: I must see him; I must tell him —alone—about the sealing wax. About Creda and Pace. About my fingerprints on the revolver. About the letter.

And as swiftly she questioned her impulse; the few things she knew or had casually observed might be significant only in her own mind. And it would be so terribly easy—as with Creda's interrupted note to Jim—to do more harm than good. To tell Sloane of the letter would only prove that Creda had written it; that she had actually been writing it, probably, when she was killed. The wave of perplexity caught and held her. Almost certainly, however, she would have gone eventually to Sloane with her story (such as it was) of her own will. But as it happened she was soon to be summoned to Sloane's study for what proved to be a really official inquiry.

For five minutes after Sloane walked out of the lounge, leaving a shaken and rather stunned audience behind him, the sheriff and several of his deputies arrived. Clattered up to the front door in an old but extremely powerful automobile and came in—all of them weary, all of them haggard, all of them hurried.

And they remained.

It was noon when they arrived. It was perhaps midafternoon when (after a long conference between the sheriff and Sloane, while the other three men joined the cowboys in their, thus far, fruitless search for Roy Wilson) the inquiry began again.

She was not the first person to be called into the study. And no one was sent for until after the sheriff and Sloane had made a long, slow detour of the cabin in which Creda Blaine died and had spent some time inside the cabin itself. And had followed this tour (which was witnessed rather uneasily by the little cluster of those waiting on the porch) by another long conference again in Sloane's study.

It was not pleasant, waiting while Sloane, apparently, acquainted the sheriff with every detail of which he had possessed himself.

Dorothy Woolen perhaps was the only calm and unmoved one among them; she got out a great piece of cross-stitch embroidery and worked on it, slowly, painstakingly all that afternoon. Her blonde head and pale face was bent constantly over the fine stitches she took; yet Eden was curiously certain that her mind went right on recording, and her eyes—somehow—seeing every look and gesture and motion on the part of the rest of them.

But there was nothing to do but wait. They smoked a great

deal and talked very little and watched the changing light on the distant rim of mountains. Averill wrote a note or two, seated at the long table in the lounge. Later she and Jim walked out along the path, walked slowly, talking in low voices. Eden watched them go, Averill's sleek black head so near Jim's shoulder, her slender figure graceful in every demure, gentle movement under the sleekly fitting gray linen.

Eden watched and tried not to watch. They reached the cluster of pines and walked on and at last turned onto the road leading to the mile-distant gate and disappeared in the dip of the arroyo. She was not conscious of her face betraying anything of her thoughts until Noel, lounging on the porch railing near her, said in an odd voice: "Eden."

She turned with a quick movement, reminded only then of his presence. He was sitting on the broad railing, his knees drawn up and his arms around them, looking very boyish in spite of the touch of gray at his temples and the fine lines around his blue eyes.

"Noel! I'd forgotten you were there."

"So I thought," said Noel gently. "Eden dear, may I say something?"

"Of course, Noel."

He dropped the end of his cigarette over the porch railing, glanced toward the blue shadow of the arroyo where Averill and Jim, walking so slowly, talking so intimately, had disappeared, and then looked at Eden. Dorothy was at the other end of the porch, some distance from them, her blonde head still bent over her embroidery; Pace and Strevsky were not in sight. Noel said in a low voice so Dorothy could not hear:

"Eden, my dear—you are not just a little taken with Jim, are you?"

Eden tried to reply evasively.

"What a question! Jim is to marry Averill."

"That's it," said Noel earnestly, blue eyes still watching her anxiously. "It would be no good, you know—I mean, you'd just be letting yourself in for trouble. Averill would never give him up, especially to you. Averill," said Noel simply, "can hate longer and better and—and meaner than anybody I know."

"I know," said Eden slowly. "Let's not talk, Noel. I keep thinking of Creda. What do you suppose will be the end of this?"

"God knows," said Noel, sighing.

Brilliant sunshine poured down from a bright sky; the shadows under the pines and under the great cottonwoods were blue as the haze over the mountains. Through the cluster of pines at the south end of the porch Eden caught a glimpse of the cabin where Creda had died—quietly, because she was unable to scream for help, bound in that bloodstained chiffon scarf.

Again, as she had done already many times, Eden searched her mind and memory about the scarf, her own scarf, once clean and delicate and softly scented. Now an ugly thing, sinister, a silent witness reposing, had she but known it, on a shelf in Sloane's study along with a revolver and a note. Touched once, exploringly, by the sheriff's thick fingers. Speculated upon endlessly.

Somewhere under that brilliant, hot sun the little steward took his secret way; all that day they searched for him. Little Roy Wilson with his childish mouth and his curly blond hair. And they searched, too, because Chango insisted upon it, for a hatchet. A newly sharpened hatchet, he told them; with a notch on it to show it belonged in the lean-to storeroom where he kept stove wood.

After a long time Averill and Jim, still strolling, still talking quietly with an appearance of the utmost mutual understanding, returned. Jim saw the three on the veranda, glanced once at Eden and went directly into the house and did not return. She had no chance to warn him of the note Creda had written, even if she hadn't persuaded herself, by that time, that she had been mistaken; that the crumpled paper Chango had given Sloane had not been, after all, the curious letter Creda had inexplicably begun to write, and had failed, not so inexplicably, to finish. And for that letter Jim must have an explanation. There could have been, in spite of the suggestion in Creda's letter, no league, no understanding between Jim and Creda.

She told herself that and believed it. Aside from everything she knew or thought she knew of Jim, the fact remained that he couldn't have been in a conspiracy with Creda to wreck the engine he had made and, in the process, to murder two men.

Time went on. The shadows of the cottonwoods grew slowly longer and pointed toward the east and the rim of eastern mountains began to take on a shimmering crimson glow as the sun sank lower. Once Chango came to summon Averill to Sloane's study and later (a long time later, it seemed to Eden) Noel was sent for. He returned, looking extremely tired and curiously disheveled, as if he had been rubbing his hands through his hair and worrying his tie.

"God," he said explosively. "Well, that's over! If there's anything Sloane and this sheriff don't know about me, then I don't know it myself." He lighted a cigarette with unsteady hands, took a long puff of smoke and sat down disconsolately on the railing. "I wish to God I knew how my revolver got there. Do you know what I'd like to do, Eden?"

"What?"

"Take that plane that's waiting out there and fly away—away to the ends of the earth. Anywhere away from here."

"You can't," said Eden practically. "The fuel line is cut."

"I know," said Noel and smoked and brooded.

"But I'd take you with me if you wanted to go," he said at last with a flash of his normal, charming smile.

"I wouldn't be permitted to leave," said Eden somberly. "I'm almost the First Suspect. If Pace is out of the running."

"Don't joke like that."

"I wish it were a joke."

"Miss Shore, please," said Chango's voice at her elbow. She turned with a jerk, knowing what was coming.

"Mr. Sloane wants you, please. This way."

Noel got up, too, and laid his arm lightly around her shoulders and kissed her cheek. "Buck up, my child," he said. "They can't eat you. We've all got it to go through."

She tried to smile and followed Chango.

Sloane was waiting, and the sheriff. Chango ushered her into the small room, offered her a chair facing the two men and withdrew, closing the door behind him. Sunlight poured through the west windows and lay hot and clear upon the worn brown rug and the shelves and glinted against a microscope on top of the shabby, roll-top desk. Sloane who had risen when she entered resumed his seat before the desk, tilting back in the swivel chair. The sheriff, a big, well-fleshed man with a tired face and pouched eyes, gave her a scrutinizing look and took out his handkerchief and wiped his glistening forehead and bald head.

Sloane said: "Miss Shore, I want you to tell us the whole story of last night over again. This is Sheriff Utley and I want him to hear it from your own lips. Slowly, if you please, and in detail. But first, I want you to look at this."

"This" was a once crumpled, now flattened piece of paper with words written on it in a large, careless handwriting.

It was the note Creda had written; the note that had been removed from Eden's own pocket. Yet—yet it wasn't that either! For there was more, much more, written upon it than the line or two she remembered with such clarity.

She looked at it incredulously and caught her breath in a sharp little gasp. Both men noted that and she realized it. Sloane said:

"I'm told by Averill Blaine, and by Noel Carreaux, and by Jim, that that is in Creda Blaine's handwriting. Have you seen it before?"

"Yes," said Eden and instantly cried: "No—no. This isn't right."

"Read it," said the sheriff suddenly.

She gave him a startled look; surely they knew it by heart. But she read, faltering a little in spite of herself.

"Dear Jim. Cold-blooded murder is too much. I won't do any more, I can't. Jim—you must believe me—and let me go. I give up my share of the money willingly to you. I promise you not to tell no matter what——"

It stopped there—trailed away in a line of ink that had not been there the night before. Eden cried sharply:

"But it's not right. It wasn't like that. It's all wrong."

"So you've seen this before?" The sheriff leaned heavily forward. "Your fingerprints are on the revolver, Miss Shore. You found the woman dead. Your scarf choked the life out of her. Now then, why did you do it?"

"But I didn't," cried Eden, in a high, unsteady voice. "I didn't!" She turned toward Sloane with her hands thrust out beseechingly. "You must know I didn't do it! I had no motive. And Jim—this note isn't right. He couldn't have been what Creda says—he—why, he's your friend! You know him."

A look in the detective's eyes stopped her. It was a cold, strange look which removed him definitely and finally from a world where friendship counted and appeal had power. He said, although that icy look made it unnecessary:

"Friendship has nothing to do with this, Miss Shore. Please remember that, and Jim himself offers no explanation."

CHAPTER/18

Eden thought rather desperately: I must pull myself together; I must arrange what I have to say and I must make my statements clear and simple so they will believe me.

She leaned forward a little, speaking earnestly. "But I found that letter last night; in the cabin where I found Creda. I—took it and slipped it in the pocket of my white coat. Sometime last night it was taken from there; I don't know who did it. But it was not like this when I found it. The middle part is the same. But words have been added to it."

Sloane said nothing and the sheriff said: "What words?"

"These." She pointed. " 'Dear Jim' and all the words after 'believe me.' "

The sheriff took the note from her fingers and read it slowly and ponderously again.

"You claim then that whoever (according to your story) took this note from you deliberately added enough to make a case against this Cady fellow?"

"The note as she claims to have found it is enough," said Sloane dryly. "That leaves, do you see, 'cold-blooded murder is too much.' (Evidently referring to the plane crash.) 'I won't do any more, I can't!' (Which, in so far as it can, confirms my theory that Creda Blaine was a part of whatever conspiracy there was.) And 'Jim—believe me' certainly refers to Jim."

"But it's the rest of it that seems to make it clinching," said Eden quickly. "Her handwriting would be so easy to imitate."

Sloane said: "How long have you known Jim Cady, Miss Shore? I was under the impression that you met him first when you came to St. Louis for Miss Blaine's wedding."

Eden hoped the warmth in her face was not a flush.

"That's quite true," she said stiffly. "But I saw the note, you see——"

"Why did you remove it?"

"I don't know."

"You gave me to understand you touched nothing."

"I—but that seemed to me——" She stopped there, helplessly.

"It seemed to you, I suppose, to incriminate Jim. It occurred to you then, too, that a situation whereby a man may wish to receive the entire proceeds from his own invention rather than a mere salary for the time he worked on that invention is not outside the realm of possibility?"

There was a shadow over the detective's face as he spoke but his eyes remained as coldly inhuman as two small blue icebergs.

"No! Nothing of the kind occurred to me. I—I was frightened—indescribably shocked. I—I had no clear thoughts. I—it was on the desk you see when I saw someone watching me——"

The sheriff, who had been tilting back in his chair, let the two front legs down with a bang and the detective leaned forward and said: "What's that? You said nothing—— *Who was it?*"

"I don't know. I'm not even sure there was anyone. I didn't—didn't think of it," said Eden quite honestly. "There was so much else and it—it was only a motion—felt rather than actually seen——"

"Listen, Miss Shore," said the detective rather tensely. "Suppose you begin at the beginning and tell everything——"

"But the letter. It is wrong——"

"Suppose there were two letters. Suppose she started the other one, the one you found, and left it. And wrote this one complete."

"But that——" Eden thought of Dorothy. "How did Dorothy Woolen happen to have it? Why was it in her room? What does she know of it?"

The detective rose and pulled the shade to keep the level rays of the sun from his eyes and said over his shoulder,

130

"She insists that she knows nothing of it. Now, then, Miss Shore, we're waiting. Start please with the time when you left the lounge last night."

Eden looked at the implacable shoulders of the detective, at the sheriff who, broodingly, looked back at her, took a long breath and began.

The sun crept lower and blue and purple shadows grew at the base of the mountain rims and in the hollows of the arroyo and under the cottonwoods. For they stopped her now and then to question, exhaustively and repetitiously, and it took time.

So she and Jim Cady had strolled down to the clump of pines along the drive, had they? They had been altogether alone? Had they talked of anything in particular? Oh, just chatting—had Jim mentioned the plane crash? Oh, he had. Well, what had he said?

Instinctively she kept the knowledge of the thing that had happened there in the soft shadow of the pines from them. It had no bearing upon murder. It was a thing separate —and besides, just then, she couldn't have borne to tell anyone. Noel had dimly perceived it; she hoped no one else.

She went on, and the questioning went on. It was a little difficult getting around the brief conversation she and Averill had had in her room, but she managed it. They questioned her over and over again about the time during which she had been alone in her room, next to the room where Creda was murdered. They dug down into her memory and consciousness with prodding, sharp tentacles, demanding answers.

But she remembered only what she remembered. Averill had gone away, still wearing her yellow cloak. There had been voices, women's voices she thought, and then silence. Silence until there was the sound of a drawer pulled open. (Yes, it might have been the chest of drawers being pulled away from the wall, but she didn't know why.) And silence again, and then those stealthy, tiptoed steps, entering, pausing, leaving again and closing the door afterward.

And that was all. At length they permitted her to go on. Her own entrance and horrified discovery; the thing that must have been the revolver which she thrust aside without looking when she knelt beside Creda (they listened to that in unrevealing silence); her effort to pull the scarf away. They interrupted her there.

"You knew it was your scarf?"

"Yes, of course."

"What did you think when you saw it there?"

"I don't know. I suppose I wondered who had taken it. I didn't think—I couldn't."

"Why didn't you remove it?"

"I——" She hesitated and repeated: "I didn't think of that either. Why should I? I didn't murder her. My only thought was to help her if—if I could. And to call someone."

"You removed the note to Jim Cady?"

"Yes."

"What happened next?"

They questioned her at length, as if they were waiting for it, about the half-glimpsed face vanishing into the deep shadow of the pines. Who was it? She didn't know? Well, exactly what had she seen? Oh, it was just an impression of a face. Could it have been Strevsky's? Perhaps. Roy Wilson's? Perhaps, again. Major Pace's? She couldn't tell; there was just a motion and a white, blurred oval vanishing. And a sense of surveillance.

But she would be willing to swear, if need be, that someone had been outside the cabin, watching from the shadow of the pines. Y-yes; yes, she would be willing to swear it.

"Go on."

But when at last she finished they questioned again, going over every item and every step. And then went back to St. Louis. Went back even to her little apartment in New York—so incredibly distant, so completely outside the world that had enfolded them, shutting out every other existence. Yet hinging so definitely and strangely upon that distant past.

That gave her the chance she needed, however, to tell them of suspicions that were merely suspicions, of half-formed ideas—of facts that were not quite facts. So she thought Creda and Pace had already known each other; why? Exactly why had she failed to believe Creda's denial? And what was this about a key?

They seemed covertly excited about that, although Eden herself had all but forgotten the key in the welter of what seemed to her more important events that had intervened. Sloane rose and paced the floor.

"The St. Louis police say that the night watchman at the Blaine plant swears nobody entered the plant the night before the crash," Sloane said to the sheriff. "But it's a big place; there's only one man at night; night watchmen have been known to go to sleep on the job before this. But I don't see what Creda Blaine herself could have known of the engine. It isn't everybody who would have known of the engine. It isn't everybody who would know exactly what to do to cripple the plane, or exactly how to mend the break with the diabolic skill that was employed. Wax——"

"There was wax missing from the library table. The table where Averill says she placed the plans for the engine. Red sealing wax."

It angered Sloane. He turned swiftly toward her and

pounded the desk top with the flat of his hand and swore deeply. *"Why haven't you told me all this before? Why have you kept these things secret? Why have you——"*

"Wait a minute, wait a minute, P. H.," said the sheriff easily. "There's not been much time, you know. God damn it, the woman was murdered only last night."

Only last night, thought Eden incredulously. It had been, as a matter of fact, only thirty-six hours or so since the great silver plane had landed them in that fantastic, distant, mountain-rimmed world; a lonely world, beautiful, queerly thrilling, and at the same time frightening. And she seemed to know it as intimately and as familiarly as if it had been years.

"I'm done with this thing," said Sloane, still white. "You take it over, Utley."

"I can't. You know what I've got on my hands." The sheriff was weary and undisturbed. "I know how you feel, P. H., when it's your friend—Cady, I mean. But you can't help it." He rolled a cigarette expertly, lighted it and said reflectively: "I remember how I felt when I had to arrest Apple Johnny Redback. We'd punched cattle together as youngsters; ridden in many a roundup. Were with the same outfit; how Apple Johnny could sing." He sighed a little and pulled his sagging body upward. "But I had to go after him, just the same—you remember? That was two years ago in January— we had a thaw. A bullet from—one of my men's guns got him." A ghost of youthful, singing Apple Johnny seemed to tug lightly at the sheriff's arm. He moved restively, said: "It's all in a lifetime, P. H. Can't be helped," and dismissed the ghost. "Now then, Miss Shore, anything else?"

There was nothing. But they kept her there, nevertheless, questioning over and over again—her scarf, the note in Creda's writing, the silence in the cabin and those furtive tiptoed footsteps. At the last they asked her whether she had had any quarrel with Averill, and Eden hesitated and said at last, because she had to, that she had no quarrel with Averill. It was not the letter of the truth; it was in a deep sense, however, fact itself. But she did not try to excuse it with specious reasoning. She simply lied, flatly, because there was nothing else to do. Because Creda had worn Averill's yellow cloak; because she had died in Averill's room; because her face had been veiled.

Because all at once, starkly, the significance they would give those facts if the knowledge of her quarrel with Averill and the reason for that quarrel were laid before them, became comprehensible to her. Stood out sharply and stiffly in her mind. She was dull with fatigue by that time, but she saw that clearly as she had not seen it before.

For that would be a motive.

And there had to be a motive. If the murder of Creda was intentional or if it was a failing attempt upon Averill's life, there still had to be a motive.

It was an endless circle. Eden straightened her drooping shoulders wearily and stared at the tip ends of her white slippers and tried to brace herself for the next questions.

But there were no more. For Chango came with trays of silver and china and proceeded to lay a small table with dinner for the sheriff and Sloane, and they told her she could go. But not without admonishment. Through the open door the sheriff said loudly: "But try to remember, young lady, who it was you saw in the cabin last night." And Sloane followed her to the door and stood there, watching her as she went upstairs.

It was night by that time. The sun dropped down behind a distant mountain rim and instantly twilight came with only a lingering touch of light in the sky and crimson upon the Sangre de Cristo peaks at the eastern horizon.

Dinner was late and rather an ordeal; no one wanted to talk; the candles flickered on the table; and Chango gave them scant attention, reserving his real efforts for the two men dining alone in Sloane's study. He did tell them that the searchers were returning, two or three at a time, and that so far Roy Wilson had not been found. Nor, added Chango, little eyes glittering, the hatchet.

One of them had, however, found a rather curious thing, but he had taken it immediately to Sloane and even Chango knew nothing of it then.

Jim said almost nothing; he looked taut and white; he had offered, Sloane had said, no explanation for Creda's dreadful, scrawled letter. But perhaps there was no explanation. There could, in fact, be no explanation for Jim to give them. So Eden reasoned.

Once she caught his eyes but the look in them told her nothing.

And certainly everyone—except perhaps Dorothy, who ate and drank with her usual calm and hearty appetite—showed the effects of the nerve strain and tension of the past few days.

After dinner they separated. Eden walked aimlessly out to the long porch; the stars were out by that time, remote and bright. Stars that, last night, she had thought to hold in her own grasp. The path stretched invitingly away into the cool and quiet night, with the clump of pines showing black and thick. She had an impulse to walk along the path and, indeed, had started down the steps when Noel came along the path, stopped beside her and said: "Going for a walk, Eden? How did you come out with the masterminds?"

"I don't know," she said slowly. He started down the steps

as if to accompany her and, as she paused at the top of the short flight with her hand irresolutely on the railing, he stopped too and looked up at her. The light from above the door into the hall fell dimly into his face. He said: "Come along, Eden dear. Let's stroll a bit. Besides, I—I really want to talk to you."

The soft light and the pleading look which was suddenly in his eyes reminded her all at once of a younger Noel. And of a younger Eden. How long ago, now, that childish little romance seemed.

The thought of Jim had lain like a cold weight in her heart all that day. Noel's presence was irresistibly comforting, his kindness and affection inexpressibly warming.

"Dear Noel," she said and put her hand out toward him in an impulsive little gesture. He took it and as impulsively and rather eagerly caught it to his cheek.

"You look," he said quickly, "like the Eden I used to know. Like the girl I loved. Like the girl—like the girl I still love. Eden——"

She didn't withdraw her hand. She didn't move but stood perfectly still on the step above him looking down into his suddenly youthful face, smiling a little wistfully, a little tenderly, touched by a recaptured and gentle memory.

"Noel—you can't mean that. It's too late——"

"It's never too late," said Noel. "And I do mean it." He came closer impetuously, still clasping her hand tight. "I do love you, darling. Believe it or not, I've always loved you. But I——" Someone crossed the hall inside with a brisk ring of footsteps. He frowned a little. "This isn't the proper time or place. But then I never do things at the proper time and place. Come along, Eden; let's walk down the path and I— you'll let me tell you. Will you?"

Down the path toward the pines where she'd walked the night before with Jim? With the same stars looking down from the night sky?

But this was, she remembered suddenly and with a shock, exactly what she had come for; this was why she'd left New York; this was why she'd accepted Averill's invitation. Because she had made up her mind to induce, by whatever means she could discover, the very words Noel was uttering. Well, she ought to feel pleased. She ought to accept the opening he had provided. She ought—definitely, instantly, adroitly, to settle the thing then and there. For certainly nothing had changed except that her need for Noel—for kindness, for care, for security—was even greater than it had been.

The outside world still existed beyond that lofty, mysterious rim of mountains. Afterward she would be thankful for Noel.

She said gravely: "Yes, Noel. I'll come with you."

135

"Eden——" His face became sober; his eyes bright and purposeful. "Eden," he repeated. "Does that mean——"

She must say it quickly. Instantly. While she could say it. While she could remember that that was the decision she had come to, thoughtfully and quietly, before she had met Jim and enchantment had fallen upon her, blinding her eyes and her senses.

"Yes, Noel."

She could not read the look in Noel's face. And footsteps came rapidly again along the hall and someone stepped onto the porch and banged the door behind them and it was Jim. He paused for a moment, while she half turned to look at him. His face was in the shadow, with the light behind him; he did not move or speak for a perceptible moment as if he were taking in every possible implication of the little tableau.

Then he said, his voice quite without expression: "Sorry. I didn't mean to interrupt. I only wanted to ask Eden about —about this letter Chango found. Sloane says she got hold of it first. God knows, I don't know anything about it. Will you," he asked with chilly politeness, "tell me where and how you found it? Anything at all——"

Noel went up the steps again, drawing Eden after him.

"As a matter of fact," he said cheerily, "you did interrupt an important moment. And a—a particularly happy one," he said, smiling at Eden and drawing her hand closely through his arm. "However, Jim, don't worry about that confounded letter. Oh, yes, I know about it; they've questioned everybody probably. But it means nothing. They can't possibly take it seriously. Good God, you wouldn't sell out your own people! You wouldn't wreck your own engine and steal your own plans. It's crazy. Even Sloane and the sheriff must see that."

"Nevertheless," said Jim, "that's what they seem to think. Even Sloane. I hoped that Eden could tell me something that would help explain it."

Noel looked at Jim, looked at Eden and shrugged.

"All right," he said lightly. "I'll leave you two alone to thresh it out. But remember, Eden, what you promised me." He turned away with a wave of his hand and a smile at Eden. Jim said: "Will you come in here, please; the big dining room seems to be unoccupied."

She preceded him into the house and into the long dining room, with its chairs stacked on tables and its windows bare, pending the arrival of the dude season. The light from the hall streamed in, but there was no other light and it gave her a sense of isolation.

"Whoever found it added to the letter," she said at once. "I'm sure of that," and told him quickly and anxiously all she knew of it, watching his face as she talked.

When she finished he did not speak for a moment. Then

he said: "I don't understand it, Eden. Creda couldn't have written to me like that. And if someone else did it, then— why? And who? I can't think of anyone who would do that to me. Well, thanks, Eden. I——" He spoke rather stiffly and said: "I do thank you for telling Sloane all you knew about it and trying to help me. It was good of you."

"Not at all," replied Eden as stiffly and was struck with the absurdity of her reply. That, to Jim.

"Well," said Jim, "I—suppose that's all——" He made a kind of motion toward the door as if to end their short talk and Eden moved quickly to leave. But quite suddenly he caught her hand and swung her back to face him.

"Eden, why did you do it? Why did you try to hide that letter?"

She looked up helplessly into his face—loving him and wishing she could stop. And all at once he gave a kind of groan and caught her hard in his arms.

Her heart was pounding frantically. But before she could more than realize the unexpected thing that had happened, he released her again. He looked white in the half-light and a little stern. And said: "What was that?"

"I heard nothing." Nothing, she wanted to say, but her own mad heart beating.

But he turned away from her and went to the door and looked up and down the hall.

"Funny," he said in a troubled way. "I thought someone —well, tiptoed along the hall. There's nobody there now." He gave her a deeply perplexed look. And became under her very eyes a stranger again—remote, cool, distant. But regretful.

"I'm continually in the position of asking your forgiveness," he said stiffly again. "You'll have to forgive me this latest outburst, too. Don't try to understand. I hope you'll forget this, too."

It ended the thing. She walked out of the room beside him as composedly, she hoped, as if nothing had happened. Down at the end of the hall Averill stood at the open door into P. H. Sloane's study, talking to Sloane. She turned and glanced at them, a slim, demure figure in perfectly fitted gray linen.

Then Eden was caught and appalled by the look in Averill's eyes as they met her own, for it was sheer, bare hatred. Cold and—which was queer—purposeful.

Jim left Eden as if the sight of Averill had been a chain pulling him toward her.

Noel was waiting. But Eden thought, I'll get my coat, and she was a little ashamed of seizing upon the pretext for an escape.

She ran up the stairs, pursued by the look of purpose in

Averill's face, definitely disturbed by it. But what, after all, could Averill do that she had not already done? She entered her room in a kind of daze. As she entered it, it occurred to her that there was something wrong—the door was open. Hadn't she closed it when she left the room? But it didn't matter.

Without closing it she walked over to the dressing table and stood there absently before the low mirror, too low for her to see her own image, only her white dress and bare arms in the small circle of light from the lamp, and her hands absently touching and moving the little powder box.

The instant in Jim's arms again had shaken her more than she would have believed possible. Was she, Eden Shore, going to let herself be assailed like that—and by a man who had told her he didn't want her? That it had been a mistake? That he was to marry Averill?

Well—forgive, he'd said. And forget.

It was a slight motion in the mirror that caught her eye. The door behind her was moving slightly. Then her eyes became focused and could not move aside from a thing that was there, beside the gently moving door, in that shadowy, obscured reflection.

It was a plain wooden handle, rather worn, curved. She saw only the end of the handle—not the thing to which it was attached, nor the hand that must hold it.

It moved slightly, catching the light, riveting her eyes.

In the still moment with the stars and mountains outside, a coyote howled away off in the night. It was answered by another, as if they had found prey, and all their wolfish instinct had arisen.

CHAPTER/19

Off in the distance the coyote called eerily again. And Eden moved.

No one ever knew what would actually have happened if she had not. There was no possible way to know, only to guess. But from somewhere she did draw the power of motion.

She tried first to scream—or thought she tried to. No sound came from her throat. And, eyes still riveted to the unsteady, worn wooden handle highlighted against nondescript but bulky shadow, she was conscious of only one compulsion and that was escape. She must force her muscles to respond to her will. Scream; escape.

It was as if someone outside herself were in command of her own body.

So she tried to scream—or thought she tried to—and moved. She moved probably in the direction of the door. But instantly her hand caught on something which entangled her wrist and tugged sharply against it; there was a light crash, another louder crash, a sound of splintering glass and a sound like the report of a small revolver—and simultaneous and complete darkness in the little room. Darkness and confusion. Sounds—feet running lightly, a door banging—more sounds.

It was a moment of unutterable swiftness and confusion. She was still standing beside the dressing table, held as if transfixed by darkness and terrible uncertainty. And there were footsteps again along the passage, heavy, running footsteps—not light and furtive ones fleeing in the darkness, as for a fractional moment other footsteps had fled. She tried again to scream and perhaps succeeded for the bedroom door that had banged flung itself open again and someone shouted: "Eden—Eden, where are you?" and it was Noel.

Other footsteps were running, too—she could hear the clatter, the shouts, the questions. And the light flashed on again in the little room, this time it was the overhead light, and Noel saw her and cried, "Eden, good God, did he hurt you———"

Sloane was there, too, and Jim. And Averill. All crowding in the door of the little bedroom. On the floor at her feet lay the dressing-table lamp, shattered, the bulb in a hundred pieces, the ivory silk cord jerked from the wall socket and, now, disengaged from her wrist. She pulled it over, then, as she moved.

"*Who*———" she whispered.

Jim cried: "Eden—Eden, what happened?"

"It was Wilson," cried Noel. "I saw him. Running down the hall toward the back———"

"But, Eden———" Jim was touching her, thrusting Noel away, putting his hands upon her arms, her throat. "Eden, did he hurt you? For God's sake say something."

"I'm not hurt. I knocked over the lamp. He—there was a hatchet. That's the only thing I saw. The hatchet—with the light shining on it, then there was a crash———" She was shuddering, burying her face on Jim's shoulder.

"I thought it was a gun," cried Noel. "It must have been the bulb breaking. I was halfway up the stair."

Sloane was in the hall, shouting: "Chango! Pete—search the house! Don't let anybody get away—it's Wilson———"

He disappeared, running, shouting directions. The sheriff's voice from below took up the refrain. All at once men were everywhere—spreading the alarm—searching.

Averill came nearer and put her hand on Eden's arm.

"Did you see him? Was it Wilson? Do you really mean he had a hatchet?"

Eden all at once was trembling so she could scarcely talk.

"That's all I saw," she said jerkily. "He was in the shadow of the door; there was a—a shadow—as if he wore a coat. And a wooden handle like the handle of a hatchet. That was all."

Hours later, when Sloane questioned her again, it was still all she could remember. And by that time the search for Roy Wilson had perforce been given up until morning.

They had not found him. Jim, Noel, Strevsky—even Pace had joined in the search while Averill and Eden and Dorothy waited in the lounge, huddling together, watching from the windows and the hall, listening.

They did not know, even, how he had escaped. There was a side door at the foot of the back stairway. And on the stairway they found two things.

One was a gray topcoat, belonging to Pace. He admitted it frankly; but denied any knowledge of how it came to be where they found it. He had left it in his room, he said; that was all he knew. No, certainly his room was not locked. Why should he lock it?

"Did the man you saw wear this coat?" asked Sloane, holding it so Eden could examine it.

But she didn't know.

"It's possible. There was—just a dark shadow."

"But he could have concealed his face or his clothing with this coat?"

"Yes."

The other thing they found was a hatchet. Lying on the stairway as if it had been dropped in flight.

But according to Chango it was not the hatchet he had missed. For this one's worn, wooden handle had no notch in it.

"Not," said Noel later, "that I can ever quite believe a Chinese. No matter how frank Chango looks and speaks you always feel he may be holding something back."

But that night he clung to his story with fervor and so far as Eden could see Sloane appeared to believe him. The hatchet that had disappeared at the same time Roy Wilson had disappeared had had a notch in the handle. This one had none.

"But why," said Averill, "would he murder Creda? So far as I know I never laid eyes on the boy. Certainly he didn't know Creda. Unless he's gone stark, raving mad——" She paused and shrugged her shoulders.

There was a silent moment of extremely unpleasant conjecture. Sloane turned to Noel:

"You're sure it was Wilson," he said.

140

"How can I be absolutely sure?" said Noel. "He was running along the passage up there. Just flashed across it—how can I be sure? I'd heard the sound of the bulb breaking. I was thinking of Eden—I didn't stop him; I couldn't have. But I—I thought it was Wilson; I was sure of it then."

"And you're not sure now?"

"When you question me like that, no. I mean I can't remember anything exactly and definite—like yellow, curly hair or—or clothing. But that was my first impression. My only impression. I shouted out something—I don't know what. And he vanished and I ran to Eden's room. I had to—see about Eden first."

Averill said: "Why should he want to murder me?"

"But it wasn't you," began Jim. "Creda——"

"Creda in my yellow coat. Creda in my cabin. Creda with a veil over her face," said Averill with quiet, deadly stubbornness.

Sloane said: "You'd better all go to bed. It's past midnight. There'll be a guard around the house tonight. In case he returns."

The sheriff got up heavily, put down a glass that had held a very long whisky and soda and sighed.

"I've got to go, P. H.," he said. "I can't help it. I'll leave a couple of deputies, if you want 'em. And I'll be back——"

"You can't go," said Sloane. "You've got to stay over——"

They walked out to the porch together and were still there, talking in low voices, when Eden and Averill went upstairs.

Noel, sitting dejectedly on the lower step of the stairway smoking, got up rather reluctantly to let them pass. His dashing look was decidedly blurred; he looked tired and his full age with the gray patches at his temples and the lines at the corners of his eyes very clear under the light.

"Better lock your door tonight, Averill. You too, Eden. Yell like hell if anything scares you. It's what I intend to do." He stopped and brooded and added a little bitterly: "My revolver! If Sloane would lock me up I'd feel safer, anyway. I wish to God Jim hadn't brought us out here."

"You aren't the only one who wishes it," said Averill crisply. Dorothy came into the hall and Noel roused himself and said gallantly: "I'll take you to your room, Dorothy; it's down at the end of the hall."

Eden, closing the door of her little bedroom, lighted now with no shadow lurking behind the door, remembered the tender little scene Jim had interrupted.

Tender, yes, and gallant on Noel's part.

But it was only gallantry. Only sentimentalism. Only Noel. With his adventurer's look, his extravagant talk, his dashing, spuriously youthful mask. Under it he was a little futile, perhaps. Never what anybody could call intellectual; never quite so romantic a figure as he had once been but always amiably helpful, always gallant.

It would surprise him, she thought with a rather mirthless little smile, if she took him at his word.

As she had made up her mind to do. And then—instantly in Jim's arms—found she couldn't.

What had Jim thought, she wondered, about the things he must have overheard. Knowing Noel he couldn't have taken it at its face value! But suppose he had; it was nothing to him what she did, whom she married or determined to marry. Or didn't marry.

She wondered suddenly if she would ever—years and years from then—marry anyone. And instantly she told herself smartly that she would, certainly, sometime.

But something deep inside of her resisted. Marriage was a thing that lasted; a thing that had its own obligations, its own demands. And one of those demands was the utmost, unswerving loyalty. And how could you be loyal to anybody else when your heart belonged and always would belong to—to Jim, she thought, and put her hands on that stubborn heart as if to control it.

In a few days, in another week at the most, he would go as completely out of her life as if he had never existed.

She was thinking of that when Dorothy Woolen came and knocked and asked in a low voice to come in.

She opened the door and locked it again after Dorothy entered.

"There's something," said Dorothy promptly, "that I want to tell you. I haven't told Sloane. But it—I think you ought to know. In case you need it," she said, watching Eden with blank, totally expressionless eyes. She wore an unexpectedly coquettish baby-blue dressing gown and her pale hair was in two long, childish braids down her back. But she didn't look childish; her shoulders were too heavy, her jaw too thick. She said coolly: "Shall I go on?"

"Y-yes."

"It's about your gray chiffon scarf. You see—Averill Blaine had it. She picked it up from the floor, there on the plane. She —something roused me and I awoke just in time to see her walk along the aisle and bend over and take your scarf from the floor. She looked at it as if she wondered whose it was and then put it in her pocket. In the pocket," said Dorothy slowly, "of the yellow coat she was wearing. She—please try to understand me, Miss Shore. She is my employer. But I feel that she will not tell anyone about that scarf and how it came to be there—so that whoever murdered Mrs. Blaine probably saw the scarf in her pocket and simply made it serve his pur-

142

pose. But I think you ought to know. If you want me to, I'll tell the detective but I would rather not. My job——"

"Thank you. I understand."

But Dorothy hadn't finished. She had more to say and she found it difficult. She started to speak, hesitated, started again.

"It's—about the plant, Miss Shore. I—well, you see, it occurred to me (I typed the wills, you see) that since Mr. Blaine and his wife are both dead, Miss Blaine stands to inherit all their property."

"But—she——" began Eden slowly.

Dorothy would not let her put it in words. She rose quickly.

"I only wanted you to know that. And about the failure of the engine; that is no loss to Averill Blaine since she intends eventually to sell it, when it is rebuilt, to Major Pace. Just the same. And for the same amount of money. Only now she'll get almost all of it. That—that's all, Miss Shore. Except, you must believe me, I have no motive in telling you this. It just happens to be a matter of record. Good night——"

CHAPTER/20

She went quickly to the door, anxious now she had spoken to be away. Yet there was no friendliness, no warmth in the girl's bland, pale face.

Eden closed the door and locked it again and stood there for a while lost in thought.

Averill had been one of the last to see Creda, certainly; she had loaned her the yellow coat. And then, Averill said, she had returned at once to the lounge. But how could anyone be perfectly sure of what had happened during that little interview between Creda and Averill? She herself had had a glimpse of the violence that lay below Averill's habitually demure manner. Averill had taken the scarf; if Creda were unconscious anyone could have strangled her—it didn't take a man's strength. Anyone—knowing Creda's inability to scream when frightened—could have made that first attack with a knife.

But Averill couldn't murder anyone! Revulsion caught Eden sharply and strongly.

Averill's reason for not telling about the chiffon scarf was quite comprehensible.

But she hadn't murdered. Eden felt sure of that. She had enough money without Bill's money and Creda's; she had enough power, which Averill loved more than money.

No, it wasn't Averill.

She resolved, however, to tell Sloane about the scarf. In

all probability he wouldn't believe her; but she had to do it.

Roy Wilson. Was it actually the little steward who had stood there in the shadow, waiting for her? Waiting for *her!* Why?

Morning came, incredibly bright and hot by nine o'clock with the sun and sky brilliant and not a creature moving on the sweep of pasture and grazing lands all around the ranch house.

They had not found Roy Wilson. There had been no further disturbance during the night and they had made certain that the steward was not anywhere about the ranch house, the cabins, the corrals and barns. That much they could be sure about. But nothing else.

It was after breakfast that for that long, oddly baffling interview, Sloane summoned Eden to his study. The sheriff had gone, he said; he had had to go but he would return. And to her questions he replied briefly that they had not found Roy Wilson.

"You are certain it was Roy Wilson?" he asked her.

She wasn't certain, of course.

"I didn't see him. I only saw the—the handle of the hatchet. Nothing else."

There was a little silence while the rancher-detective's far-seeing, blue-gray eyes searched quietly into her own eyes. He looked tired that morning and the easygoing manner which had so neatly suited his rancher role had gone. For the first time she saw him as Jim must have known him, taut, hard-working city detective, a little weary, altogether disillusioned, very tired of people and their tragic frailties. There was something almost inhuman in his look that morning.

But he wasn't quite inhuman. He was still enamored of his chosen pose for he took from his desk a little flat package of cigarette papers and a small bag of tobacco and proceeded to make himself a cigarette. It was not made expertly but the making seemed to accord him some inner satisfaction. He licked the paper, rolled it and lighted it.

"Oh," he said then. "Will you have a cigarette, too, Miss Shore?" But he passed her a box that stood on his desk and was lavishly supplied with machine-made, expensive cigarettes.

"Miss Shore—can you think of any reason why Roy Wilson—or anyone—would consider you a danger to him? Think."

"No. No—there's nothing."

He paused, watching her, smoking his somewhat wobbly cigarette, thinking.

"Look here, Miss Shore. It seems to me that, without knowing it perhaps, you may have a key to this business. For that reason I'm going to tell you something—rather arrange some things you already know in perhaps a different order. I'll do it briefly. And I—frankly, I want your confidence." (Frankly? There was nothing frank, nothing appealing in his look.) He went on:

"It goes without saying (and I'm sure you've come to the same conclusion yourself) that some one of your party is responsible for Creda Blaine's death. Invisible, malevolent beings do not exist, no matter how convenient such a being would be at this point. I had nothing to do with her murder; my boys are out of it. I am absolutely sure of that. Besides, it stands to reason that whoever killed her had a motive, and a motive for murder has to be a deeply personal and urgent motive. No, whoever murdered her has to be one of eight people. Wilson or Strevsky; Pace, Jim Cady, Noel Carreaux, Miss Woolen, Miss Blaine. You, yourself. You do understand that, don't you?"

He paused briefly and as she didn't reply continued:

"Now, then. We have considered each one in turn. We've tried, deliberately and carefully, to build a case against each one." He smiled briefly, there, and said: "Playing no favorites. Pace, of course, is the first and prime suspect; he has an alibi, yet from what you tell me and because I believe that Creda Blaine's murder is somehow bound up in the circumstances of the plane crash, I can't quite rule him out. Yet I can't build a definite case against him; I have nothing exact to go on. And I'm stopped at every turn by that alibi."

He paused again, smoked thoughtfully for a moment and said: "Wilson, I suppose, is next. But there quite definitely is no case. Wilson's disappearance, his return, and the—thing he attempted last night—all point to him. But if Wilson killed Creda Blaine, his motives are outside the realm of reason. It's possible, of course, that that is the explanation. A homicidal maniac. Yet coming so directly after the plane crash and the—shall I say, provocative circumstances of that crash, Wilson as the murderer in no way offers a—a cipherable figure in the sum of it. Also Wilson as the murderer, following the plane crash but introducing an entirely different element (a motiveless and accidental element, really) is outside probability, too. I suppose it could happen just like that. But I can't help feeling that there is actually a chain of purpose, each link building upon the other or at least related to the other.

"If Wilson is the murderer his running amuck just like this is definitely a thing apart, an extraneous incident. Not a link at all. And it seems reasonable to me that Creda Blaine's death must have a relation to—well, to the plane crash."

"How?" ventured Eden.

"I don't know. Unless there was actually, unknown to most of you, a net of espionage in which, as I've said before, she became entangled. Perhaps before her marriage; perhaps, indeed, she met Bill Blaine while pursuing her somewhat equivocal vocation (which does certainly provide ready and generous money for anyone who's sufficiently barren of scruples to engage upon it; espionage is after all one of the two oldest professions). Well, suppose when she needed money she knew where and how to get it; Cady says Bill Blaine talked—whom would he talk to any more fully than his wife? It's altogether possible that she reported to Pace and Pace paid her—perhaps under another name which would account for her surprise when he was introduced to her as Major Pace. It's possible, too, that she secured the key to the plant in order to let Pace into the plant; perhaps he ordered her to give him the key and did not tell her what he intended to do—namely to so disable the engine that a crash would be inevitable. Then if he had the plans it would be so simple for him to withdraw his offer to buy, since the engine had failed, and to leave with the plans and with the money. Two hundred thousand dollars is no small sum of money; murder has been done for far less than that. Furthermore, Pace could still sell the plans, if he wished to, to another government than the one he claims to represent, whatever that is. Thus adding to his gains. Nothing could be simpler; this is not a time when there is very scrupulous inquiry into the hows and wherefores of information—especially exact information about anything so universally needed as a good, light, cheap airplane engine. Armament demands being what they are—well, I'll stick to Pace. Suppose then Creda Blaine was horrified when he returned the key to her and in a few hours' time, early the next morning—you did say the flight was early——"

"Very early. Earlier than they had planned because the weather reports said showers."

"In a few hours' time the crash occurred and instantly Creda blamed Pace. Possibly she told him she would have no more to do with his schemes; perhaps she accused him, perhaps she threatened exposure. This would give him a strong —oh, a very strong motive for murder. It would be a sound hypothesis—except for one thing."

"There isn't anyone else," said Eden. "He must have done it."

"You agree. Well, of course, the flaw is that he did not escape. He came with you, presumably to a wedding. He promised to wait until the plane was rebuilt and gave every evidence of doing it. If he had the plans, if he had worked out this scheme as I've outlined it, he'd have gone at once. He'd have been on the high seas by this time—his money and the plans in his pocket. Instead he's here."

"Perhaps he came with the intention of killing Creda. Perhaps he was afraid to let her live with the evidence she must have had against him."

"That wouldn't have mattered once he'd made his escape. He could have lived as he chose, where he chose. He needn't have returned to America ever. Besides—there's the alibi."

He sighed, rolled another cigarette and went on: "Pace, Wilson, Strevsky. Ludovic Strevsky, brother to Michael Strevsky who was killed in the plane crash. He may be out for revenge; I don't like his look myself; he may have suspected or even known that Creda Blaine was involved in that plane crash. But—if that's true, what about the plane crash? Who planned and executed that neat little maneuver? I've tried to build up a case against Strevsky, too. But again I have no evidence. That leaves Cady and Noel Carreaux; you and Averill Blaine and Dorothy Woolen. It seems to me it would be difficult for a woman to secure the key to the plant, avoid the night watchman, reach the plane, manage to get at the engine and cut the fuel line and mend it so expertly with wax (and cut it expertly, too, near the engine). And for what motive? Averill Blaine would be injuring her own property, her own interests. She was insistent about selling the engine; she was determined, even when it failed, that Pace was still to buy it. Dorothy Woolen has no interests in particular involved; she has an alibi for the time of Creda's murder; she sat in a chair opposite me and never moved the whole time I was at the piano; again I can't build up a case against her. And Carreaux is in the same position as Averill Blaine; he wanted to sell the engine; he would be injuring his own property if he connived at destroying the engine and preventing the sale; and he has an alibi as Pace has. At the same time his revolver was found beside the dead woman and he has a very lame story to tell about that."

"My scarf," said Eden and told him. She told only about the scarf; she did not mention the further suggestion Dorothy had made.

Even so, it seemed to her there was a skeptical look in Sloane's face as he listened. And he said only:

"If Miss Woolen is right, the discovery of the scarf was a matter of luck for whoever murdered her." He paused briefly and then went on: "So far as I can see there are three ways to account for the presence of Carreaux's revolver," he said. "Someone removed it from his bag with the intention of killing Creda with it when opportunity offered itself. Or Creda herself removed it, knowing she was in danger and hoping to protect herself. Or—it was not removed."

"But then Noel——"

"If that theory is the true one, Carreaux had it himself, intended to murder Creda with it, but changed his mind when he saw the chiffon scarf. The revolver would make a noise, would bring everyone at once. Whoever murdered her was strongly aware of the need for silence. Thus the knife, in what I think was an abortive first attempt to kill her. Thus the scarf—fortuitously discovered—to complete the job. If Carreaux did it, he simply forgot the revolver—murderers do forget; it's why we catch them. Besides a fold of Miss Blaine's coat had fallen over it. If someone else had that revolver it was left there purposely; it had not been fired but it would detract attention from the murderer. If Creda Blaine herself had the revolver, the chances are the murderer never knew it was there. Certainly if Creda tried to fire it she was unsuccessful. And the only fingerprints on the gun that are not blurred beyond recognition are your own, Miss Shore."

"But I didn't," began Eden with a gasp.

The telephone on his shabby, laden desk rang five times, interrupting her shrilly. He said: "That's long distance," and took down the instrument. "All right," he said into the telephone. "Oh, it's my call to St. Louis. All right, put them on."

Eden rose. "I'll go," she said but he stopped her.

"Wait—it'll take them a few moments." He reached into a pigeonhole of the desk and brought out two things. A small kitchen knife and a square piece of pasteboard with printed figures on it. "Did you ever see either of these before?"

The pasteboard looked like a baggage check. The little knife was just a small, wooden-handled paring knife. Sharp. She stared at it and shrank a little away.

"It's the knife that was used in the first attempt to kill her," said Sloane quietly. "It took place, if I'm right, outside the cabin. In the shadow of the pines near where we found the knife. Those small rusty stains on it, if you'll look closely, are blood; there are no fingerprints on the handle. It is impossible to discover who took the knife from the kitchen; it is never closed—anybody could have done so, at any time (hours perhaps previous to the murder) without being seen. If I reconstruct the crime correctly, and I think I do, she escaped, ran to the nearest cabin and tried to barricade the door. And fainted. And her murderer followed her, entered the cabin, finished the business with the gray chiffon scarf. And tiptoed away again. That is, if you have made no mistakes in your own telling of what you heard, Miss Shore; all this is on the basis of your story being accurate."

"It is as accurate as I can make it. I've told you everything I remember."

There was a flicker in the detective's eyes. "No," he said, "you haven't. You omitted one of the most important events of that night—oh, hello. Yes. Yes, this is Sloane; you've got the report about the baggage check? All right, let's have it."

She watched him, fascinated, while he listened to the distant voice which, five feet away from the telephone, was only a metallic rattle. He made a few notes swiftly; a few equally brief replies. And after a while said, "Thank you" and hung up and turned on the swivel chair to look at her.

"That," he said, "was about the baggage check. One of my boys found it near the plane; I don't know whether it was lost or thrown away. In any case it seems that the night you left St. Louis Jim Cady deposited a large package, wrapped in paper and tied with string, in the checkroom of the airport from which you left. At my urgent request the police opened the package and found plans and blueprints for an airplane engine which has been identified by one of the plant employees as the engine that crashed."

"Not—Jim———" whispered Eden. And realized suddenly and rather dreadfully that of all those names Jim's had been the only one not explored. It was a too significant omission. Sloane said: "You care very much what happens to him, don't you, Miss Shore? The night Creda Blaine was murdered (wearing Averill Blaine's yellow coat, in Averill Blaine's cabin) Cady said to you, 'I'll settle with Averill.' *Didn't* he?"

Eden's throat closed so she could not speak. Sloane said:

"Your face admits it. And on the heels of that you had an interview with Averill Blaine during which she told you that she intended to hold Cady to his word and that furthermore his whole career was tied up with her; she could, in other words, make him or break him because his whole past and future was in the Blaine plant and she, now, largely owns the Blaine plant."

"She said—part of that. Not about the plant."

"I'm afraid it's her word against yours. She told me last night (just before you found Wilson upstairs) that she felt she had to stop what was merely an infatuation on Cady's part. And that your interview was not at all friendly. That it was, in fact, quite violent. That you, in fact, struck her. Across the face."

"That's not true!" cried Eden almost frantically. "It was Averill. She struck me! And besides that was later—after Creda was murdered. It's not true as she told it. You must believe me———"

"Your word against hers," said Sloane. "I can't tell truth by the sound of it. The point is, did you or did you not enter into a conspiracy to kill Averill Blaine and murder Creda accidentally instead?"

Eden was on her feet.

"No, no! It's impossible—it's cruel—without a shadow of evidence—I couldn't have done it! Jim couldn't! You—you know him. He's your friend. And Averill *can't* accuse him."

Sloane interrupted. He rose and went to the door.

"He was my friend," he said. "And Averill does not accuse *him*. You admit then that you yourself had a motive for wanting Averill Blaine out of the way?"

"No, no!"

"You were overheard. By Creda Blaine who, when she borrowed Averill's coat, told her of your somewhat romantic scene with Cady. That is not, of course, evidence that is admissible to court; but inadmissible evidence often points the way to truth."

She remembered the rustle back of the pines; she remembered Jim saying "What was that?" But she hadn't wanted to kill Averill—or Creda. It was as if a nightmare were closing tighter about her.

"But I didn't murder her," she cried desperately. "I—I never thought of it—I couldn't murder anybody!"

"I didn't ask you if you had set out cold-bloodedly to murder anybody," said Sloane, his hand on the doorknob. "I asked if, in the heat and anger of the moment, you lent the— assistance of your silence to anyone. To Cady—to be exact."

"No, no," cried Eden again in horror, twisting her hands together. "You must believe me. You must listen. You must——"

"Did you know Creda Blaine had borrowed that yellow coat? Answer me."

"No——"

"Did Jim know it?"

"No—I don't know."

"That's all now, Miss Shore." He opened the door.

"But Jim didn't—Jim couldn't——"

"That's all," he said. "Thank you." And she was in the hall and the door was closed behind her.

And Jim himself came from the lounge.

"Jim——" She said it breathlessly, almost frantically; he must defend himself. He must explain to Sloane his reason for checking those plans, his reason for keeping silent about it. He must instantly, promptly demolish the case Sloane had built against him—so strong a case that Sloane did not even tell her fully of it, but was content instead to build and demolish the case against each of them, leaving only that stacked-up evidence against Jim to stand. Creda's letter; the little pasteboard check. The dust of suspicion that Averill, in trying to implicate Eden, had cast upon Jim. Unintentionally perhaps; she had accused only Eden, not Jim; but nevertheless she had supplied Sloane with an alternate motive.

Jim spoke first. He looked very white and, somehow, angry. But he said smoothly enough: "I've been thinking, Eden, that I ought to apologize. About last night. I'm afraid I interrupted —— May I be the first to offer you and Noel good wishes?"

CHAPTER /21

The curious thing was that it seemed so unimportant. So trivial really that she brushed it away with a feeling of impatience; it was as if Jim himself couldn't possibly credit his own words.

Instead of replying, she said quickly: "I've been talking to Sloane. Jim, has he told you about the baggage check? Surely he must have done——"

"You didn't," said Jim, "let much time go by."

"Time?"

"Between affairs of the heart," said Jim promptly. "Or perhaps it wasn't of the heart. The stage lost a good actress in you, Eden."

She caught her breath sharply as if a dash of cold water had been flung against her face.

"That's unfair, Jim!"

"I suppose it is. Somehow I wouldn't have expected you to forget so promptly and so easily. So you and Noel are to be married?"

She put up her head.

"In any case my marriage doesn't concern you."

"How right you are," said Jim. "Do forgive me——" And stopped and said in a different, graver voice: "And I mean that. I know as things—are—between us I've no right to say a word. I only want to know—do you love him?"

She couldn't answer for a moment: it was silent in the hall, silent in the lounge. Out on the porch someone spoke to someone else and they could hear a murmur of voices without distinguishing words. Then she put back her head so as to look squarely into his eyes and said: "You have no right to ask that, Jim."

His face did not change. There was no way of knowing what the look in his eyes really meant.

And there was a rustle above and steps coming slowly down the stairway. It was Dorothy Woolen; she came gradually into sight, her white sports shoes and sturdy legs, the hem of her bright blue dress; she stopped for an instant as she saw them and looked down over the banister with utterly blank, expressionless eyes. Then she put one hand to the pale yellow braid above her broad white forehead and said to Jim:

"May I speak to you, Mr. Cady?"

Jim looked surprised and then, quite distinctly so Eden perceived it, a flicker of something like understanding crossed his face. He said: "Excuse me, Eden. Yes, of course,

151

Dorothy," and went quickly to meet her as she came down the remaining steps. His voice was warm and oddly sympathetic.

Eden said quickly: "Jim, you must talk to Sloane. There's something—he's got a baggage check. He telephoned to St. Louis——" She glanced over her shoulder to the closed door of Sloane's study, at the end of the hall, and lowered her voice. "They say—the police, I mean, that you checked—Jim, I know how mad it is—but they say you checked the plans. The plans for the engine——"

She stopped as if her voice had died in her throat. For Jim was looking straight into her eyes and he knew about the baggage check; knew about the plans; knew what the St. Louis police had said. She was sure of that; there was sharp, instant comprehension in his face. Yet Sloane had talked to the police only a moment or two ago, when she was in the room with him. It was true then, what Sloane had said; and it couldn't be true. She went to Jim and said almost pleadingly: "It isn't true, Jim."

"And suppose I say it is true."

"I still," said Eden slowly, "don't believe——"

Something eager and swift flared in Jim's eyes.

"Eden," he began. And Dorothy said, moving colorless lips:

"Miss Shore, I couldn't help overhearing as I came along the hall above—is it true that you are to be married to Mr. Carreaux?"

The eager look left Jim's face. He turned to Dorothy and said:

"Yes, Dorothy. I was wishing her happiness."

Dorothy came down the remaining steps, paused a moment, looked full at Eden with completely blank, flat gray eyes, and said: "I understand you were engaged to him long ago."

"Why, yes. Once long ago. Not—you don't understand. Not now——" She didn't know what she had been about to say; denial, expostulation, anything. There was no time. For Noel came swinging in from the porch, followed by Strevsky. He was excited, blue eyes blazing. He cried: "Strevsky did it. He cut the fuel line. He's going now to tell Sloane."

"Lud, for God's sake, did you do that?" demanded Jim, seizing Strevsky by the arm.

He looked sullenly back at Jim.

"Sure, I did it. The first afternoon we were here. Do you think I wanted anybody to get away before your detective found out who killed my brother!"

"But——"

"Oh, it's all right now, boss. I fixed it this morning. So we could go after Wilson. If he did it, the little sneaking——"

152

"You fixed the break?"

"Sure. It's okay now. And I'm going to tell Sloane."

He detached his arm from Jim's grasp with an effortless little twitch and went on gracefully and swiftly as a leopard to Sloane's study door, where, without knocking, he disappeared.

"It was a mistake to bring Strevsky," said Jim slowly. "I thought I could control him."

"He's a primitive bird. If he got it into his thick head that Creda was in any way responsible for the plane crash and his brother's death——" Noel stopped abruptly, thought and said: "Do you suppose Strevsky's the fellow? The murderer, I mean?"

There was an instant's silence. Behind them and beyond the closed door of Sloane's study they could hear a murmur of voices. Noel said: "After all if Pace is out—I'd rather it'd be Strevsky."

Jim smiled without much mirth.

"I oughtn't to have brought him," he said. "But I had to have someone who felt as I felt about the crash and who would go along with me."

"You oughtn't to have brought any of us here, Jim," said Noel rather wearily. "That was the mistake. Coming here. Not telling any of us what you thought and planned. Bringing us all out to this Godforsaken and God-forgotten place. Rimmed in with mountains as if it was another world——" He checked himself sharply.

They had moved, talking, onto the porch. Sun poured down. Pace sat at one end, smoking and staring with enigmatic eyes at the blue mountain wall in the distance. Averill sat at the other end, her neat black head with the even white part showing bent over a letter she was writing. She looked up, too. Attracted as Noel had been attracted by that flying figure in the distance.

Then they all saw it—and watched, suddenly arrested and rigid, as if in that first instant of perception they knew the truth.

Eden was never to forget the sight of the horse and rider rising into the sky from a distant slope; hurling toward them through sunlight and heat; swerving to avoid prairie-dog holes; stirring up small clouds of sand. The thud of hoofbeats became louder; the horse stopped with a swirl and stood there heaving and sweating, and the man was out of the saddle, running along the path, spurs jangling as he reached the porch and flung across it, shouting: "P. H.! We've found him! P. H.!"

It was the cowboy they called Charlie.

And Roy Wilson had been found. An hour before noon with the sun beating down hard and hot upon the sand and the sagebrush and two tall spikes of flowering soapweed rearing at his feet as if to mark the spot.

He was in the dip of an arroyo a mile or so distant from the house, and there was a fringe of sagebrush and cactus above him. He was on his back with sightless blue eyes staring at the brilliant blue sky and his childish mouth open and drawn.

He had been dead for some time.

One of the boys, ranging through the brush, found the thing that killed him and it was Chango's hatchet, stained, with a notch cut in the handle of it.

And he had been dead certainly for twenty-four hours.

That was the next fact that emerged.

"Blood's dried, P. H."

"And the condition of the body?"

The man, panting, shrugged and mopped his arm across his wet forehead.

"If it was a calf I'd say twenty-four hours at least. It's probably been more——"

"I'll come along."

Sloane paused and his eyes swept the circle of faces. All of them were there, drawn by the news of Wilson's murder. Even the pilot, Strevsky, had horror in his eyes and Pace, at Eden's elbow, lifted his cigar with a trembling hand and lowered it again as the detective's eyes met his own, lingered and then went on. And stopped at Jim who stood near, with Averill's hand linked in his arm.

"You'll come, too," said Sloane, addressing Jim. "Have them bring a horse for Mr. Cady, too," he told Charlie, and said to Jim: "You can ride?"

"You ought to remember," said Jim evenly. "We've had many rides together."

The detective accepted the challenge as evenly.

"Perhaps I've remembered too much."

Jim's eyes narrowed. He dropped Averill's hand from his arm and stepped forward to face the detective. For a sharp instant they stood, curiously alike in their tall, lean bodies, both sun-bronzed, both taut, both tensed against encounter. Both shrinking from and yet demanding a clearing of the slate between them, a balancing of old memories and old ties with the immediate, unlabeled but terribly urgent demands. Jim was the first to speak.

"Look here, P. H., you'd better explain. Let's have things clear between us."

"You're the one to explain. I've given you a chance and you refused."

"I didn't refuse. I told you only the truth."

"Not the whole truth. What about these plans? You said they were gone. You——" He stopped, looked at Jim and said more quietly: "All right. Since you ask it." He glanced at Charlie and said parenthetically: "There's somebody with Wilson?"

Charlie looked worried. "Ed."

"Ed? Well, he'll stay there awhile." He turned back to Jim. "The fact is, I like my cases to be complete before I make an arrest——"

"Arrest!"

"Arrest. In this case, naturally, humanly, I would like to have a case so complete that there would never, anywhere, be a question of it. It would be better for us to have this thing out alone——"

"Why? There's nothing these others can't hear. I've known since yesterday when that letter of Creda's was found what you thought."

"What I feared," said Sloane rather heavily. "What I would have avoided if I could have done so."

"Go ahead," said Jim. "State your case."

"You know what it is. It doesn't need stating. You refused to sell the engine. You admitted that. It would have been (in an odd, inverted way) to your admitted advantage if the plane failed. Well, it did fail. You brought all these people here and told me there was something phony about the crash and begged me to investigate it. On the surface it was the act of an innocent man; it looked like that to me and to these others. But there was also evidence that the plane had crashed, which was not held by you alone; it was shared by a man who had been with you when you discovered it; a man of certain mechanical knowledge and a man who was not likely to forget; that man is Strevsky—and he instantly demanded revenge for the death of his brother. Was your action in coming to me, then, a result of your own wishes? Or was it an expediency calculated to shut Strevsky up forever and to convince him that you yourself had no part in the plane crash——"

Strevsky looked startled, opened his mouth and closed it again.

Jim, gray below his tan, said: "That's not true."

"Wait, you'll have to admit there are those two ways of looking at what you did. Now, then; your engine was worth a lot of money—Pace proved that. Suppose you decided that inasmuch as you yourself had built that engine, you alone ought to have the money for it. If the thing is once sold to Pace you lose out forever. Well, then, what could be simpler than to fix the engine to crash as it was fixed? Thus destroying the only model and preventing its being offered for sale to anyone, particularly the government you expected to sell it to, for months to come. It would take months to rebuild from the copies of the plans possessed by the factory. In the meantime you would have those months in which to sell your own plans—with no competition from anyone—the Blaine Company or Pace because the engine itself had crashed."

Pace wriggled and said suddenly: "But they would have copies of those plans, too. They could sell without a model as easily as Cady could sell."

"I see you've thought it all out," said Sloane. "The point is time. The first one to sell and to convince the buyer that his offer was in good faith stood to make a lot of money. And the inventor, the man who actually built the engine, would certainly have an advantage over anyone else when it came to finding a market. Always provided the model was destroyed."

"Go on," said Jim with tight lips.

"All right. Then this letter——"

"That was not written to me. I don't care what it says, there was nothing between Creda and me to justify the thing she wrote. Besides——"

"Besides, Miss Shore came to your defense and insisted that letter was not as Creda Blaine wrote it. Well—that's something for someone else to settle; I've sent it to be analyzed by handwriting experts. In the meantime I have to go on the only theory that explains it; there is no other course open to me. But even so, I was anxious to give you the benefit of the doubt; in spite of the years during which we've seen almost nothing of each other, I found myself——" The detective paused and said: "Reluctant to believe you had become a murderer."

"P. H.——"

"I'm not finished. Why did you tell me the plans were lost? Why did you tell me the plans had been stolen from the drawer in the library table? When you yourself, without troubling even to conceal your identity from the checkroom attendant, deposited those very plans in the checkroom of the airport the night you left St. Louis?"

"Jim!" cried Averill sharply. "Jim—you took the plans! You—it was you who were in the house that night—that's why you were late at the airport. You went back to the house while we waited for you; you took the plans and——"

She stopped as sharply as she had begun to speak. Slowly, as wax hardens so the hardening can almost be seen, her small face set itself in rigid and implacable lines. She said almost querulously: "You did it. You killed Bill. You killed the mechanic. You wrecked the engine. Because you wouldn't sell it. You——" Her thin voice was increasingly angry and unsteady: "And you killed Creda because she knew. She knew and wrote to you; and you watched while I gave her my coat. You didn't come into the house. You stood there in the shadow and heard our talk and watched through the window of my cabin and I gave her my coat. And after I'd gone you killed her and——" There was a small yellow flame in her eyes. She whirled to Eden and cried shrilly: "And you helped! You saw him and you helped——"

"It wasn't Jim!" gasped Eden. "It wasn't Jim——"

"Then you know who it was! You told the sheriff you saw —and pretended you couldn't remember who it was you saw. Well, who was it, then? Why don't you tell? We all heard the sheriff tell you to try to remember whose face it was—as if you could forget anything like that! The reason you won't tell is because it was Jim——"

"It was not Jim. Averill, stop—you don't mean what you are saying. You mustn't——"

Jim said: "Thank you, Eden. Averill——"

"Not now," said Averill, quickly, eyes smouldering. "We'll have this out later."

"Your private quarrels can wait," said Sloane. "Just now——"

"Just now," said Pace unexpectedly and with determination, "there is something I want to say. There are things you must know. You can't touch me; up to now I've kept silent; I am discreet; I must keep my coats clean of this affair. If you'll promise me immunity——"

"I'll promise you a long jail sentence if you don't tell anything you know," said P. H. Sloane savagely.

Pace smiled a little.

"Oh no, my dear sir. I'm innocent. There's nothing you can prove against me. I have no stolen plans. I have an alibi for the time when this poor, pretty woman was murdered. You cannot charge me with intentions that came to nothing; intentions which had their birth in—patriotism," said Pace as coldly and as smugly as a snake. "And I am of a mind to tell you a story. All in the interests of justice. Besides," he looked at his cigar and added with simple honesty, "besides, I cannot stay here longer. I must be about my—mission. And if my little story can aid in the progress of justice——"

"God damn you," said Jim.

Alarm flared in Pace's eyes.

"You must guarantee my own immunity," he said to Sloane. "Someone might fail to understand my motives."

"I'll guarantee nothing," said P. H. "But if you don't tell what you have to tell——"

"Don't threaten," cried Pace hastily. "Don't threaten. I offered to tell, freely and of my own will. Very well, then." He flicked the ash from his cigar, smiled a little and said with the utmost neatness and conciseness: "You are quite right about Creda Blaine. She was for years one of our sources of information. A pretty, one would say harmless, little wench, with a shrewdness. Ah, yes, a shrewdness. Too bad she was murdered. Well, then, she married one of her—shall we say merely to be clear, one of her victims. But after marriage (it is as you guessed, Mr. Detective, with that acute brain of yours), after marriage she found herself still, occasionally, in need of money. Therefore she managed on three occasions to provide us with bits of information. Bits only, but we pay well. She supplied them through me whom she knew by another name." He said it modestly with a self-deprecatory air. Jim, fists looking hard and able, took a quick step toward him; Pace jerked back, shot a glance at the detective which demanded protection and went on more rapidly: "She was unable, however, to secure the entire plan for this new engine. Which we wanted very much; a valuable engine," he interpolated with a flicker of congratulation toward Jim who did not respond, and Pace went on even more hastily: "Therefore, since she failed, we were obliged to take steps. Even if necessary to buy the engine. I came in person, myself. It was a delicate bit of business." He paused there as if to rearrange certain facts. "Well, Creda Blaine recognized me when we met; if I had had the opportunity I should have warned her I was now Major Pace. However, we had an immediate understanding. We went for a walk after dinner and she understood at once that I must have her help; otherwise —well, I daresay you understand that, too. In the end she agreed to supply what I wanted."

"And that was?" said the detective.

"Only a key," said Pace airily. "And her own escort to the Blaine factory. We left the house, I expect, about two o'clock in the morning."

"Creda!" gasped Averill. And Eden remembered that wakeful night; footsteps past her door, the sense of a sleepless house.

"And when you got there what did you do?" demanded Jim.

Pace spread his hands outward.

"Nothing," he said and sighed. "You see someone got there first. And it was someone she saw. I don't know who it was. I wish she had told me because then I would know who murdered her."

There was a charged silence. Then the detective said: "What do you mean, someone got there first?"

Pace lifted his eyebrows.

"Just what I say! We reached the plant; the watchman was snoring in a cool spot under some trees. We simply went to the front door and entered. That was all. She went ahead of me to see that the coast was clear. (I had told her, merely, that I must see the engine.) When she came back she was frightened. She said someone was working at the plane; that whoever it was had an electric torch and was doing something to the engine. She said, I believe, that it must be a workman. But she wouldn't let me go to see for myself. She said we had to leave at once. I—I believed her. There was truth and genuine fear in her manner. I know, now, that she recognized someone. There was nothing, then, I could do. We went back by taxi as we had come. No one saw us enter the house. She kept the key. I admitted defeat. Naturally I didn't want to buy the engine if I could help it."

"Then you really meant to fix the engine and steal the plans."

Again Pace lifted his eyebrows.

"Whatever I meant to do (and mark you, I admit nothing) I failed. Except that the plans alone would have been no good to me if there had existed a complete and thus saleable model of the engine. Besides," he added with a sigh, "when I looked in the library table for the plans—where I had seen Miss Averill place them only a few hours earlier—the plans were already gone. No," he sighed again, "I failed. All the way around. But that's my whole story. And you can't touch me."

"Who was in the plant?"

"I don't know. I told you that. I don't know. She didn't say. But she was terrified. Blue with fright. Undoubtedly whoever it was killed her." He put his cigar at last to his lips, drew on it, frowned when he discovered it had gone out and reached for a match.

The curious thing was that his story sounded true in every detail.

"Was it Cady?" said the detective suddenly and harshly.

"I cannot say. I don't know. It may have been."

"It wasn't," said Jim. And Pace, having found a match, interrupted:

"But there is the letter she wrote before she died, addressed to him. 'Cold-blooded murder is too much,'" quoted Pace. He added thoughtfully: "It must have terrified her when (after she kept silent about what she had seen, because naturally she didn't dare tell under what circumstances she had seen it) the plane crashed and killed two men. One of them her husband. I'm sorry she had to die. However," he shrugged, "her usefulness was at an end.

"P. H." It was Charlie, speaking a little diffidently at the detective's elbow.

"What? Oh! Yes, we'll be right along. You've got horses?"

"Yes, boss. Maybe we'd better be getting back to Wilson."

"Right. You'll come along, Cady?"

"P. H. You've got to listen. I checked those plans; yes, I found them in the house after the others had gone. I went back to look for them. And I didn't tell you because I had to convince you the crash was phony and the disappearance of the plans helped. I intended to tell you later that I'd found them. But I had to have your help—I had to interest you——"

"Do you admit you took the plans from the library table?"

"No. No, they were stolen. But I found them still in the house. Hidden in a drawer of an unused bedroom. Whoever took them would have had to come back for them. I checked them simply for safekeeping until we returned. And—oh, it may have been a mistake. If they'd been hidden anywhere but in that damn bureau—I mean if it had been a more ingenious hiding place, so it looked as if somebody'd stolen them, I'd have told you. But if I told you the truth you'd say they were simply mislaid. And I knew damn well they weren't. It was a crazy impulse—perhaps coming out here at all was crazy—but I had to do it. The way I did it. I had to make you believe me. If I was wrong I'll take the consequences."

"Consequences," said the detective softly. "But that includes murder. Creda Blaine. And now young Wilson."

And Charlie said, rather plaintively: "I told Ed we'd be right back, boss. You know Ed. He kinda hated staying there with Curly. Alone."

Oddly it brought the thing to an end if not a conclusion. P. H. said shortly: "You'll come along, Cady. Anyone else——"

In the end, as if every one of them had to see for himself, all the men went—Jim and Noel riding easily and well; Strevsky, all his grace gone, sitting like a block of wood on the saddle, grasping the horn anxiously but determinedly; Pace riding with unexpected ease and certainty. It was queer to see them leave in a group, following Sloane's tall figure on a sleek bay mare, followed themselves by several cowboys who looked as if they'd been cut in one piece with their horses.

Averill, standing by the railing of the porch and watching them leave, turned at last toward Eden, gave her a long enigmatic look and without speaking entered the house. Dorothy Woolen, a silent, recording figure, had already disappeared so quietly that Eden did not note her going.

She stood still, watching the group of horses and men grow smaller and smaller in the distance, thinking of the suddenness with which the scene had ended, and of the questions that ending had left unanswered. The last horseman disappeared over the distant slope. Silence and heat settled down upon the ranch and claimed it. Silence and heat and emptiness. Averill did not return. Chango, whose beady, inquisitive eyes and flapping white apron Eden remembered vaguely as having hovered about for the past quarter hour, had disappeared, too.

She sat down listlessly in one of the big chairs, leaned her elbows on the porch railing and tried to summon reason out of chaos. But the trouble was Jim's explanation of the missing plans; his lack of explanation about the letter. She believed him. But perhaps no one else.

Sloane had said the consequences included murder. Creda. And now Wilson.

She thought back, touching certain memories cautiously as with frightened, cold little finger tips. The plane crash—flames shooting earthward from a bright sky, where a skylark had mounted and sung. As bright a sky as the sky that day—that stared down into the blank, blue eyes of the little, curly-haired steward.

They were not pleasant thoughts. She rose restlessly and walked slowly, thoughtfully down the path. She paused in the cool shadow of the pines and remembered again. Irresistibly, with a heart that ached.

How merciless, under that demure manner, Averill actually was! How cruelly able to govern emotions, to direct her will! Averill could have murdered. Had she so willed it.

Suppose—suppose she had willed it!

It was so sharp and clear a thought that, despite (again) her own instinctive denial, she had to consider it. She walked on slowly, thinking.

The sun high above traveled slowly on, past its height, toward a descending arc. Brilliant sunlight poured down upon the ranch which looked small and unimportant in all that expanse of sand and sagebrush rimmed in distantly by mountains.

Eden walked on, lost in thought. She turned away from the path leading to the gate and in a long circle skirted the house, went past barns and corrals and stopped for a while in the shade of the great cottonwoods.

Off in the distance, shimmering in the sunlight, lay the great silver plane.

Without thinking, perhaps because of a subconscious desire to assure herself that this tangible link with the outside world still existed and had being, she left the shade of the cottonwoods presently and walked slowly toward the plane over the hummocky land, flat as her hand at one moment and tumbling into and out of a dry stream bed the next.

It was hot and the sun poured relentlessly down, leaving no shadows except that of the cottonwoods behind her and the outline of the plane's wings flat upon sagebrush and sand.

She hadn't remembered it was so far to the plane.

When she reached it the house and corrals looked small and unreal, like a distant mirage in the heat-laden air.

She touched the side of the plane; it was hot, warmed by the sun. The steps were down and after a while she pulled open the heavy door and entered the cabin. No one, of course, was there. The aisle tilted a little but the seats looked inviting and comfortable. She went to the front of the plane, paused, moved slowly back again and stopped at the seat she had occupied on that night flight. She had sat just here. With Averill in her yellow coat ahead of her so she could see the black satin cap that was Averill's hair. Who had been across the aisle? Dorothy? Or Pace in his red shawl?

She sat down in the seat she had occupied during the night in the plane and then because of the sun moved to the other side. The leather cushion sank softly downward. Pace had sat here—or Dorothy.

If only the plane could speak! If only the metal furniture, the neatly upholstered, thin leather cushions could tell her what had been witnessed during that night.

If she were a detective perhaps she could discover some clue, some tangible bit of evidence in that plane where they had all sat through the night, thinking what thoughts, planning what plans, arriving at what desperate, ugly decisions?

But there was nothing. Blank, clean leather and steel. Small windows letting in sunlight. Nothing human; nothing that was evidence.

Time passed without her consciousness of its passage. There was no sound anywhere. She wondered once what the men were doing; what they had found; if they had drawn any conclusions at all from the circumstances of the little steward's death.

He had sat in that plane, too, dozing childishly with his mouth open, in the end seat.

There was some special significance about his murder.

Her mind touched it, was caught again in the swirl of other thoughts, then returned, fumbling for that significance.

How silent it was! She might have been the only living thing in all the world. It was curious how distant the ranch house seemed, how remote she was from it and from human life. The desert stretched away from the windows, flat, empty, shadowless.

Roy Wilson.

But if Roy Wilson had been dead twenty-four hours then he had not stood in the shadow behind the door, shielding his face with a coat, holding a hatchet in his hand!

And in the same instant she discovered that she was not alone on the desert.

The bright black shadow of the plane, stretched out on the ground below, moved a little. Rather the shadow itself did not move, it only changed its outline a little, briefly. As if something moved somewhere and cast a shadow, thinner, smaller, like the shadow of a man, which glided into being and then blended itself in the flat black shadow of the plane.

A man! But there was no one at the ranch except Dorothy and Averill.

162

CHAPTER/22

She listened. She tried desperately to hear over the beating of her heart which thumped so loudly she thought whoever stood outside in that bright, empty desert must hear it.

Thoughts raced through her mind—none of them coherent. She'd been a fool to come so far from the house. Why had she done it! Why had she lingered there, lost in thought! Above all, who was it?

And did that someone know she was in the plane?

It became the all-important question.

There was for a moment or two no sound of motion outside the plane. Then there were footsteps—light, hurrying around the plane. She tried to see below and couldn't. Whoever it was passed—if he actually passed at all—too close to the plane. It was as if he were reconnoitering. Why?

And who was it?

Probably it was no one she need fear. She tried to tell herself that. The frantic pounding of her heart was sheer nerves, nerves and a sense of isolation in that bright empty world. And perhaps a memory of someone—not Roy Wilson—who had stood in the shadow, waiting for her.

It was as if a paralysis held her and restrained her from moving, from calling out, from making the faintest betraying motion.

He was now at the front of the plane. There was a slight quiver and jar running along the plane as if he had touched it—rocked it—how did you start a plane?

She rose cautiously to peer forward. And then he passed a window and she caught the briefest glimpse of an outline that was familiar. Familiar—then who?

He was coming into the plane. She sank down again in the seat, cowering instinctively as a hunted animal cowers. She couldn't see his entrance. But she heard it. Quick steps— still light and curiously stealthy—or did she imagine that stealth?

There was another jar, heavier, and less sunlight in the cabin. He'd taken up the steps, then? And closed the entrance? Odd. But there was no time to think for he walked quickly along the aisle and she saw him as he brushed past. And she sat up and cried on a great breath of relief: *"Noel——"*

He stopped as if someone had struck him and turned slowly, almost rigidly, toward her.

"Noel—thank heaven, it's you! I couldn't see—I thought— crazy things. I was terrified. Noel——"

She was babbling, her voice high-pitched and unsteady.

"Eden. You!"

"Noel, I was terrified. It was silly of me—but it's so far from the house I couldn't see it was only you."

"What are you doing here?"

"I just happened to walk this way," she said, still speaking rapidly and nervously. "Noel——" Something in his manner, in the way he looked at her drove her into confused explanations. "Noel, I only happened—I was taking a walk. I—what is wrong?"

After a moment he said slowly, watching her: "Nothing."

"But, Noel, you—you look so strange."

His brilliant eyes darted from her face to his wrist watch and back again.

He said: "Why did you tell Jim we were to be married? Why did you tell Dorothy?"

"But, Noel——" She shook her head queerly, as one shakes water out of his eyes so he can see the better. "I didn't—he only guessed."

"Did I mention marriage? Did I say I wanted you to marry me? Did I say anything that gave you a right to tell them that?" He stopped, looked at her and said: "You fool."

Queer she couldn't get to her feet. It was as if an invisible hand held her pressed into that deep seat.

"Noel——" It was only a whisper—not quite that.

He glanced swiftly again at his wrist watch.

"You've brought it on yourself. I can't help it. I couldn't help any of it once I'd got started. It wasn't my fault. And now I've got to finish what I've started." He paused, looked at her as if he hated her and said: "In a way it's justice. If you hadn't told them and turned Dorothy against me——! I never thought of marriage. I only wanted to make sure that you kept anything you knew to yourself. I didn't know you were in the other room when Creda—when I—when I had to do it. Good God," he said furiously. "Why couldn't you stay out of it! Why did you tell them you saw someone—me, of course. Or the steward. Why did you play cat and mouse with me so I never knew whether you were willing to keep what you knew to yourself, or going to tell them you saw me?"

"But I didn't——"

"You met me halfway—yet you never told me I was safe with you. Dorothy believed in me. She lied for me; you didn't. But she'll tell them the truth now. I saw it in her eyes. So I came back. Well, it's your own fault. I can't stop now."

She had to get out of the plane. She had to get out of the deep seat—she had to force open that door—she had to escape——

"Stay where you are. You've brought it on yourself. I—I'm

too tired," he said with the strangest effect of simplicity. "I can't think any more. You'll have to come with me." His bright eyes darted around the plane and fastened on a small locker at the rear.

She tried to stand. He pushed her back in the seat and opened the locker, watching her all the time, and took out a squarish bundle, secured with leather straps. He slung it quickly over his shoulders, fastening it with trembling but very quick fingers.

"But that—that's a parachute——" She must have said it aloud.

"Of course. Get up. Quick——"

She had to rise. She couldn't do anything else.

"Walk up ahead—I mean it—do you understand? Don't drive me to—do anything. If Creda hadn't driven me! She thought I killed Bill for her. Because a year ago I showed her some attention. Vain little fool! Take that seat at the right. Do as I say——"

She did it. She was an automaton. She was walking in a frightful dream.

He slid into the seat beside her. There were controls, instruments, she stared at them helplessly and didn't know what one of them was for. He adjusted the cord of the parachute.

"There's gas enough still. Queer—when we left the St. Louis airport I thought, we've got more gas than we need. The plane's heavy—— *Don't move!*"

Whatever she'd been about to do, she stopped.

He was mad. No, he was terribly, desperately sane. The lines in his face were sharp and there were dark pockets around his eyes. The easy, facile charm of his smile had had the power of disguising that hagridden look.

"Noel—*why*——" she said, her voice as thin as paper.

"Obvious," said Noel. His shaking, nervous hands reached toward the instrument board. "I was tired of being without money; I was born to have money—as I used to have."

He was certainly starting the engine. Adjusting this lever and that—a little uncertainly, frowning as if trying to remember. He had a pilot's license he'd said; but he hadn't flown much.

"Let me out—please, let me out; Noel—what are you doing! Noel—I beg you——"

"Don't—where's the starter—oh, I see."

"Noel—you've got to let me out! I won't stop you—I can't —Noel—where are you going? What——"

Her voice would have been unrecognizable. She had no thought, no strength, she could only beg, implore, plead.

"It's your own fault," he said. The engine started.

The throb of the engine completed chaos. She didn't faint;

she was aware of the throb all through the plane. The engine wheezed and died and the propeller became a propeller instead of a glistening arc. He swore and pulled and pushed at levers and started the engine again with a roar and this time the plane moved and—and how loud the engine beat. Loud and irregular and horrible—only it wasn't the engine! It was revolver shots—unutterable confusion, glass cracking and shattering—the plane jerking, half turning in a great staggering whirl.

She never knew exactly what happened. All at once Noel was leaning in the strangest way against the controls. The plane had stopped. Had the engine died again—had Noel's hand cut off the ignition? There were people—she could hear shouts. And waves of gray clouds swirled around her, gray as the chiffon veil that had choked Creda's life out.

Eventually something solid was holding her secure above the swirling veils that threatened to engulf her.

She was being made to move; half-carried along a narrow aisle. Sunlight blinded her. There were voices and she couldn't distinguish what they said; then she was lying flat down, with a great silver wing above her, shielding her from the glare of the sun.

"Is she all right?" That was Sloane's voice, she thought dimly. Sloane—how had he got there?

The pillow under her head moved a little; it wasn't a pillow, it was someone's arm. Jim said: "I think so."

"Miss Shore, it's all right. You're safe. It's all over."

She wouldn't open her eyes. But she put out her hand and Jim took it and held it to his face.

"Eden——"

"It was Noel." She thought she was shouting it. But Jim said: "What did you say, Eden? I can't understand——"

"It was Noel." She made an immense effort to explain and said: "Noel."

"Yes, Eden. I know. Sloane knows now. You can tell him about it later."

There was a long silence. Then she made another effort and said:

"Dorothy—told——?"

"Dorothy; yes. She had lied about his alibi; he got up while Sloane was at the piano, walked out the window and came back—afterward. He wasn't gone long; only Dorothy saw him. She had faith in him in spite of what she had seen. She—poor Dorothy——"

"She protected him?"

"Yes. Until she realized that—that he'd lied to her when he made love to her. Until she heard us talking there in the hall this morning. That was what she wanted to tell me. But she had no chance to tell me until we came back to the house.

Just now. And you were gone, and Noel, and we remembered that Strevsky had repaired the plane. So we got here. In time."

"Was that how you knew?"

"No. Eden—don't talk—just let me hold you. Oh, my dear———"

"I must know, Jim. What happened?"

There was a short silence. Then his voice: "Sloane—I was riding beside him; it was as we rode out to Wilson. He had me come up beside him so we could talk. And he—Eden, he asked one question. It was queer. Like a searchlight. He said: 'Why did you make the trial flight so early in the morning?' I said, 'On account of the weather reports; showers.' He said, 'And did it storm?' I said, 'No; it was clear all day.' And he—he said, Eden, 'Who got the weather reports?' And I remembered it was Noel; he kept going to the telephone the night before. That was when we decided to make the flight early, before the storm. And then we—we looked at each other. And Sloane said, 'Anybody who fixed the engine would have to make sure the engine had no chance to heat up before the plane was in the air.' He said, if the flight took place late in the day, the engine would likely have been started and tuned up a dozen times and the heat would have melted the wax; or some mechanic would have discovered the break. But the flight had to take place early, Sloane said. And I saw it, too. But we—we had to explore it. It could have been Noel in your room last night; that would have been simple—all he had to do was throw the coat and hatchet down the back stairway and turn around and run back and 'rescue' you. The only reason we could see for that was because he was afraid, all along, that you had seen or heard something in the cabin when Creda was killed; you said you saw a face, all of us heard the sheriff tell you to try to remember. He, Noel, must have been frantic to know exactly what you saw, exactly what you thought, and whether or not you intended to tell it."

"Yes," said Eden, "yes."

"I think he started something it was hard to finish; he built himself a Frankenstein; once he had stolen the plans and caused the crash he had to go on. Creda had seen him at the plant—she must have told him. Dorothy says he and Creda had had some kind of affair, trivial or I would have known it, a year or so ago. Creda would flirt with a snow man. And it meant, probably, nothing to Noel."

Something out of a nightmare repeated itself in Eden's memory.

"She thought he fixed the engine because of her. To free her from Bill."

After a moment Jim said: "It's queer. The net was of his

own contriving. Charm—Noel always had that. It was like a mask. And like a weapon which he did not scruple to use. Oh, I don't mean you; if you believed him you deserve to be disillusioned. Although," said Jim grimly, "not this way." He held her tight to him and added, "But I'm sorry about Dorothy. She—it's not nice for her. Her face used to light up like a Christmas tree when he spoke to her."

Presently Eden said soberly: "It had to be Noel. Creda wrote to him, telling him cold-blooded murder was too much and that—that you knew. She must have begun to write 'Jim, believe me, knows something and they'—we all read it as if she were addressing you. Noel must have taken it from my pocket and added to it, deliberately trying to make them believe it was you."

His arm tightened and lifted her so her head pressed against his shoulder.

"You didn't believe it," he said, his mouth close to her face. "Don't talk, Eden. Nothing really matters now but you —us."

Sloane's voice came as if from some distant existence. It sounded tired but taut, too, with excitement.

"Shall I send somebody for you with a car?"

"No—we'll come. Later."

Eden opened her eyes and turned to look and Jim pressed her firmly back into his arms so she could not see.

"It's in the past, Eden," he said. "Don't look, don't even think. They've all gone now," he added presently. "After a while, we'll walk back to the house. Sloane will want to know anything Noel told you. But don't talk now. Except tell me———"

"Tell you———"

But he didn't finish. He said, instead, smiling a little: "Shall we go?"

He helped her to her feet. The sun was still golden; the sky still blue. The great silver plane stretched its wings above them. Away off in the distance a blue mountain rim was like a wall. The plane shut off their view of the cottonwoods and the house; Jim looked down at her and took her in his arms and kissed her—kissed her as if it were breath and life and existence—kissed her as if he never would stop.

But he did stop. He stopped and looked down at her without speaking and at last took her hand lightly and they went back to the ranch house.

It was that night that Eden had another long talk with Sloane. The intervening hours she was never able to remember with any degree of certainty. There were conferences, telephone calls, cars coming and going; the sheriff arrived, and an hour or so later departed, his automobile clattering swiftly away, waking echoes from the twilight-edged mountains.

She had told Sloane everything she knew; Dorothy, she thought, had talked to the detective again, too; she saw her emerge from Sloane's study with her face as blank and white as a piece of marble. Averill waited, too, and questioned. She was still assured, still certain of herself. She asked Jim if he thought the Blaine Company would suffer from the publicity.

"After all," she said, "Noel was a vice-president and owned stock." She shook her head slowly. "I can't understand it. He didn't make much money, it's true. Nothing compared to what he once had—what he was born with. But he made enough to support himself so long as he didn't buy—well, yachts and polo ponies and——"

"But those were the things he had to have. Or at least as much as whatever price he could get for the engine would allow him. You know yourself, Averill, he was only a cipher. He did what he was told—that's all. He—I think it goes deeper, perhaps, even than greed. When he was rich he was somebody—and he'd been rich all his life until he lost his money. He knew exactly how much—how little rather—we valued him. When Dorothy showed him the letter offering money for information, it must have been the opening wedge. It showed him a way to make money; he would prevent Pace's buying it by disabling the engine himself, for the deal was to be closed that day; he had to work fast. And then he would sell the plans to the highest bidder. And if he remembered the number of the post-office box it would give him a line on a possible purchaser. Although," said Jim soberly, "purchasers for that kind of thing are not hard to find these days."

Averill looked at him speculatively.

"If we can hush the thing up," she said, "the plant may not suffer from it. And I don't see why we can't. Jim, I want to explain something——"

"My dear, there's nothing to explain," said Jim cheerfully.

"Oh yes, there is, Jim darling." Averill was never more demure, never so sweetly winning. "Surely you didn't believe me this morning when I—we must have a long talk. We are free now, aren't we, to go on to the plantation?"

"Yes," said Jim, "we can go any time."

But someone came in just then and asked for Jim and he went out.

There was a confused kind of meal served sometime during that interval by Chango. And at seven o'clock the little new moon came serenely above the mountains and by nine was bright and gentle, away up in the blue sky.

"What have they done with him, Jim?"

"Sheriff took him to the hospital. I—doubt if there's much chance. It's better that way, of course."

After a long moment Eden said: "He was like a different man—there in the plane. He—perhaps we never really knew him."

"He was not the kind of man one knows. We thought we knew him because there seemed so little to know. He's easygoing, always agreeable, always pleasant. Never seemed burdened with brains or force of character." Jim stopped and then said: "And he was always charming. He relied on that. With Dorothy—with Creda, when she met him that day and told him what she knew."

"When she met him———"

"Wilson saw him leave, walking out toward the arroyo, and he saw Creda go in the same direction a little later. He told Noel, trusting him as he didn't trust Sloane or me. It was Wilson you saw that night, Eden; and Noel saw him, too. Wilson didn't see Noel, but Noel leaped to the conclusion that Wilson had seen him and, when they talked late that night, that Wilson's aim was to make money from Noel. I don't think Wilson saw Noel murder Creda; I don't think he had any such plan in his mind. It's a case of the wicked flee where no man pursueth. Noel was in a state to doubt everything and everyone."

"How do you know Wilson told him anything?"

"Wilson told Strevsky that he'd seen Noel and Creda go for a walk that afternoon; they went separately but in the same direction and out of sight of the house. Strevsky, thickheaded and set on Pace as a suspect, never told anyone, didn't consider it important. To him Noel was a boss and all right. Wilson told Strevsky, too, that he'd been strolling around near the cabin that night when Creda was murdered but he was afraid to tell Sloane for fear Sloane would suspect him. He asked Strevsky what to do; Strevsky said to keep mum about it. But Strevsky didn't come out with any of this until we found Wilson's diary. A little, flat book which Noel overlooked. Or rather didn't take time to search out. God knows how he managed to get Wilson away from the house and murder him. He wouldn't tell that."

"You mean he has confessed?"

"I don't know," said Jim slowly. "He and Sloane and the sheriff were alone a long time. Whether or not he's told the whole story, they've got a complete case. I do know though (Sloane told me) that Noel saw Wilson and thought Wilson knew. So he had to kill him. But he missed the little diary. Wilson had written a few lines along with dates with girls, and the amount of money he'd put in the savings bank and the fifty-five cents he'd lost in a crap game. He was nineteen. He said he'd been walking near the cabins; that he had seen you find Creda and didn't tell Sloane for fear of getting into trouble. And that he thought he'd better ask somebody else's advice. He said, 'Mr. Carreaux is always kind.' "

Sloane came along the porch and said: "There you are. Everything all right, Miss Shore? I'm sorry you had such a scare. But it was nip and tuck really. You see Carreaux was riding in the rear of the rest of us—he gradually dropped back and returned. If he was seen any of the boys thought merely that he'd changed his mind and decided not to go with us. When we saw that, we came back."

Jim said: "P. H., will you tell Eden the whole thing? And me?"

The rancher looked out into the still night, with the serene new moon climbing the southern sky. After a moment he sighed.

"It's about as we figured it out, Jim. We've got a partial confession. We've pinned down facts that were surmise. He saw Creda in Averill's cabin; when it's lighted it's clearly visible from this end of the porch and thus from the window where he sat. It's also very near if you cross through the pines instead of going by the path. He saw the exchange of coats, so he knew Creda was wearing the yellow coat. He'd been watching his chance for she'd been fool enough to tell him she knew; she'd started to write her note in the cabin; he simply walked out the window; he must have come to the cabin window and told her to meet him outside and she did, leaving the note. The circumstances of the murder itself are as we guessed though I could get very little of it from him. He had his revolver; he had the knife; he appears to have been frightened, nervous; it was bound to be a blundering kind of thing, as it was. When he came into the cabin after she escaped him, his revolver in his hand, knowing he had to finish the blundering job he'd begun, she had fainted and he saw the chiffon scarf. That made the murder silent and quick. He forgot the revolver. It had fallen under the coat. He wasn't particularly smart, although he had a certain amount of cunning. At any rate, he simply returned to the lounge the way he had gone; I was at the piano; the thing hadn't taken long, ten minutes at the most; no one except Dorothy saw him. I had my back turned toward him; so had Jim and Averill. Pace was sitting in the other window embrasure and couldn't have seen him. So Dorothy lied and gave him an alibi."

There were the quick, light taps of heels across the porch. Averill came up beside them and put her white slender hand on Jim's arm.

"Let's walk, Jim darling," she said. Her voice was soft and very sweet; she put her black smooth hair against Jim's shoulder. He looked down at her and said: "All right——"

Eden, trying to listen to Sloane, watched them leave. Along the path, toward the shadow of the pines, Averill's slender figure pressed close against Jim.

It was a long time before they returned. Sloane talked steadily. As if he were checking and arranging the whole story in his mind, finally, rather than informing her. She must have heard what he said for she did realize that surmises and conjectures appeared now as facts, proven, or about to be proven. But she didn't really listen. And apparently he expected no comment.

"There will always remain," he said, "a point or two that is obscure, that will always be explained by implication. Exactly how, for instance, he and Wilson managed to get away from the house the night of the murder without being seen; how he killed Wilson with Chango's hatchet; how he returned alone, again without being seen. It was a very dark night. I suppose he simply carried the hatchet, hidden under his coat, and invited Wilson to walk with him."

A slight commotion arose at the door; a car swept up to it, its lights glancing ahead. Major Pace and two bags appeared on the threshold. Pace came toward them; he had his gray overcoat over his arm, a cigar and a fedora in his hand. He spoke to Sloane, he spoke to Eden, he bowed and went away. Getting into the car, vanishing into the night. As mysteriously as he had come.

The lights of the car and the beat of its engine gradually diminished.

And Averill and Jim returned, walking slowly along the path. At the steps to the porch they separated. Averill went inside, the light shining for an instant on her smooth black head. Jim came toward them.

Sloane rose and said: "So that's all, Miss Shore."

Jim said: "Not quite all. Eden——"

Sloane had walked away; he stopped under the light to roll himself a cigarette with anxious, loving care and then he, too, disappeared.

And Jim directly, without preamble, took Eden tight in his arms.

"Will you marry me?" he said.

"Jim——"

"I didn't mean what I said, about its being a mistake, Eden, you must have known that. I couldn't help it; it was Averill; she said she would tell Sloane that you and she had quarreled——"

"She did tell him that."

"She said she had evidence that would involve you; she—— Eden, you've got to understand. Averill is an opportunist, and she had the stronger hand. I don't think in her heart she ever believed you murdered Creda. But she resolved to turn the circumstances to suit her purpose." His voice was a little rueful; she felt rather than saw through the dusk a little grin on his face. "I can't flatter myself that it was my personal attraction; Averill has pride and ambition and she—she hated being a loser, especially to you, more than she loved me. Eden——" His voice became sober, "I want you to know this; I became engaged to Averill before I saw you. She never loved me but she was jealous of her possessions. I don't know exactly how our engagement came to be, except her father wished it. At any rate, it's all over now and in the past and, Eden——" His voice broke a little. He held her close in his arms and said unsteadily: "I love you so——"

The little new moon away above traveled serenely along its prescribed course; what is destined to be, is destined. Jim said presently, "Tomorrow we'll fly back. Averill is going on by train. Dorothy is going with her. There'll be just you and me and all the sky and stars around us."

The night was cold and clear and the stars bright. The distant mountain rim looked silver.

"We'll come back," said Eden softly, her voice a bare whisper in the silent night.

"Together," said Jim. "You haven't answered me, Eden. Will you marry me?"

A pause.

"Yes, Jim," very low.

Another pause. Then:

"Tomorrow, Eden? P. H. can fix the license. Will you—tomorrow?"

After a moment she turned in his arms and lifted her face. He said a little huskily: "If that's my answer——" And stopped.

It was as if the clear stars, the serene little moon in the dark blue sky, the distant silver rim of mountains, all the night and many nights belonged to them.

DIRECT YOUR OWN DESTINY
The Path Toward Greater Success and Happiness In Love, Marriage, Human Relationships, Financial Dealings Lies Ahead

What do the next five years hold for you? Will you find the lover of your choice? Will the glamor and success you've always dreamed of, at last be yours? If you are single, will you marry? If married, will it last? Will you achieve great wealth? Will rapid advancement come to your career? Will the next five years bring you peace and contentment?

The stars have the answer. This amazing book is your own personal and private forecast for the next five years. It reaches into the secret depths of your future and extracts the final answers to your hopes and dreams.

Don't waste a minute. Send for your copy of YOUR PROPHECY: FIVE YEAR FORECAST FOR ALL THE SIGNS TODAY. Priced at an incredibly low $4.95, it's a 288-page hardcover book, one you will be proud to own and treasure for years to come.

Accept this free trial offer. Just fill out the coupon today and mail it, along with your check or money order for $4.95. We'll pay the postage and handling charges. Keep the book 10 days, and if not completely satisfied, return it to us for a free refund.

Astrology Book Dept.
POPULAR LIBRARY INC.
355 Lexington Ave.
New York, N.Y. 10017

Please rush me YOUR PROPHECY: FIVE YEAR FORECAST FOR ALL THE SIGNS. I enclose $4.95 for each copy ordered. After 10 days, if not completely satisfied, I may return the book for a full refund.

Name_____

Address_____

City_____ State_____ Zip_____

Clip and Mail This Special Shipping Label and...

```
SHIP TO:
_____
       PRINT YOUR NAME HERE
_____
              YOUR ADDRESS
CITY _____
                STATE      ZIP #
CONTENTS: 6 INDISPENSABLE PAPERBACKS
```

We will send you all six of these widely-acclaimed reference paperbacks for only $4.25

A $26.30 HARD-COVER VALUE

PERFECT FOR HOME, SCHOOL OR BUSINESS OFFICE!

SEE OTHER SIDE ▶

Let these Get-Ahead books help you write better, read faster, speak more effectively!

Here's an unusual opportunity for everyone who is determined to get ahead in business, socially or at school. Just print your name and address on the special shipping label printed on the opposite page. Clip it out and mail it together with the coupon below. We will paste your label on a package containing six valuable get-ahead books jam-packed with the powerful ideas, practical helps and short-cut steps you need for improving your writing, reading and speaking skills right now. These books cost $26.30 in their original hard-covers. Now, they're yours for only $4.25 in practical paperbacks. Here's a brief glimpse of what you get:

(1) Better Writing
Shows how to get your thoughts on paper easily, quickly, more clearly and forcefully.

(2) Faster Reading
Proven-successful ways to increase your reading speed and help you understand and remember more.

(3) Speaking Effectively
Tested ways to improve your English, sharpen your speaking skills, sway an audience, add power to talks.

(4) Synonyms & Antonyms Dictionary
Provides exact words you need to express your written and spoken thoughts. Easy to use.

(5) Increase Your Vocabulary
How to expand your vocabulary quickly. 30-day new-word-mastery technique.

(6) Desk Dictionary
632 pages of clear, complete, up-to-date definitions, pronunciations, usages, origins of words. Illustrated.

MAIL THIS COUPON WITH SHIPPING LABEL NOW

---FREE TRIAL OFFER---

Popular Library
355 Lexington Avenue
New York, N.Y. 10017

Send me postpaid, all six get-ahead books, in handy desk-top slip case. I'm enclosing $4.25 and, if not fully satisfied, I may return the books in good condition within 10 days for a full refund.

Name_____
Address_____
City_____
State_____ Zip_____

Be sure to enclose shipping label with coupon

What a good time for all the good things of a Kent.

**Mild, smooth taste.
King size or Deluxe 100's.
Exclusive Micronite® filter.**

Kings: 17 mg. "tar," 1.0 mg. nicotine;
100's: 19 mg. "tar", 1.2 mg. nicotine, av. per cigarette, FTC Report Aug. '71.

© Lonillard 1971

What a good time for all the good things of a Kent.

Warning: The Surgeon General Has Determined That Cigarette Smoking Is Dangerous to Your Health

Cozy 'n Kent!